LYDIA

by Pip Wright

With all my thanks,

Pip Wright

Published by **Pawprint Publishing** 🐾
14, Polstead Close, Stowmarket, Suffolk   IP14 2PJ
First published as a limited edition of 500 in October 2005

Acknowledgements are due to a number of people
without whose help, the publication of this book would not
have been possible. In particular, thanks are due to
Des Herring & Stuart Bowell. Also, thanks to the staff at
the Suffolk Record Offices at Ipswich and Bury St. Edmunds.

Other books by Pip & Joy Wright:
The Amazing Story of John H. Steggall, 'The Suffolk Gipsy'
Newspapers in Suffolk **(6 vols.)**
Grave Reports
Witches in and around Suffolk
Diary of a Poor Suffolk Woodman **(with Léonie Robinson)**
pub. by Poppyland Publishing

Front cover picture by Henry John Yeend King
Picture on back cover reproduced by kind permission
of Peter Stibbons, Poppyland Publishing

Printed by **Polstead Press**, Station Rd. East, Stowmarket,
Suffolk IP14 1RQ

PART ONE

The morning of 27th June 1826

*Even when you have seen it all before, death doesn't come easy.
It was true, the crowds gathered around the porch of Cotton church
were no strangers to funerals. Too many had buried infants before
they'd even been weaned. There were those that day who stood,
tears in their eyes, reminded of their own personal tragedies
already acted out in that place. I saw them all seeking to share
their grief and find consolation in one another.
They did not notice me. At least no-one acknowledged the fact that,
shrouded in shadows, I stood apart from the rest of them, observing
from the cover of an ancient yew.
Why should they? Locked in their own shared sorrow they had
no time for the outsider in their midst. They had come to bury their
own. I had to pay my respects to Lydia in my own, less public way.
It was sad. Of course it was sad. This was a funeral. But this
one was worse: it was Lydia's funeral. She was twenty-seven. She
left a husband and three children, five sisters, a mother, a father and
a former lover.
Let's not forget the former lover! All of the others whose lives
had been touched by Lydia could exercise their public grief, and
that would be right. I was only an onlooker, but my misery was no
less real. Nevertheless it would have to be buried along with Lydia.
I could hardly take my sorrow home with me.*

i

Those who had been close to Lydia at her time of death congregated close to the church porch. Looking haggard with disbelief, the husband-turned-widower, Samuel Blomfield, stood holding the hand of little Harriet as the sky threatened to thunder out its disapproval. Young Johnny, aged six, stood apart as if more separated from his mother than anyone else there.

I couldn't take my eyes off him. He was the son I could not acknowledge and a living reminder of all that Lydia had meant to me.

Lydia's parents, Robert and Anne Saunders, having struggled to raise six of their seven children to maturity remained silent, bowed, old and pathetic, as if the only thing holding either of them up was the other. Burying infants was one thing. That was hard, but it was God's will. This was a daughter, grown and in the prime of life, which made it so much worse.

The congregation processed inside, as clouds thickened after weeks of warmth. Doubtless, the all too familiar service ran its inevitable course. Prayers and platitudes. Comfort for the bereaved. Lydia's body had been borne to St. Andrew's Church encased in the simplest of coffins. To an uninformed observer, this was just another pauper's funeral.

Chapter 1

September 1785

A row of scythes, the blade of each carefully bound round with strips of waxed cloth, bore testament to the fact that the harvest was over. A honing stone hung in a sack nearby. It had been a wet summer and far too many days had been lost, but working round the clock and some late drying wind had seen a successful end to it. The men were well satisfied.

Now it was the turn of the women. A horkey was arranged for Michaelmas. Still two weeks away, it would be a feast for a king, or at least a Lord of the Manor and his Steward. It would celebrate an end to another good harvest and the hiring of workers for the coming year. There were tenements to let and beasts to be slain rather than feed them all through what might prove to be a long hard winter. So nothing would go to waste. This was a time of preservation - the salting of beef, bottling of fruit, brewing of beer and the smoking of hams. September was the month of plenty. All too soon, it would be only a thin memory.

Anne Stannard was hard at work with rest of them. Though unskilled at butchery, she had been brought from her usual, more menial tasks to assist in the cutting and salting of half a bullock. Her deft hands took to the task and as long as one of the men was on hand to keep her knife sharp, she was able to follow the bone and waste less than others with far more experience.

At twenty-seven, but looking far younger, Anne attracted the attention of a number of the men. As fast as her knife became blunt, someone would be on hand to sharpen it using a hand-held stone, or on the wheel that stood in the corner of the barn. Even the step at the back doorway, which faced out across the moat to the meadows beyond, had a hollow from years of such use. Each time she received help or instruction in her unfamiliar task, she would smile sweetly and then turn her attention back to the job in hand.

Cotton Lodge was always an isolated place. It was where many of the labourers had been born and spent most of their childhood, but even to them felt remote. It was no easier to approach it by road than by using the well-trodden footpaths that led to it from a variety of directions. Midway between the villages of Cotton and Mendlesham, at the point known as Hayes Corner, a track left the road at a sharp angle. This track soon dwindled to nothing, and from then on, reaching the farm involved an amble or canter across meadows and between pollarded trees. In times past, this had been the home of a wealthy Catholic family and its very isolation had been of benefit to them.

The main house, of some antiquity, had been built inside a moat encompassing nearly an acre of land. Even then, it assumed a faded grandeur. Beside it and still within the moat, in one corner, stood a smaller dwelling, perhaps even older. Across the causeway, to the west, a mass of assorted buildings had grown up around a roughly paved square. These comprised barns, stables and outhouses as well as mean, crumbling dwellings, which served as tied cottages to those workers who needed to live close at hand. House servants generally had accommodation in The Lodge itself, but those who looked after the horses, the gardens, the livestock, or managed the dairy and the laundry occupied these roughest of homes.

Usually the yards would be the province of the women and those too elderly to work in the fields. Now the harvest was in, the area around The Lodge was alive with men and women of all ages, some working with purpose, others just trying to give the appearance of busy-ness. Now and then, the master would appear and activity would seem to double. But for all concerned, it was a feel-good time: the sense of a job well done and a time of well-deserved celebration.

Though unmarried, Anne could not afford to take seriously the attentions of any of these men. She already had a child and in the due course of time expected to marry the father. Robert Saunders had been courting her since they had both worked at a large manor house on the other side of the village and close to her parents'

village of Wetheringsett.   But he was a journeyman, hiring himself
a few months at a time.

Eventually, he would settle, have a tied cottage and they would
wed.   The baby was named Elizabeth after his mother.   It was as
good as saying to the world they were engaged.   In the meantime,
her parents would look after the child.   She would work at Cotton
Lodge and send home as much of her wages as she could afford.
Her parents had their doubts as to Robert's sincerity, but for now, as
far as Anne was concerned, she was betrothed and a little flirting
was as much as she was prepared to offer.

"Thass a right good job you done o' tha'."
This was praise indeed from Mrs. Diggins, housekeeper to the
Steward.   Anne glowed with satisfaction.

This was not one of her usual tasks.   She was a 'maid of all
work', which meant she lived in the big house and could be called
upon to do a variety of jobs.   The advantage was she was dressed
and fed, so most of the meagre income she received was her own
and could be sent to her parents to look after the child.   She had
been in service nearly half her young life and was becoming
invaluable to her employers.   Now it seemed butchery was yet
another skill her clever hands could master.

A silence fell over the working team.   They were aware of a
grandly dressed military man, sword at his side, entering the room.
Pell Heigham made an impressive figure.   Anne, at five foot three,
was as tall as most in the room, men included, but Heigham was a
head taller than that.   As second son, he would never aspire to the
inheritance promised his elder brother, but having purchased his
commission and assumed authority over a proportion of the family
estate, he was here in person to witness the fact that all was safely
gathered in.   He would not remain for what were, after all their
festivities.   A mere two hundred acres were worth no more than a
fleeting visit.   The Steward, from two paces behind, bowed and
scraped as if entertaining royalty.   Mrs. Diggins, the Housekeeper,
flapped and fluttered like a broody hen.

Anne found herself turning her ears to listen to the conversation. It wasn't easy. More used to the broad dialect of Mid-Suffolk, the aristocratic twang was hard to understand.

"What is this building?" Heigham asked.

"They call it the old dairy, but it's south facing and not much use as that in summer."

"My guess would be it was part of the original house - do you see those mullions?" Heigham pointed to an unglazed window high up at one end of the room. "Also, it has fireplaces and a chimney. It seems a shame to let it get into this state. I wager it would make good servants' quarters and give you more room in The Lodge." Heigham turned and looked at Mrs. Diggins.

"That nephew of yours and his family have been working over at Rougham. You're short of workers out here. Why don't we repair this place and move them in. You must have a few spare men can turn their hand to building work now the harvest's in."

Mrs. Diggins was clearly delighted, but unsure how to demonstrate her gratitude.

Anne Stannard listened avidly. Her Robert had been working over at Debenham, six miles away, and she'd seen less of him than she'd liked. She was still hoping he'd be coming to the horkey a fortnight hence.

Never the most reliable, he'd be likely to start out with good intentions but be waylaid at the beer-house at Mickfield and get no further. However, he had done a bit of building, and if only she could find him a job at The Lodge, then she could see him more often.

She knew better than to speak right now, but her chance would come soon enough. She was in Mrs. Diggins' good books. She would speak to her when the time was right and Mrs. Diggins would speak to the Steward. Content, she set about her work with gusto, a smile like a smirk still covering her face.

"Look at her - like the cat what got the cream."

"She's thinking of her young man, thass what."

She didn't care - they could mock all they liked, but she could see a time when they'd be a proper family; she and Robert, in their own cottage with little Elizabeth, and maybe more.

"Are you gonna dance with me at the horkey, Anne?"

That was Nehemiah Mullinger - old enough to be her grandfather.

"She 'un't dance with you bo' - she 'un't dance with nobody but her precious Robert."

"Wass he got what I 'in't?" Nehemiah jokingly protested.

"He's a rum'un that Robby Saunders."

"He's a Saunders and he's from Bacton," laughed Mary Lovatt. "An' we all know there's rum owd folks come from Bacton."

"Is yar Robert coming to see you tonight then?"

"Maybe he is, maybe he 'in't."

Anne tossed her hair provocatively.

"Even if he do, you 'un't find a lot of privacy round here now the corn's bin cut," cracked Matthew Turner. Anne blushed.

"Leave the poor girl alone," scolded Mrs. Diggins. "She's a right to a bit of peace and quiet from you lot. She's worked harder than the lot of you together. I wouldn't blame her if she never spoke to any of you again, let alone danced with you."

* * * * * * * * * * * * * *

The threshing floor was swept clean. Bales of straw were strategically placed around the edge. What passed for a band was tuning up and running through its limited repertoire. A makeshift bar had been constructed with barrels of ale and skins of home-made wine. Jugs of cider - still, but potent - stood on a plank supported by two trunks of ancient willow. Couples were already arriving. They brought their own tankards and cups, some newly made for the event, carved from a solid piece of wood or of heavy leather stitched by the cobbler and made sound with waxing of the hide and tarring of the stitches. These were for the most part crude vessels but they served to transport liquor from jug to stomach with as short a time-lapse as possible between the two.

Those who arrived singly, hoped to be heading homeward with company that night. The warmth of an Indian summer and a good supply of drink would see an end to any remaining inhibitions. Young and old alike were coming with high hopes of a thoroughly satisfying evening. Old toothless men, widowed but still hopeful;

5

young pubescent girls, confused by their own bodily changes; lusty young men, now relaxed after the rigours of the harvest; potential old-maids, hoping for one last chance at happiness.

Anne arrived early, as the drink was just beginning to flow. It was but a short walk across the farmyard from her shared room up in the attic of The Lodge to the threshing barn. You could still hear the music, though the shouting of the caller was seeking to obscure it. As numbers and voices grew, the fiddle, flute and drum of the musicians had to work harder to raise the volume of their dozen or so tunes.

"Hey Anne, don't forget, you promised me a dance."
There were several voices uttering such sentiments.

"I'll dance a 'strip the willow' with you," she promised. The way they danced that, you moved partners at each change. That way she could satisfy all of them. She felt cheered and elated. Robert had promised he would be there. It had been a week since she'd seen him at her parents' house in Wetheringsett, which lay half way between his and her places of work. Little Elizabeth, nearly two, had been excited to see them both, and it had been a magical time.

"Come yew on Anne - you can't just hide in a corner like the dried-up old biddies." That was John Driver; about her age, and fancying his chances. She looked back at the corner where she had been sitting.

It was true - most of the women there looked like perpetual wallflowers. She had been the only pretty one there. Dressed as best as they knew how, they still managed to look dowdy and spinster-like by comparison. Anne sparkled and attracted all the attention. She could wait no longer for Robert to arrive. She lifted her long skirt and made for the dance, making sure John Driver knew that a dance was all he would get that night. He could hold her hand, but when he tried to hold her closer, she slipped tantalisingly from his grasp.

Enviously, the old maids in the corner she had just vacated, looked on. Mrs. Diggins, the housekeeper was there. Her husband had been a soldier, they said; died young. Now, her children grown, she seemed wedded to the job. Her nephew, William and his wife, newly arrived, were already dancing. William's sister Sarah, only five years Anne's senior, looked a generation older and sat colourless and unappealingly alone.

As the volume of sound increased, you had to shout to make yourself heard and voices rang round the rafters of the old thatched barn. One or two had metal pieces set into the heels of their boots and you could hear the clack of the metal on the stone tiles of the threshing floor. John Driver made another clumsy attempt at familiarity as it came to swinging your partner. He grabbed at Anne around the waist and placing his hand around her rear tried to kiss her, pulling her to him as he did so. Anne was having none of it.

"You behave yourself!" she yelled, "Or you can go find yourself another partner."

He did, and soon he was whirling Elizabeth Fenning around the floor with far more abandon than Anne would have stood for. As the evening wore on and the drink took its toll, couples wandered off into the darkness to do what couples do under such circumstances. Anne was still waiting for Robert. Bitterly disappointed, she found herself talking to the rejects of the event. She tried to speak to a lonely looking Sarah Diggins, but their small but significant social gulf was enough to ensure no real conversation could be had. They had nothing in common.

Resigned to an earlier night than she had planned, Anne wandered sadly back toward The Lodge alone. She let herself in by the side door and climbed the ancient oak staircase that led to the upper floor of the old house.

A nearly full moon had risen and she found her way without further light than that which streamed in through the diamond leaded panes of the larger windows. Most of the live-in servants were accommodated above the outbuildings attached to the northern end of the house, but Anne and two other girls had been afforded the pleasure of a large loft space in The Lodge itself. It was bitterly cold in winter and you could die of dehydration in the middle of summer, but in between times it was quite cosy.

Anne guessed the other two girls wouldn't be back for some

time yet.   Two sisters, still in their teens, Hannah and Martha Gillings, shared the attic room with Anne.   Each had her young man and it was a fine night.   Anne undressed in the dark.   Little light filtered into her attic.   No sooner had she slipped, in her underclothes, between the coarse pieces of linen that served as sheets, than she heard the door open.

"Hannah - is that you?" she called.   No answer.

"Martha - you're early."   But it wasn't Martha either.

She trembled and then went to scream as a figure lifted the covers and slipped in beside her.   He smelt strongly of beer.   He clasped a hand over her mouth.

"I told you as how I'd come - see.   I hope you 'in't give up on me?"   He unclasped her mouth and kissed it, almost violently.

"Robert - but you can't come in here.   I'll get dismissed."

"No you 'un't.   Cos no-one know I'm here - see.   An' them silly little girls what you share with 'un't be back for hours yet. An' by then I'll be gone."

"Are you sure?"   As she said it, Anne was aware of a tacit consent on her part.   She could hardly play the coy little innocent. They already had a child, were promised in marriage and they did love each other, didn't they?

"When are we going to get married?"

"Soon - don't you worry.   I got it all sorted out.   I reckon I'll get a job with a cottage this year - a good job."   He smiled and though she couldn't see him, she knew he was in a good mood.

"I hope you 'in't bin a-dancing with all them other boys."

"I did have a dance or two," she confessed, "but I wouldn't let 'em hold me - not like I let you."

"I should hope not," he smirked.   "You be my gal - see."
He stayed just long enough for their satisfaction and her safety.
He had gone long before Hannah and Martha came giggling in.

"You got yourself an early night," laughed Hannah, so drunk she could hardly stand.   "I thought you'd be having a look at the sky by now.   You get a lovely view of the stars lying on your back," chuckled Martha, in case the euphemism was lost on her roommate.   Anne said nothing except, "I'm glad you had a good time."

8

Chapter 2

Summer 1786

Whether it had been the night of the horkey, or one of a number of subsequent nights when Anne's room-mates had stayed out late, by Christmas it was evident the damage was done. Home at Wetheringsett for a full three days with John and Mary Stannard, Anne knew she had to own up to the fact she was pregnant again and no nearer to being married than two years previous. She wasn't looking forward to telling her mother, who had no time for Robert Saunders and certainly would be in no mood to bring up another of his bastards.

By the time she had been home a day, and had plucked up the courage to speak, she needn't have bothered. Mary Stannard may only have birthed one live child, Anne, but she had had enough miscarriages and stillbirths to recognise the signs.

"You're with child ag'in, 'in't you?"

It wasn't really a question.

"And I suppose thass a-goin' to be Saunders again."

Anne looked sheepish.

"When 'you a-going to realise he 'un't marry you unless you force his hand? Go to the parish and get a bastardy order. That way at least he'll have to pay what he owe this time. When's that due?"

"Summer sometime."

"Well you needn't think I'm looking after this one. Lizzy's lovely and I don't mind her one bit, but I'm too old for babies. I can't cope."

She sounded fierce, but Anne knew her mother too well. There hadn't been a boy born in their family in two generations. It had always been her greatest regret that she'd not had a son. Here was a chance at least of a grandson.

"I suppose you're wanting a boy?" Her mother seemed to be

warming to the idea already.

"I thought I'd call him Robert..." Anne tried her luck. "...but if it's a girl, we'll call her Mary." She was being as diplomatic as she knew how.

Arrangements for care of the child could be delayed. In the meantime, it was Christmas Eve and her body remained slim and lithe as ever. It would be some time before she would need to tell Robert.

* * * * * * * * * * * * * *

That had all been back in December. Winter had come and gone. Hedges had been trimmed, ditches cleaned out, crops planted and the corn was now high. Flocks of fieldfares pillaging the hawthorn were a distant memory, as was that Christmas when Robert had appeared with a duck for the feast and a hand-carved doll for his daughter, Elizabeth. For Anne he had brought a necklace of green stones, and there were also gifts of scented waters for Mary and tobacco for John. Expensive items. No one asked how he had come by them.

By February, when her condition was becoming obvious, Anne told Robert. He seemed pleased enough and again promised he would marry her 'when his ship came in,' whenever that might be.

Towards the end of June, Anne's employers were urging her to return home. But as she was not grown too large and still felt fit enough, she continued to work at The Lodge, though she was excused the heavier tasks.

At first, Mrs. Diggins, the housekeeper, seemed irritated by her presence, but since her niece Sarah had shouldered more of her responsibilities, she tolerated the situation. Sarah Diggins took it upon herself to ensure Anne should not tire herself too much. It was as if she was determined to protect this, the child she was sure she, Sarah, would never have.

There was a kind and caring melancholy about her, and Anne now saw her more as a soul-mate than the distant and haughty woman she had once believed her to be.

10

It had been growing warmer for several days. Anne was becoming less mobile and had let her skirts out about as far as the fabric would permit. Surely her time must soon arrive. Several of the ladies around the farm had opinions on the matter. Anne may have been unsure of the date of conception, but there were plenty with the experience of a dozen or more confinements who were prepared to offer advice as to when the child would be born. Already most of those dates were past.

One thing that concerned Anne was the fact she hadn't felt the child kick for the best part of a week, and though old Sophie in the Laundry assured her this was quite normal, somehow it didn't feel right.

Nothing had been resolved about who should care for the child once he was born (Anne was sure 'he' was a boy). Robert had assured her parents he would be more reliable over payments and would look for a permanent job nearby. They wished they could believe him.

The yards in front of The Lodge were quite empty for much of the day at that time of year. There was haymaking, shearing, digging potatoes, hoeing and all manner of jobs to be done in the fields. Children and women were employed on stone-picking and bird scaring. As usual, Sarah Diggins was keeping a close watch over Anne.

From one of the hovels across the yard, a woman emerged, dragging a string of children with her. It was Betsy Barnes. She cradled a baby in her arms. It was screaming inconsolably.

"Have you seen my 'usband? He's forgot his snack. I've got this lot to feed and I don't know where he is."

"I think I heard someone say Joseph was up the Great Kiln Field," said Sarah. "Robert Francis had a fence down and they were afraid his animals would get in among the beans."

"But that's half a mile off," cried Betsy.
The other two felt sorry for her. Joe could be a violent man if things didn't go his way.

"Here, give it to me," said Anne, "I'll take it to him. I'm not a lot a' use round here."

"You can't walk that far," protested Sarah. "Not in your condition."

"I'll be more comfortable on my feet; I get the cramp sitting down," laughed Anne. "I'll take it easy. He won't get his food that quick, mind."

Pulling the cloth bag over her shoulder, Anne began to plod methodically across the yard past the newly formed hay-ricks; when suddenly, she cried out and the other two saw her fall to the ground, as if in pain.

"Quick, get her inside," called Sarah. "Get her up to my room." The contractions had begun and it was as much as the pair of them could do to steer Anne up the narrow staircase onto the bed in Sarah's room. Betsy Barnes's baby was still crying, but Anne's moans were louder.

Sarah was terrified. Help she would, but this was outside her experience and she was afraid of what might happen if Betsy left her to manage the situation alone.

"Where'll we find a midwife at a time like this?"

"Where's old Sophie?" asked Betsy. "She'll know what to do."

"She's dollying for them at Hayes Farm."

Agitating the washing dolly was a job for older women who were still physically fit. Betsy turned to the largest of the children there, a girl of about six with matted hair and a threadbare dress.

"Git yew up the track to Hayes Farm and tell old Sophie we need her right now! You understand?"

The child, though young and having the air of one who was simple-minded, understood, whether by virtue of the words or the urgency in her voice.

"You run now - and tell her Anne's child's on its way."
The last few words were shouted as the child made haste.

Anne was hardly aware of their efforts as they strove to boil water and find clean pieces of cloth in anticipation of the imminent birth.

To Sarah and Betsy, it seemed an age before old Sophie entered the room.

"Let's have a look at her - oh yes luvvie, it's on its way alright. I'll get my bag."

"But where are you going?" Sarah was concerned that the child might arrive before she came back.

"There's things I need, luvvie," old Sophie said mysteriously. "Things you 'in't got here. Things only old Sophie has in her birthing-bag. Don't you fret. This one'll be a little while yet."

That was the worst time for Sarah. Betsy Barnes disappeared, taking her tiny tribe with her, and it was an eternity of spasms and cries before the bag pushed its way into the room followed by old Sophie.

"Should I send for the surgeon?" Sarah asked.

"Don't be sorft, luvvie. Surgeons 'in't for the likes of us. And anyway, by the time he get here, we'll have us a bonnie baby boy."

It was true; labourers couldn't afford doctors' fees, which were measured in guineas. Apart from that, they'd not trust a man to see to them at such a time. Old Sophie had acted as midwife a hundred times and most mothers and children had lived to tell the tale. It was unlikely that any expensive surgeon with all his medical training could equal the success of old Sophie and her bag of secrets.

However if they had believed the birth was close, they were mistaken. By nightfall the pains were greater and more frequent, but the labour continued. Word was sent to Wetheringsett to let her mother know her time had come. Anne was exhausted, but still there was no child. Robert, it appeared, could not be found.

Being mid-summer, sunrise came early. Briefly the pains abated and they all took a nap. But then Anne screamed and woke Sarah who shook old Sophie awake. The child came quickly then, but the old midwife had seen enough stillbirths to recognise this child would not live more than a few minutes.

"It's a little girl, but she's a poorly thing. I can baptise her if you like." From the depths of her bag, she produced a small bottle of holy water, blessed by the Rector and supplied for such an event.

"What will you call her luvvie?"

Anne wept, unable to answer.

"Come on luvvie, you wouldn't want her to go to her maker

without a Christian baptism, would you. It'll be a proper job. I'll even see it's put in the parish register."

"Mary! ...I ...I said if it was a girl... she'd be called ...Mary."

Sarah held Anne's hand as old Sophie removed the stopper of the bottle and anointed the head of the lifeless child. She wanted to ask if it was right to baptise a child that was clearly already dead, but couldn't bring herself to. Soon after the sign of the cross had been applied to the child's inert body, they all caught a brief hour or two of sleep. It had been a long night.

*　*　*　*　*　*　*　*　*　*　*　*　*　*

If the child had lived, it would have been normal for Anne to have returned home to her parents' house in Wetheringsett and stayed there till she had been properly confined and churched, a process of up to six weeks. As it was, she intended to rest up with her parents only briefly and was determined to return to Cotton Lodge far sooner. There was little to hold her at Wetheringsett - a mixture of pity and silent disapproval from her parents; a child who hardly recognised her and who called John and Mary 'dad and mum.'

Robert hadn't been seen or heard of for weeks, until he turned up unexpectedly one afternoon, a fortnight into July. He tried to explain his long absence, but Anne didn't want to know. A depression had gripped her that made her insensitive to reason.

"I b'in working night and day. I di'n't know the little'un 'ud die. I b'in making good money to care for the both of you."

It was no use. She couldn't bear him near her: he had to leave her be and try instead to explain himself to the unlikeliest of confidants, Anne's father, John Stannard.

"I don't understand it. I b'in doing what everyone wanted. I 'in't touched a drop in weeks and it 'in't because I 'in't been thirsty."

John Stannard for once could see a whisper of sincerity in Robert.

"You'll have to give her time. Mary and me lost... ooh I don't know how many babies... before we got one to survive. But it

14

never got no easier. And you still miss 'em - the little 'uns you never had."

"I say to her not to worry and maybe next time that might be a boy."

"I can see how that mightn't have been the best way to say it."

"So what am I s'posed to do?" Robert was at a loss.

"You know what that say in the Rector's big book? 'Mary, base born daughter of Anne Stannard, baptised and buried, June 1786.'"

"So?"

"Look lad - I know thass the Cotton way - have a kid or two and then think of getting wed. Our Anne's in good company and there's plenty more in the register like her. But don't you think thass about time you got it right. Afore there's any more little 'uns, she need a husband."

"I did say when I got a job proper with a tied house and all..." Robert began. But John Stannard interrupted him.

"I've spoke to Reverend Close: Anne's in no state to return to Cotton Lodge but she say thass what she's gonna do and there 'in't no changing her mind. But from what I hear, the Steward's gittin' 'owd and there's no place for folks what 'in't called Diggins up there. From what I can see, Mr. William now run the place, and half the parish too. Now..."
He paused to prepare for the main point of his speech.

"There's a position coming up at the Manor..."

"What, here in Wetheringsett?"

"Rector say they'll be needing a married couple - from next Easter. He'll put in a good word and book the wedding if you do want."

Parting with this information gave John Stannard an immense sense of relief. Now, he had to see if Saunders was as good as his word.

"Do you think she'll still have me - she dun't seem to like me much at the moment?"

"Are you surprised? Oh she'll come round, and she'll need you more than ever. Give her time. I can't promise much of a wedding mind. We've never had a lot put by."

"Oh don't you worry 'bout that. I'll call in a few favours and we'll have a grand do. You'll see."

Within a few days of this conversation, Anne did return to Cotton Lodge. Sarah Diggins was delighted to see her, but noticed a change in her. It was as if she had, at the age of twenty-eight, made the transition from childhood to adulthood. Some of the sparkle and bravado had gone, but there was in its place an inner strength that would serve to see her through harder times than this.

For all that, it was not easy for her, returning to Cotton. Every corner, every face seemed to remind her of the one tragedy in her life so far, and despite Sarah's continued kindness, Anne knew she could not remain at The Lodge.

Reverend Close's assessment of the situation was fairly accurate. The Heighams who owned Cotton Lodge were in no hurry to replace the Steward, though he was becoming frail and had handed ever more responsibility over to William Diggins, who was acting as a kind of farm Bailiff. William was a shrewd business-man, well-versed in the changes that were coming about in agricul-ture. Also, he was educated, good with accounts and working hard as an Overseer of the parish. He had no time for those that couldn't or wouldn't earn their meagre pay. His answer to the poor and destitute was to package them off to the 'House of Industry' over at Wortham, as Cotton had no parish workhouse of its own.

Throughout that winter, Anne and Robert planned their future. They had already been to meet the Master at Wetheringsett Manor. Robert would work in the stables. It wasn't strictly true, but he claimed to have worked as an ostler before. He was sure he could handle the work. Like Anne, he could turn his hand to most things.

The cottage they were to have was a wreck when they first saw it, but they weren't too dismayed. With help from friends and family, it could be put to rights. The first time they climbed the rickety open staircase, there were two owls sitting side by side, snuggled up together on the roof timbers. It seemed a good omen.

16

Sarah Diggins saw to it that Anne grew in strength over those winter months. It wasn't too difficult. Inside The Lodge, the diet was rich and wholesome and most days there was plenty left over. Anne was introduced to all kinds of delicacies that had never come her way before - one day it would be partridge, another it could be cold tongue or haunch of venison in caper sauce. By spring when meat would have been a rarity in her parents' house, Anne was glowing with health whilst others around her exhibited all the usual signs of seasonal malnutrition.

In spite of the organisation involved, the wedding was a simple affair. It was a Tuesday afternoon and practically everyone attending had sacrificed a lot just to be there. Employers were reluctant to lose half their work force at a time of high activity on the farm. It was early April and plenty of fields still had to be ploughed, harrowed and sown. In spite of that, it was a good turnout. The day was full of spring promise and Wetheringsett churchyard was alive with primroses and violets.

A peal of bells rang out. They were proud of their bells, which were rung, as were those at Cotton, from an ancient tower at the Western end, open to the worst of the weather. On this occasion, it wasn't to prove a problem as, being well past noon, the sun sloped in on their efforts. John Stannard was one of the proud ringers that day, only leaving his bell-rope and donning his jacket when the bride was driven up in horse and cart by none other than William Diggins. It was just a simple hay-cart, but it had been recently painted and was swathed in spring flowers.

If anyone had wondered about Robert turning up on time, they needn't have worried. He had worked overtime for weeks, just to have the whole day off. He had in fact been sitting inside the church for a good half-hour before the curate arrived. The Rector would conduct the service, but Rayner Bellman liked to check everything would be just so. He had been curate there for a number of years but lacked the money and connections to secure for himself a parish. He was a fastidious man and a slightly nervous one. He was surprised, as anyone would have been, to discover this

17

well-known 'jack-the-lad' sitting as if in a trance, awaiting the arrival of his bride and the wedding guests.

The bride herself looked the proverbial picture, dressed in a gown that had been used countless times in their family. Little Elizabeth had the luxury of a new dress. As bridesmaid, she was in her element. Mary Stannard had turned her clever hands to this simple, but stylish garment. Mending and making for several wealthy customers, she had come by a number of samples of fabric, which had served to turn her grand-daughter into a princess for a day.

The service itself was short; many were expected back at work within the hour. Anne and Robert led those that were able to follow back to their newly renovated cottage for some refreshment. When they had begun that day, the house had been bare of furniture, save a bed, a table and two chairs. By the time the guests had left, as was the tradition, the cottage was amply furnished, much made by skilful hands under rush-light through the long months of winter.

The last to leave the reception was Sarah Diggins. More conscious than ever of her loneliness, she hung on until the bitter end. Her brother had driven the cart back, straight after the ceremony. Sarah intended to borrow a pony from a friend and as it would soon be dark, wanted to be beyond the Norwich Turnpike and on more familiar territory before dusk.

"Come and see me," she said. "Please!" her eyes implored.

"Of course," Anne said, and she meant it. "Just as soon as I get a day off."

But it would be another three years before the two of them, seemingly so close, should meet again.

Chapter 3

New Year, 1790

Anne sat close to the open hearth in the room that served both as kitchen and living room. In less than three years since the day of their marriage, she had turned the tiny, draughty cottage into a cosy home. There was a baby in the cot and another well on its way. Another Christmas had come and gone, and a full pot hung over the glowing embers. Life was good. Robert may not have been a perfect husband, but at least he was a good provider. As long as you didn't ask too many questions as to the source of the supply.

Nevertheless, Anne was worried. Her father always said, "You are only as good as the company you keep." The company Robert usually kept arrived in the form of Harry Thurlow, a disreputable sort of character, who so far had avoided serious brushes with the law. Unfortunately, he was a braggart of a man, too free with his mouth when the drink was inside him, and adventurous to the point of recklessness.

Anne hated it when he sat in her kitchen recounting tales of doubtful veracity where he, Harry, always seemed to come out best. He'd been there several times throughout the Christmas period, when accounts of his poaching exploits were to the fore. Robert seemed to hang on his every word. Anne was far more sceptical.

"So we start a-whistling from all different directions and the keeper - he get so confused, he run into his own man-trap. Lord, you should'a heard him holler. Lost a leg so they say - but of course we di'n't hang about to find out - grabbed the pheasants and buggered off."

Then there had been the nights when Robert hadn't come home at all... not until the next morning, usually with something for the pot. He was drinking a lot too, though for once, they didn't seem short of money. Still, there were times when she would lie alone in their bed, worrying. Anne had heard of men going to sleep at the side of the road as they staggered home from the alehouse, and never waking up, on account of the frost. Robert and Harry had taken to supping at the Oak at Mendlesham. Who knew what devious plans were debated over a few jugs of ale.

Anne could only catch hints of where they made their expeditions. One evening, she had heard Gipping Wood mentioned. This was Tyrell land, jealously guarded by keepers with guns. Anne felt vulnerable. Farm labouring was dangerous enough. Plenty in their parish had been widowed by accidents or by carelessness. And she had this over-riding fear that if it came to it, Harry Thurlow would come out of it smelling of roses whilst Robert languished in gaol or worse.

So, now they were gone again. There had been talk of a Fair for New Year over at Stowmarket. It was a good step, but you could walk it in two or three hours if you put your mind to it. The frozen ground helped make the Hundred Lane passable for the first time in weeks. If she had felt they were only heading that way for a bit of fun, it would not have been so bad. No, it was what Harry had said about everyone in the town going there, servants and all. What he was presumably referring to were grand houses being left empty, and ripe for the picking.

Hadn't she pleaded with Robert not to go - claimed she was feeling twinges and pains; hadn't she appealed to his better nature? But then Harry had dropped all those hints about men who were tied to their wives' apron strings, and they'd gone off laughing together with no suggestion of when they'd be back. The way they went, there'd be at least six inns and alehouses to visit before Stowmarket.

After a jug at the Horseshoes at Mickfield and another at the Ten Bells, they headed for the maltings at Stonham. Robert was feeling tired and they weren't yet halfway. He'd been working long days, and been out most nights. He was already beginning to wonder if this was a good idea.

"Harry, have you ever nicked a horse?"

"Oh no bo' - you don't touch horses. Some judges'll hang you

20

for horses. Horses is for nobility - if folks see the likes of us on a horse, they want to know where we took it."

As they reached the brow of the hill, they could see the malting buildings stretched out beside a cross roads along the turnpike. To one side, the road rose steeply and halfway up the hill stood the Angel. It had stables behind, and was a popular stopping point for carriers and tradesmen. The richer clientele and the stagecoaches tended to stop at the Pie Inn, half a mile further along the turnpike.

The Angel was basic even by their standards, but for Robert and Harry it was an opportunity to see if there might be the chance of a lift. A drink and a listen, and they were in luck. A tinker, on his way to the fair at Stowmarket, was able to make room for them. It was hardly any quicker than walking, and twice they had to get off - once to allow the old horse to pull the wagon uphill, and once to help control it on the steep downward slope into the town.

Robert hadn't been there for over ten years, and in that time the small town had grown beyond recognition. The malting towers punctuated the skyline as they reached upwards from the river valley.

The track, still frozen, ran past a grand and ancient house coming to a fording point across the river. Fortunately, the river was low. It had been a dry winter and the old horse made easy work of pulling the well-laden wagon through and up the other side. They parted company with the tinker, overtipping him with a generosity fuelled by their earlier intake of alcohol.

Then, striding up the main street as if they owned the place, the two colleagues marvelled at the grandness of the shops and town houses, some of which rose to three storeys. It was past mid-day by this time and it was easy to follow the crowds to the green area of common-land which Robert recognised from his youth as the place where he'd once played a violent and terrifying ball game known as Kamping. He'd lost a tooth that day, as he recalled, to the thugs of Stowmarket. Well, now perhaps it was pay-back time.

An array of brightly decorated stalls caught Robert's attention. Momentarily, he forgot the reason he'd come and was wondering what might serve to placate Anne on his return, when he noticed

Harry was in conversation with another, shabbily dressed fellow.

"This is Pikey," said Harry. "He's been looking around for us - found just the place."

Pikey was an unpleasant-looking, feretty-faced individual. Whether his nickname was a corruption of his real name or a description of his nature and appearance, wasn't made clear. One thing was sure, he didn't inspire confidence.

Up to this point, Robert hadn't been aware that their group was a three rather than a two. He felt slightly resentful, and wondered how much more he had yet to find out. The little group wandered away from the crowds and in the seclusion of a lane, a plan emerged.

"There's this big house in Ipswich Street - goes up and up - cellars too. It belongs to this rich type called John King - owns a corn chandler's and a malting." Pikey informed them.

"How do you know all this?"

"Got friendly with one of the servants, di'n't I? She told me all about it - 's filled with good stuff. They'll all be off at the Fair most of the afternoon. We want to go now while the place is empty."
Harry was all for heading that way at once, but Robert was more cautious.

"How can we be sure they 'un't come back yet?"

"Well, this John King - he's got an old mother, almost blind. They've took her with 'em. She can't go very quick. It'll take 'em ages to get her back." Pikey seemed confident enough. But if Robert was unsure about Pikey, the feeling was clearly mutual.

"Have you done one of these places before?" he asked.

"Of course I have, you know I have..." began Harry.

"Not you - him!" Pikey said, pointing at Robert.
Uncomfortably, Robert shuffled from foot to foot, unable to come up with an appropriate response.

"Alright - listen!" Pikey spoke as if laying the law down to a small child. We break in the back where the servants go in. We only take what's easy to shift and don't be too greedy. If you get caught with more than ten pounds worth on you, it's a hanging offence."

Robert's head was in a whirl. Suddenly, this was serious. A bit of poaching was one thing; poultry-thieving or liberating the odd barrel from behind the brewery were his line. All at once, he felt out of his depth and was none too sure he wanted to learn to tread water.

But there was no going back at this stage. As for keeping it under ten pounds, he could hardly believe there was that much money in the world.

A network of lanes ran behind the King's Head, emerging halfway up, along a street of inns and assorted shops. At the top of the street were a number of taller buildings. Mr. King evidently lived in one of these.

Robert and Harry followed Pikey up an alley between two of the larger houses. They turned left into a paved yard. Pikey tried the door, which not surprisingly was locked.

"Perhaps we'd better go - if we can't get in," said Robert, somewhat relieved. The alcohol-induced bravado of earlier in the day had given way to the fearful anticipation of arrest and all that might entail.

"Don't you worry 'bout that bo'," laughed Pikey. Spotting a key that was visible on the other side of the half-glazed door, he picked up a broken tile from the corner of the yard, and without fear of the noise it might make or who it might attract, smashed a pane to enable himself to turn the key, affording them access to the building.

Passing first through service rooms, they headed upwards and to the front of the house where more valuable booty might be found. Harry pulled open drawers as he passed through, pocketing spoons and other cutlery. Pikey seemed more selective.

"You can leave that stuff where it is. The good silver'll be locked up, but I'm sure we can break our way into whatever cupboard they've hid it."

Grabbing a heavy iron poker from beside a smouldering fire, Pikey made for a locked cupboard built into the corner of what might have been a butler's pantry. It didn't take a lot of force to open it, revealing a vast array of the finest glass.

"Leave that - too hard to sell on - take the silver serving spoons though - we can melt them down. Bring the tea-caddy."

Just following instructions, Robert tried to find room in a pocket for some of the items Pikey was pointing out. Anything that couldn't be well concealed, he left where it was, as they moved on.

"Well, lookee here," called Harry as they came upon a dining room. Claret, brandy and port bottles stood, invitingly. Robert, who would normally have drunk with them measure for measure, found he had lost his appetite. He just wanted to be out of that house as fast as he could, preferably with a good profit in his pockets.

Leaving the others to it, he moved through a succession of grandly-furnished rooms, collecting all manner of items as he went - a silk scarf, a gold hat pin, a small pocket pistol, such as a woman might carry, and a prize to reckon with - a belt of sovereigns placed for safe-keeping between the boards of one of the beds and its mattress. He decided to keep this find a secret from the others. Confident he had his share, Robert began to work his way back towards his companions in crime. A small hip-flask went into his pocket, along with a capped pocket watch and a pair of the finest ladies' gloves.

Coming nearer to the dining room, Robert was disturbed to hear the devil of a racket coming from where he'd left the other two. His first impression was they had been discovered and a fight was taking place. Then, he realised, it was mere drunken carousing on their part. They had filled a number of the fine glasses from the butler's pantry and proceeded to drink from them, smashing them as they were emptied.

Robert was terrified that the noise they were making would give them away, but the street outside was empty. More cautious than they, he felt the need to remonstrate with them.

"Give it up will you. The Constables'll be here in force today."

"They'll be up the Fair, after pickpockets." Pikey grinned, revealing a mouth of brown teeth. "We're just letting them rich bastards know what we think of them."

As Harry Thurlow threw down another fine twisted-stem glass

so it shattered in the grate, Pikey picked up a large shard and gauged a primitive fish shape in the polished wood of the dining table. He roared with laughter as he did so.

Robert could see there was no reasoning with them. They had practically forgotten their original purpose and seemed set on wreaking as much havoc as possible.

"I 'in't waiting to get caught like you - I'm scarpering whiles I can." He meant it, and checking the road was still clear at the front, left the way he had come, determined to quit Stowmarket by any route that would avoid his being seen in that part of town.

He probably wasn't to know, but Takers Lane, to the South of the town was notorious. It was known locally as the haunt of footpads and the like, but as he made good his escape, to anyone observing, here was just a pauper in a hurry, not worth the bother of threatening. If they'd known the contents of those threadbare pockets, they might have thought otherwise.

The carelessness of the two thieves he had left behind was unforgivable, but suffice it to say, the drink gave them a feeling of invulnerability that, as it happened, was totally misplaced.

John King had indeed taken his whole family to the Fair. Even the servants had been granted the afternoon off, though two were to go with the family to supervise the children and help with old Mrs. King, his invalid mother.

The old lady had begun to feel the cold, and a young girl called Naomi had been sent back for a warmer shawl. Hearing such goings-on inside, she had hurried back to John King, who, together with two constables and two of his employees (who just happened to be around at the time) made haste to catch the thieves before they could escape.

It was a short but violent confrontation. Pikey attempted to use a bottle as a weapon, but John King carried a lead-loaded walking stick, which was more than a match for the staggering thief. The blow that laid him low was one Pikey was unlikely to recover from. Harry went quite quietly after that.

He faced a bitterly cold night in the town lock-up, just off the market square, before being escorted by coach to Bury Gaol the next morning. At the time, there was a certain honour among these thieves, and Harry saw no reason to let the authorities know there had been a third member of the gang.

By all accounts, Pikey was dead, or close to it. They'd broken in, done a bit of damage, but at least the two of them hadn't pocketed much at the time of their arrest. Harry felt that as a first-timer he'd probably get a year's hard labour and by the time of the Assize in March, he'd have served a quarter of that already.

What Harry wasn't to know was that John King had made a list of what was missing and come up with a value in excess of forty pounds. The mystery was where it had all gone - presumably, the constables believed, the two thieves had taken away the valuables before returning to drink themselves stupid and wreck the house.

On March 17th at the Spring Assize, Henry Edward Thurlow was charged with Grand Larceny, a charge which, if proved, carried the death penalty.

By the time Robert had forded the river and climbed the hill to Stowupland with soaking feet and a fearful hunger in his belly, he was shivering uncontrollably from a mixture of fear and the now bitter cold.

It was clear he could not expect to make it all the way home that night, so spotting an isolated uninhabited cottage, Robert stopped. The sovereigns in his pocket were too much of a give-away to use at any inn or hostelry. He had practically nothing left of his own money. He searched the hovel for a sheltered corner, but there was little to give him cause for cheer.

Windows and shutters blew free in the wind. Upstairs, a clear night sky was visible through gaping holes in the thatch. He struggled to find dry wood and tinder to make a fire. Awkwardly striking the flint and iron he carried, he coaxed a tiny flame, which he encouraged to consume planks from the door, in what remained of a fireplace, having first set light to the silk scarf. Probably the most expensive piece of tinder he'd ever used. But who wanted the damn thing anyway! Who wanted any of it? Robert had no idea how he was going to sell his ill-gotten gains. If he was found with them, how could he claim they were his by right?

No, there was only one answer. He had to hide them - hide them so they wouldn't be found for a very long time.

Still cold, and tired and hungry, but encouraged by what he somehow sensed had been a narrow escape, Robert lifted some of the tiles under the old brick oven beside the fireplace. Then, using John King's best silver serving spoon, he began to dig until he had a cavity large enough to comfortably accommodate his haul. Finally, making sure it was all well buried, he replaced the floor tiles. Robert banked up the fire with logs he found in an outhouse and curled up beside the flames, feeling more comfortable than he had done for some time.

When Robert didn't arrive home by first light the next morning, Anne wasn't particularly concerned. There had been plenty of nights like this and, like as not, he'd probably canter in halfway through the day with a grin across his face and a rabbit for the pot. At least with Robert, there didn't seem to be a shortage of food. Who it actually belonged to wasn't something he cared to discuss, but with Elizabeth and little Annie to feed, she didn't tend to worry, other than to warn him to be careful.

However, when she did venture out with the children to call on her mother, she met Martha Tye at the end of the lane. Martha was already in full flow delivering the latest news to anyone who cared to hear. She had quite a crowd around her.

"...The Rector and his wife... went to the fair at Stowmarket... yesterday morning... stayed with his brother overnight... came back early on account of a baptism this afternoon... dreadful goings on... robbery, housebreaking - shocking, Mrs. Close said... That Harry Thurlow, thrown into gaol - always said he was no good - mind you, he's lucky compared with the one as was with him. Knocked senseless he was... dead they said... no more than he deserved."

Anne's blood ran cold. She wanted to ask more but couldn't bring herself to face the wall of accusing looks. Already some had turned in her direction, putting two and two together. They'd all seen Robert and Harry about the village. 'Thick as thieves,' they'd be thinking. Anne half ran, half staggered towards her parents' house carrying little Annie and dragging Elizabeth. She collapsed in tears in her mother's kitchen.

It was some time before the sob-speech became speech-sob and Mary Stannard could understand what her daughter was trying to say.

"I didn't want him... to go... but he reckoned they'd soon be back and... not to... fret after him." Even then, the words were punctuated by the distress in her voice.

Mary tried to sound hopeful, though on the strength of the information, she had to conclude it really did sound as if Robert's luck had run out.

Ever practical, Mary hadn't time for moping over what might or mightn't be. "I'll look after the little 'uns. You get yourself on home. You don't know it's him what's dead. And if he do be all right, then you know as well as I do he'll be cold and wanting his meal like men do."

There was no arguing with her, and anyway Anne had always been the dutiful daughter. Carefully avoiding having to speak to anyone, she headed back, feet crunching on the frosty grass of the track leading to their cottage.

And there he was. Slumped in the chair beside the fire, but what a change. He shivered and clung to her and wept in a way she'd never seen. Then he told her - the whole story; nothing left out. Everything!

Well, nearly everything! The removal and subsequent burial of the loot remained his secret. Perhaps he was attempting to protect Anne from any repercussions; maybe it was his own little something for a rainy day. But that remained Robert's secret. He swore blind he was telling Anne the whole story, and she in her innocence, believed him. Except of course, it wasn't the whole story. How could he possibly have known what had happened after he had left John King's house? Was it true what Anne had heard. And if so, would Robert's part in the robbery be revealed?

Languishing in Bury gaol, awaiting the March Assize, Harry Thurlow had nothing to gain by implicating Robert. Still oblivious to the value placed on the stolen items, he preferred to be seen as a petty house thief. The local Constables were pleased at their success, and believed that Pikey's demise might serve to deter others tempted to break the law in their town. John King, probably one of only a few in the district to have insured his house contents against theft, was surprised about the missing items but not unduly concerned about their loss. He assumed the two thieves must have taken one lot of loot from the house before returning to vandalise the place out of jealousy or spite.

Two months later when Harry tried to explain there had been another accomplice, no-one was very ready to believe him, and still trusting in his receiving a lesser sentence, elected to offer a plea of guilty. The Judge, having read the details before him, advised the prisoner in the dock that this was a very serious charge and it would not be in any way to his advantage to persist with such a plea. Confused by the legal language and formality of the court, when the indictment was read again, Harry stuck with his plea of guilty.

Assize week in Bury St. Edmunds was a grand affair. Those of the landed gentry who possessed town houses brought family and a retinue of servants. As well as attending the Court, there were balls, entertainments and a week of social inter-action, climaxing with a firework display among the Abbey ruins.

John King, still wary of leaving his Stowmarket home unattended, did however arrange accommodation for his family and himself to enjoy the festivities. King was against the idea of his wife attending the court. He felt she and the children should not be exposed to the language and the behaviour of the prisoners and some of their more vocal supporters.

In the case of Harry Thurlow, there were no facts to reveal other than the extent of the crime to which he had pleaded guilty and to enable Mr. Prendergast, Thurlow's counsel, to call witnesses who might attest to his good character. The learned Judge having complied, a church warden from Mendlesham and a local farmer who had once employed him attempted to testify as to his honesty and good nature. But ten weeks of gaol had knocked the charm and swagger from the man in the dock, and it was a sorry figure who stood there. He failed to match the picture of 'hail fellow well met' that they described and their attempts were always going to fall on deaf ears.

The Judge, in his most solemn voice, then asked the prisoner why sentence of death should not be passed upon him. Harry, for the first time realising the situation he was in, began to yell out, "Get Saunders, he'll tell you where all the stuff is - he took it, not me." Then he dropped to his knees and pleaded with the Judge to be as merciful as he could.

"I have," proceeded the Judge, "appraised you of the awful circumstances in which you find yourself. You brought this upon yourself by entering the house of an honest business man, stealing items to the value of over forty pounds."

"That's as false as God is true!" yelled Harry.

"...before returning to pursue violent outrage and drunken depredation upon the property of John King of Stowmarket. It is, therefore my duty to pass the dreadful sentence of the law upon you, leaving you not a hope of mercy."

"Come off it, your Lordship, I 'in't that stupid. I never took all that - it must be Saunders - get him - he's the one what done it while Pikey and me got a bit drunk."

The Judge continued as if he had heard it all before.

"Therefore, after two Sabbaths have intervened, you will be led to an ignominious death and be ushered into the presence of the Almighty. Lose no time in false hopes, I implore you; seek out the advice of a Minister of our Holy religion and through mercy implore the forgiveness of the Creator."

"Mercy - mercy - you call this mercy?"

The remainder of the Judge's words were spoken to the accompaniment of screams of protestation from Harry Thurlow.

"The sentence I pass upon you is that you should be taken ("No your Lordship!") ...to the place from whence you came ("Please, your Lordship!") ...and from thence to the place of

30

execution, ("It was Saunders - Robbie Saunders, not me - ask anyone!") ...and there to be hung by the neck until you are dead, and may the Lord have mercy on your soul."

As the correspondent for the Bury Post wrote at the time, 'Henry Edward Thurlow was much affected by the sentence and had to be carried from the court.'

In actual fact, he didn't hang. Along with three others, before the two Sabbaths had elapsed, his sentence was commuted to one of seven years transportation. He sailed to New South Wales at the end of the year. He didn't come back.

Robert and Anne heard by way of mouth the events of the County Assize. Later, the Curate read them the newspaper account as they called to discuss the baptism of the new addition to their family, another daughter, named Mary in memory of the daughter who had died, but in hope of better luck this time. Mary seemed strong and full of life, but you never could tell.

Two days after the baptism, the Master at Wetheringsett Manor called for Robert to see him immediately. Robert waited in the unheated room that served as an office. The interview was brief and one-sided.

"It has come to my attention that the man Thurlow in Bury Gaol has been seen a good deal in your company, and even that you may know something about the robbery in Stowmarket."
Robert would have liked to protest his innocence, but the Master was in no mood for interruptions.

"At this moment the Parish Constable is searching your house for the missing stolen items. After that, whether he finds anything or not, you will be asked to vacate the property within twenty-four hours. Your tenure in this parish depends upon your continued employment here. This has now been revoked. The parish of Wetheringsett will not welcome any request for further settlement here."

Then, as if doing him a favour, though both knew this was not the case, "... a horse and cart will convey your belongings to the boundary of another parish, tomorrow afternoon. Good day!"

Chapter 4

March 1790

It had been the best part of three years since Anne had seen Sarah Diggins. She felt guilty: for a short time, though their backgrounds were very different, their friendship had been a precious thing to both of them. In Anne's defence, she had been deeply upset by the death of the child and for a long while couldn't bear so much as to think about her days at The Lodge. As time had worked its healing effect, it had been increasingly difficult to get away from the home she had made in Wetheringsett, just five miles to the East. She now had three children and a husband who certainly couldn't be trusted to be left alone to look after them. Her parents were getting older... excuses, excuses, they all seemed so feeble when she tried to justify her long absence. It was made doubly worse as she was now about to ask a favour, almost as soon as she'd walked in the door.

Sarah, who looked much the same - all of her 36 years (had she ever looked young?) - was greatly cheered to see Anne. It was a lonely existence out there a mile from the centre of the village; as far, at least, from any other large house. The winter had been wet, rendering the roads around The Lodge impassable for weeks on end. If Sarah was harbouring a grudge over Anne's long absence, it wasn't evident. Anne felt slightly cheered. She hadn't wanted to use past friendship to put a roof over their heads, but as Robert had pointed out, it seemed the only option.

"So you've another little girl now," Sarah commented on hearing the news. "And called Mary, just like the little one that...." She didn't like to say the word 'died' and looked into Anne's face to see if she mightn't have said something to upset her, but it was all right. Nevertheless a change of topic wouldn't be a bad idea.

"It's so good to see you. After all this time, I thought you'd forgotten us in this dreadful place."

"Is it that dreadful," laughed Anne. "I always thought it were a happy place, really."

"It's changed." Sarah felt the need to make her fully conversant with the way of things. She continued... "The Steward is old and frail. My brother is now the Bailiff and runs the farm. He's a good man, but he's hard on his workers. He doesn't like me having friends among our employees." This wasn't the kind of news Anne wanted to hear, but she'd let Sarah have her say, then see what could be done.

"He is treasurer to the Overseers, and his son, Will Junior, is deputy to the Parish Constable. They only see the worst side of people. They don't remember what it's like to be poor. They sup tea with the Reverend Pretyman or shoot with the Tyrells. There's a hardness of heart about the place. My aunt, old Mrs. Diggins - you'll remember her - she can't move about too well any more so they want her to leave, and for me to take her place."

"But she 'in't old - she can't have got that bad in three years." Anne was appalled. She remembered Mrs. Diggins as the highly respected housekeeper who had made the big house run like clockwork.

"Of course what my brother really wants is The Lodge. And mark my words, he'll be in there soon enough." Sarah sipped her tea whilst Anne drank hers more vigorously, unused to such subtle richness of flavour.

"Here's me going on about my life and I've not asked a word about you and that husband of yours."

If ever a time was right this was it.

"That's really what I come to see you about. You see, we're homeless. They've sent us back. Mr. Hayward at the Manor heard as how Robert had been seen with this man what went to gaol. They turned up with a search warrant - searched our cottage - di'n't find nothing - but they said we had to go anyway - straight away. Put us on a cart, and dropped us at the parish boundary, where we was out of their hair, so to speak."

If Sarah was offended by her former-friend's reappearance, cap in hand, it was not obvious. Far from it; the concern she showed made Anne feel quite humble.

"You mean, they put you and three children on a cart with nowhere to go? Where are your family now?"

"Not too many minutes away. They put us down by Boundary Farm. Robert's sheltering in a barn with the children, and the furniture."

"With a baby, in this weather! We must get you here without further ado."

Sarah, ever the one to organise people, was in her element.

"You know where to find Nehemiah - tell him to harness a pair of horses to the hay wagon and take you down Potter's Lane to fetch your family and your belongings. I'll speak to William. With the Easter hiring coming up, I'm sure we must have a cottage spare, and a position to go with it."

Sarah sounded so confident, Anne found her spirits raised in a way that she would not have believed just twenty four hours earlier. She had worried when the Constable had arrived at her door demanding to search the place. There were items in the house she had been unsure about herself, but the Constable seemed to be clear precisely what he was looking for. He was half-annoyed, half-apologetic when he failed to uncover any of the goods on his list. Then, just when she had been congratulating herself on having weathered the storm, Robert had come home to drop yet another bombshell. There had been no hope of a change of mind. No, this decision had come directly from George Hayward himself. He was a magistrate, Manager of Wetheringsett Manor, and when he made up his mind, it stayed made up.

So that left a return to Cotton Lodge, not something Anne and Robert would have chosen. Wages were less, tenements poorly maintained and in all probability, Robert's reputation would have gone before him. This did appear to be the case as the hay-cart and its passengers, their goods and chattels drew up beside the moat that ran around The Lodge. They could hear William Diggins across the yard.

"You promised them? You promised them! Just who is Bailiff around here? We have enough problems of our own without taking charge of those who by rights should now be the responsibility of another parish!"

Sarah, it appeared, could give as good as she got when faced with her brother's wrath.

"You have no cause for concern! Anne was one of the best housemaids we've ever had. Robert has been builder, ostler, shepherd, and gardener at farms all round the district. Most of the land-owners round here know him."

"Only because he helps himself to their pheasants. I have enough lazy lay-abouts on this farm without employing another."

"So who will you hire? It's nearly Easter. You sent two this winter to the poor-house because they were too old or too sick to work the way you demand. You tell me - who's going to come out here for low wages, the tumbledown shacks you call cottages and a Bailiff that treats his labourers like slaves?"

She had a point and he knew it. A number in the parish had moved away North to the mills and factories where at least the work was regular and there were jobs for the whole family.

"Well, all right - they can have the cottage beside Low Meadow." It wasn't much of an offer and he knew it.

"But that place is a ruin, there's no roadway to it. They've got a new baby - for heaven's sake."

"It's all I've got to offer right now. If he's that much of a builder, he'll put it to rights. She can help you in the house and he can report to Jacob at the stables in the morning."

Sarah was not by nature a demonstrative woman, but if she had been, she would have hugged her brother at that moment. It was true, the cottage he described was a long way from fit for human habitation, but the summer would see it put to rights and what was more, it was near at hand. Sarah would have her friend back with her.

As Anne remembered it, the cottage was a bit run-down. It stood at the end of what had once been a green lane that had become at first overgrown through lack of use, then been put to pasture as it was well fenced both sides. This had rendered any footpath that had once been there unusable for months of the year.

35

When she finally made her way across the meadows to what was little more than a shack, she felt like weeping. Close on her heels, Robert seemed to sense her despair. However, he was more confident.

"Don't you worry 'bout that gel. That 'in't as bad as that look and there'll be plenty around to help us make it right."

She almost believed him. With Mary in her arms, wet and hungry and becoming ever more fractious, Anne trudged back up Low Meadow, with its mud and its sheep dung, wishing she had never left Wetheringsett. Robert meanwhile was pointing things out to Elizabeth and little Annie who was almost asleep in his arms.

"You see that bit a wood there? Well there's enough to finish the roof timbers and I know a man as'll mend the thatch. Afore you know it we'll have us a house."

Anne could hear Lizzie shrieking with delight about how she wanted to help her father build a house. But as far as she was concerned it had been a mistake to come back. She knew it wasn't fair but she couldn't help but feel bitter towards Sarah Diggins who had promised so much, only to leave them with the sour taste of disappointment.

As she came back into the farmyard, all the bitterness welled up inside her.

"Is that it?" she sobbed. "Is that what our friendship is worth - a heap of clay lump in the corner of a waterlogged field?" She sobbed herself into Sarah's arms, the squalling baby almost suffocated between them.

William Diggins was still there, but whether he had had second thoughts or had suffered the barbs of his sister's tongue, a change had come over him.

"Of course you can't move in yet. You can have one of the cottages up opposite Hayes Corner. But it's only temporary while your man gets Meadow Cottage fixed."

William took himself off, embarrassed by the enforced change of mind.

Later that evening, Sarah was their first visitor. By this time their few pieces of furniture were in place; a fire was burning in the hearth. They had found logs and even a little coal in an outhouse. Sarah brought a basket of food, guessing they would be short. Anne felt for the first time as if she had come home.

Past their door ran the drover's track that led from Cotton to Mendlesham Green, and Robert had already gone in search of male company at the Green Man. Give him his due, he had done his bit with unpacking and settling the children, making the place weatherproof and getting the fire going. Unfortunately, Anne reflected, he was probably spending the little money they had and it would be at least another week before there would be any more.

Sarah stayed a couple of hours and in that time it became clear to Anne just how lonely and desperate she had become. There seemed little chance of her aspiring to the very things Anne herself had - a husband and children. For as she said, at her age, how was she to meet anyone?

It was a mile and a half to the Green Man and at least the same distance back. Surprisingly, on this occasion, even after a few jugs of ale, Robert's head was as clear as the evening sky long before he was back to Hayes Corner. The items he had buried beneath the floor of the tumbledown shack near Stowupland were still troubling him. It wasn't so much that he felt he should own up to his part in the robbery. That hadn't even crossed his mind. He had a family to support, and anyway, putting himself in the dock was unlikely to get Harry Thurlow a reprieve. No - it was the lure of the loot that was the problem. What was the point of working yourself to death when you knew where to lay your hands on more money than you could earn in a year? On the other hand, evading capture had been a near run thing and he wasn't confident in his ability to pass on the goods without attracting the wrong sort of attention.

At that point, as he strode home in the moonlight, Robert made a decision. He would leave the sovereigns, the pocket pistol, the gold hat-pin, the hip flask and the pocket watch where they were. That house had lain empty for long enough and would probably stay that way. What was hidden beneath its floor would be his secret alone. He wouldn't even tell Anne. And only if desperation drove him to it would he go back for the money. Deciding to do nothing about it gave him a good feeling, as though he was closing a door on that chapter of his life. It also gave him a certain comfort to realise that unlike most of his kind, he was a man of means and that if the worst came to the worst, he could still look after his family.

* * * * * * * * * * * * * *

That Summer, after working every evening for weeks well into the hours of darkness, Robert and Anne and their three children moved into the cottage at the corner of Low Meadow. It looked across the lea toward the back of The Lodge. Throughout the light night months, Sarah Diggins was a frequent visitor. Anne found a calm contentment in the place, and even after a winter's isolation, was well pleased with it. She became pregnant again that following Summer and was astonished to discover how attentive and reliable Robert had become. He still enjoyed a little night-adventuring but as far as most labourers were concerned, poaching wasn't really the same as theft - that was why it had a different name. Like scrumping apples as children, from the master's orchard, or the wives gleaning after the beans had been harvested, poaching was seen as a necessary and inevitable pursuit and certainly saw them through the hard times when food was scarce. Wages were low and you had to fill the pot with something.

The farmers complained their profits were down and they couldn't afford to pay more. Food prices had slumped and as well as tithes, taxes were being imposed to pay for the war everyone said there was to be with France. For all that, Robert noticed the Steward and Mr. Diggins didn't go short, especially when entertaining their grand friends. Anne, working once more in the big house was often involved in preparing these feasts, and would bring home all kinds of exotic left-overs, much of which Robert and the children would turn their noses up at.

"Rich buggers' food," Robert disparagingly would say at carcass of snipe or swan's wing.

He preferred the fare he brought in from the surrounding countryside. Such as the moorhen's eggs he'd pick from a watery

38

nest with a spoon tied to a stick and carried under his cap until it was time to come home. Then there were pigeons - if you found sitting birds, you could knock them out of a bush before they saw you. There were even sparrows that Robert taught Lizzie to trap from their nest burrows in the hay-ricks using a lamp and a net. They didn't produce a lot of meat, but they made fine gravy.

As a result, the family survived, and in the spring of 1792, Anne gave birth to another healthy daughter. She called her Sarah, and when she was baptised some time later, Sarah Diggins became the child's Godmother.

Chapter 5

Autumn 1794

The old Steward died in October. For some time he had been failing and had taken to living in one downstairs room. This had irritated William Diggins who had long felt the big house should be his, and he wasted no time moving his wife and himself in. Sarah came home from a trip to Eye market to discover she was the sole living inhabitant of the Corner House, though the body of the Steward was laid out in the parlour.

Anne, who had been caring for the old man throughout the final weeks, was hard hit. Worse news was to come. Old Mrs. Diggins, the housekeeper, sensing this was no longer the place for the ageing and the rheumatic, accepted her son's offer to go and live out her declining years with him.

The Steward's funeral was conducted with all the appropriate ceremony. There was even talk of the Heighams paying for a head-stone. Reverend Pretyman came from his retirement to eulogise over the man so many had respected. There was, in his sermon, just a hint of what many others were inwardly thinking; things might be very different from now on.

They were. First rents went up, then piece-work rates plummeted. Even in households where both husband and wife were working, the money earned wouldn't put bread on the table. Anne's health had not always been good and it affected the amount she was able to bring to the family budget. Elizabeth, at eleven years of age, was expected to be full-time child minder to the other children, something she did competently and without complaint. It was a training that would stand her in good stead throughout her life.

Following a miscarriage earlier in the spring, Anne's parents had come to care for her. They saw Meadow Cottage for the first time and weren't impressed.

"No wonder you're always poorly, with the state of this place.

40

Even at dry times like this you can smell the damp," John Stannard complained.

"Robert's done his best to make it cosy." Anne protested.

"Oh I'm not moaning about him on this occasion," chuntered her father. "It's your employers who should know better than to make you live here. Why the house was even built here I don't understand. You only need to look at the rushes growing in this corner of the meadow to know it's wet two thirds of the year."

They meant well, but having her parents there hadn't been much help, really. They were getting on in years and there were so many things it was easier to do herself, except she'd had two more to feed, to wash and clean for. Cruel though it sounded, she'd been glad to send them back to Wetheringsett.

"I could always have a word with the new Rector," suggested Mary Stannard, Anne's mother. She still called Thomas Methwold the new Rector, even though he'd been there for three years.

"He might find you a position in service. He's well in with the Haywards at Thorndon."

"Oh mum, you know they won't take a married woman with children."

Of course they wouldn't. There was no shortage of young girls anxious to leave their family hovels to work for the landed gentry as under-maids, in spite of long hours and poor money.

"Well if you won't, at least let us look for a place for Lizzie. She can't spend her whole life looking after her sisters, however well she does it."

They meant well of course, but they knew Lizzie was still too young. But it wouldn't be long before she wasn't, and any money she might send home would be so useful.

The day they buried the Steward, the whole farm stopped working. Even those who looked after the livestock arranged their day to enable them to walk the mile or more to Cotton Church, following the cart that carried the coffin. It was quite a coffin. George Orsbourn made it. He said it was the best one he'd ever built - intended to keep it for himself, but Heigham had offered a

41

price he couldn't refuse, so there it was on the cart, heading for Cotton church.

There wasn't much of a wake. Harvest celebrations had been only a few days earlier and William Diggins had decided two supplies of food and drink in a week were more than could be expected of him. As a result, few people hung about, and by late afternoon, most of the labourers had been ushered back to work while it was still light.

"I don't know why I feel so tired," said Anne to Sarah as they set about clearing up in the large kitchen that dominated the Corner House.

"You're not pregnant again are you?" asked Sarah.

"Good Lord, no! Though it would be no surprise to me if I was. Robert only has to look at me and I end up with child."

"You would tell me if you were… I wouldn't mind."
Anne knew what Sarah meant. She had just turned forty and was prone to tears at the thought of someone else's pregnancy.

"The trouble is he want a boy. Really bad. Oh he say he don't mind, but I know he do."

Anne reflected on her five daughters, one dead, four living, and her two miscarriages since little Sarah's birth.

"I reckon I can't carry boys; that's why I keep losin' 'em. I just wish I could birth him a son so he could larn the boy how to snare a rabbit afore he be too old to do it himself."

As they were talking, they were aware of an elegantly dressed man standing in the open doorway. Possibly in his late thirties, and with only a trace of a Suffolk accent, he asked, "Could one of you please direct me to Mr. William Diggins?" Then, when they both continued to look slightly surprised, he said, "I'm John Hart, the new Under-Steward."

The Heigham family had acted fast. They had not attended the funeral. They had not been in the county for the best part of six months, but they were kept abreast of matters by mail, and believed in moving their Stewards and estate managers around. The lands they held in and around Cotton were at a distance from the three

42

family seats that occupied most of their attention. Despite that, the ambitiousness of William Diggins had not gone unnoticed. He had ably run The Lodge and its acreage for a number of years as the old Steward had been failing in health. There was clearly no need to send him an Under-Steward now. So, what had been their intention?

If the move had been designed to irritate William, it certainly worked. The first problem was where John Hart would live. Having finally acquired the big house, Diggins wasn't prepared to vacate even a part of it. That left the Corner House, the fragment of the medieval manor house that dated back two centuries before The Lodge. Sarah could hardly share the old house with him, so it was with a measure of bad grace that William Diggins found room for his sister in The Lodge.

Feeling thoroughly unwelcome, Sarah took to visiting Anne more often. She rarely arrived empty-handed, aware of the smell of poverty that pervaded the place.

Towards the end of November, she brought a few eggs. The hens were going off the lay, and these at least would be a treat for the family who had begun to take on the undernourished look of most of her brother's labourers.

"How do you find the new Under-Steward, then?" Anne asked.

She had wondered, along with others on the farm if he mightn't prove a husband for Sarah. But there seemed to be little mutual attraction. They rarely made contact, except to share a pew in church on Sunday. And it was generally assumed John Hart had been sent to learn the running of a farm in anticipation of promotion to another part of the Heigham estate.

"Oh he's a fine gentleman, so it seems. The men and women round the farm like him well enough. Which isn't always the case with my brother..." Afraid this sounded a little disloyal she added, "...but it's not so easy to be popular when you're the master." They both knew this wasn't necessarily true, but left it at that.

On this occasion, Sarah had come for a purpose. She was used to speaking her mind and you didn't have to beat around the bush with Anne.

"Are things really as bad as they look?" she asked.

"Oh thass a bit hard at the moment, but it'll pick up," said Anne, ever hopeful.

"I mean, are you getting enough to eat? - you and the children."

"Look what Robert brought in yesterday." Anne held up the scrawny-looking chicken she had been preparing for the pot.

"Yes, but whose is it?" Sarah knew Robert of old.

"Best not to ask - anyway, you're right I s'pose. It's the only real meat we've had this week."

"I thought so," said Sarah. "Have you considered going to the Parish for poor relief?"

"Robbie says we can't - Mr. Diggins - your brother - would be whully cross - it'd be like saying to the world he pay low wages."

"But he does pay low wages - so low you can't live on them - for heavens sake - others are asking and getting it. Sam Sore had five shillings when Ambrose Canler was Overseer."

"I di'n't know that," said Anne, amazed. "That'd feed our family for weeks and buy Lizzie a coat and put coals on the fire…"

"Exactly! You tell Robert that the Parish has money - I know. I've seen the accounts from when William's brought the books home. They gave away two hundred pounds to the needy last year - and if anyone's needy it's the folk who work on this farm."

Anne, who to tell the truth had been worried sick, was greatly encouraged and determined that when Robert next appeared home, she would broach the subject with him. That was the next problem. When would he be home? Often as not he'd arrive home an hour or so after dark for his meal, then disappear with Wimble Blomfield. Once or twice he'd told her he was going back to work, but as there was no night work at that time of year, she knew it was a lie. That troubled her more than anything. He may have been unreliable, but he usually told her the truth.

Wimble, whose proper name was probably William, though no-one could be very sure, worked as a labourer at the mill. He'd pretend he was an apprentice miller, but as Robert observed, in his forties he was taking a mighty long time to learn what to do. In reality, Wimble Blomfield humped sacks, weighed the grain and swept the floors, as a result of which he was usually good for a pocket of flour every now and then.

As regards his nickname, it was original, but far from unusual. Half of the village, men especially, were known by nicknames to such an extent that their birth names were long forgotten. There was Toy Finbow, Chaffy Mullinger, Symbol Gaffer and Thursday Steggal. Everyone assumed Dandy Vinson was so named because he'd been born up at Dandy Corner but most of the nicknames had been attached for no obvious reason other than for identification purposes, as most of the men in the village had been baptised John, William or George.

Wimble Blomfield had one other thing to recommend him, besides the odd present of flour or grain. He brewed his own beer from barley spirited away from the mill. When it was warm enough he'd taken to malting quantities of it in an old shed behind his house. As a result, there was a never-ending supply of home-brew. Robert, in return, would take Wimble for night excursions in search of anything that might make a meal or turn a quick profit. The hen bound for Anne's cooking pot had been the fruit of such an expedition. She had heard the two men boasting about it as they warmed themselves up by the remains of the fire.

"D'you reckon Mr. 'high and mighty' Frere will miss that one?" Wimble had asked.

"Not a chance," Robert had replied. "They got so many birds running about Finningham, they 'un't miss a poor skinny little thing like that."

Anne hoped it was true. Poultry theft was a major issue. It had become so common that groups of landowners had formed protection groups, determined to put a stop to it. Also, sentences in court had increased, which was no surprise. If Robert and Wimble were caught, the magistrate they'd probably face would be the Right Honourable John Frere himself.

If Anne had but known it, she might have been more worried to observe Robert's reaction to something entirely different. Most nights it had been late when either man had entered the house of the other. Usually one would knock and await his friend; they would

45

sup together after the night's work was done. Thieving and poaching meant a lot of walking; best not to dirty your own doorstep. It was safest to put a couple of parish boundaries between your home and your crime.

However, Wimble was still eating when Robert knocked so he called him in.

"Sit you down while I finish my broth. I'll get one of the youngsters to pour you something."

Then, he called, presumably to a child fetching something from the indoor store. "Vir, bring Robbie a mug of ale - he look like he need it."

Quite suddenly, to Robert's amazement, there stepped into the kitchen quite the most beautiful girl he had ever seen.

"I don't think you've met my daughter, Virtue. Say hello to Mr. Saunders, Vir, where's your manners?"

Predictably she giggled, then muttered something before returning to her place at the table. It was funny, it had never dawned on Robert that Wimble would have a child of that age - she must have been sixteen or seventeen. But thinking about it, Wimble had to be forty-five, a good ten years older than Robert, so why not?

Trying not to stare at the child, (though it was hard to think of her as a child) Robert entered into the conversation. For the most part it was about gleaning. For centuries it had been acknowledged as a well-accepted perk of the poor, gathering the remains left behind after a crop was harvested. The practice had traditionally run right through to late autumn, when the discarded tops of root vegetables were collected up for the little goodness they provided. Now even this was being prohibited by many of the farmers. They claimed they were losing valuable animal fodder, though the labourers had seen enough left to rot in the fields to wonder why this most basic of rights was being denied them.

"Over at Wickham, they took them women to court," said Robert. "And the magistrate, he say they'd lock'em up if they did it again. How's a family s'posed to survive, thass what I want to know."

"Thass because them rich so and so's set all the laws. Thass why we need to part 'em from the odd bit o' poultry - share it out a bit. Work to our laws, thass what I say."

Robert looked across at Virtue and realised she was playing the same game as he was - looking at him, then looking away as he looked at her. Her face was flushed and her dark hair and eyes shone in the lamplight.

"Just so long as you don't get caught," warned Hannah, Wimble's wife.

Robert found himself wondering however this unlikely pair had produced such a beautiful child. Hannah was homely, but hardly likely to have ever looked much different; a bit like Anne in a way. Pleasant enough, but you couldn't imagine her, even in her prime, looking like Virtue. The other younger ones round the table - they seemed to belong; chubby rosy-cheeked, windswept faces, hair in tangles and clothes that had seen better days. Sure enough, Virtue looked as out of place as those sovereigns had seemed in Robert's hands.

"I hate to drag your man away from you, but I think we ought to be abroad," Robert said.

It was strange how assertive he was now. After the experience with Harry Thurlow, he now felt far safer if he was the one making the decisions. With Wimble it was easy; you told him what to do and he'd do it. Gulping down the last couple of spoonfuls, he grabbed his coat and boots and made for the back door.

Robert gave an unnecessary backward glance at the tableau round the table. He uttered a thank-you, noticing Virtue drop her gaze at the instant he looked in her direction.
Maybe she was just shy, but.... it did make you wonder.

Outside and along the lane, they made off through Bacton. At the far end of the village was a beer-house known as the Duck's Eye. Little more than a front room for drinking, it only opened as and when was required. At shearing time, it did good business, in spite of its isolated position. By late November, it took a good deal of knocking and shouting to persuade old Eli Hammond to open at all.

By this time and with a further jug of ale to encourage them, the main purpose of the evening was unravelling.

"They do say, down at Old Bells Farm, there's ducks so tame, you can pick 'em up and carry 'em home," said Robert.

"If it's that easy bo', why's no other bugger doing it?"
Good point.

"Thass cos they got dawgs."

"Well I 'in't sticking about there to get my arse bit off," said Wimble.

"I already thought of that," said Robert. "I got the drumsticks off that old hen in my pocket; should shut 'em up long enough to get us away."

It was unbelievably dark as they trudged through the knee-deep mud of Boys Lane. Now and again, one or other of them would swear as he found a deeper, damper spot.

"Hope it's worth it." Wimble didn't sound convinced.

"Don't you worry 'bout that bo' - I'll have that old duck and wrung its neck afore it get to cluck."
Wimble didn't like to point out that ducks didn't cluck. He just plodded on regardless, hoping the total number of dogs wouldn't exceed the number of titbits in Robert's pocket.

They heard the dogs before they saw them. Barely had Robert put his hand in his pocket before he heard something else too: the crunch of feet on gravel. Briefly and just at the wrong moment, a half-moon sailed out from behind a cloud and the silhouette of a farmer with his gun became as visible to them as their own outlines proved a target to him.

"Come you here," he yelled. "I'll have you!"

They didn't wait to find out if he was serious. The pair of them ran-squelched back up the lane with the dogs at their heels. That in fact was their saving grace. The farmer, for all his anger at yet another pair of midnight raiders, was reluctant to fire for fear of hitting his dogs.

If this should have served as a warning to the pair, it didn't. By the time they had reached the top of the lane, mud-splattered and out of breath, they were already inclined to view it as just an unfortunate mishap.

"Who told, you 'bout that place and them ducks?" asked Wimble.

"Someone down the Cock the other night were saying they'd had three or four on'em."

"Well thass why he were out there waiting for us, wun't it?"
For once, Wimble was talking sense. Before they'd walked back through Bacton, they'd determined they would listen less to the words of others and think more for themselves. As to the events of the previous two hours, they had almost convinced themselves they were the heroes of the hour and had only come home empty-handed through the utmost bad luck.

They reached Wimble's house first and Robert, who was shivering by now, was grateful for the chance to dry off before heading home. There was still a good fire in the hearth. Wimble removed his wet and mud-stained outer garments, before stepping outside for the privy. Robert was struggling to unlace his boots with frozen fingers when he became aware of someone else in the room.

"Let me help you." It was Virtue. She had a coat on, over loosely buttoned undergarments. If she was aware of the effect she was having on him, she didn't show it.

"Thanks," he shivered. "Thass whully cold tonight."
Wimble on returning, was surprised to see his daughter up.

"I heard you come in," she said, "and I couldn't get back to sleep." He seemed satisfied with that explanation, but sent her back to bed. Robert was sorry to see her go.

Within ten minutes, Robert was on the road home, feeling somewhat warmed. He almost hurried back to Meadow Cottage, climbing into bed reinvigorated.

"Ooh, warm yew up first afore you cuddle up to me," complained Anne. But he didn't warm up first. He clung close as he had so many nights before, but as he held her, most intimately, he was really in his mind, making love to the little dark beauty that was Virtue Blomfield.

Chapter 6

June 1795

The first time had been the worst. Going cap in hand to the Parish went against the grain. Neither Robert nor Anne had wanted it this way. Their own childhood may have been dogged by poverty, but they had been brought up to believe that accepting poor relief was one step away from sending your children to beg on the streets.

But it hadn't been that bad. What had once been a prop to support only the poorest of families was now a necessity to a fair proportion of the parish. To their surprise, William Diggins didn't seem to mind. Quite the reverse, he took a perverse delight in seeing that what he paid in poor rate was returned four-fold to his own labourers.

That first eight shillings had been so necessary. Owing back rent and without warm clothing for the children for the winter, it had been a lifeline, coming just when Robert's thoughts had turned once more to the hidden sovereigns.

After that, there had been two further payments, and there was the prospect of more now that Anne was expecting again. Desperate to produce a son, Anne was taking things carefully, something that was made easier by Sarah's attentiveness. The previous two miscarriages had come at three months. This time, she had already carried the child for five months and her condition was beginning to show in spite of the loose clothing she wore.

"When's your missus due to farrow down?" asked Wimble.

"Blessed if I know - about Michaelmas, I'd guess," said Robert.

At that moment on a warm Sunday afternoon, he was helping Wimble on his garden. Most of the men in the village relied upon supplying their own family with vegetables till well after Christmas. Robert, out of the corner of his eye was observing

Virtue Blomfield hanging out a line full of washing. Rather than enter service, she helped her mother taking in laundry. In a lot of places, it was frowned upon to wash on a Sunday, but Cotton was neither high church nor did it boast a population of staunch non-conformists. Besides, the Blomfield garden wasn't overlooked.

"Rector'll tick you off for washing on the Sabbath," called Robert.

"That he wun't - thass his sheets I'm hanging out," laughed Virtue. "You'd be surprised what you can larn about folk from their sheets," she said mysteriously.

As she stretched to hang the larger items, her skirt, already too short by half, rose up to show an expanse of leg. Robert couldn't be sure, but he was half convinced she was doing it on purpose. He was hot with hoeing and unbuttoned his shirt. He was certain he saw Virtue look his way.

"Thass whully quiet with the little'uns out the way. Where are they?" Robert asked.

"Missus took 'em to the Sunday School," said Wimble. "She say they'll larn to read and write, maybe."

"What's the point o' tha'? My Anne can write her name but she still sign with a cross when she get her pay. That don't do to get above yarself. They don't like it."

"Look can I leave you to finish those couple 'a rows?" asked Wimble. "I promised Hannah I'd get her some fat to make soap. If I don't, I shan't hear the end on it." Then leaving Robert to his labours, he called, "I'll give you a hand with yours one night this week."

That was the way it worked. Whichever garden they worked on, they tended to do it together. They enjoyed one another's company, and there were plenty of jobs that were better done by two.

There wasn't much left to be completed and Robert had merely to hoe the remaining two rows before returning his tools to the open-fronted tumbledown shed that stood beside the privy. It was a poor excuse for a building, held up more by ivy than any deliberate act of construction. But it served well enough.

"Uh - Mr Saunders, do you think you could help me?"
It was Virtue, struggling with the linen pole, a long forked prong of Ash hacked from a hedgerow.

"Here, let me," said Robert, taking the prop from her hands and deftly placing it to offer up the linen to the breeze.

"Thank you kindly sir," she purred coquettishly. "I expect you'd like some warm water to wash yourself," she continued.
He would normally have waited until he was home, but was in no mood to refuse. He followed her into the kitchen area where a fire burned under the copper, which was full of steaming water.

"Thass only had one lot of washing - it's quite clean."
She ladled a scoopful out and poured it into a bucket. Then, without waiting to ask, she rubbed soap on her hands and, dipping them in the water, began to wash him. She began with his face. With his eyes tightly closed, he could only feel where her hands travelled next. She caressed his neck, his shoulders and under his arms. She stroked his chest and ran her nimble fingers down toward his solar plexus; and she didn't stop there. Loosening his belt, her warm moist hands raised in him a desire that he hadn't known since he was little more than her age.

Like asking for poor relief, the first time was like crossing a bridge. Though the bridge to adultery was every bit as enticing as the bridge to charity and a whole lot more fun. Even the most inexperienced of girls knew from an early age what adults did, given half a chance. There was little privacy when upwards of a dozen might share two bedrooms.

If her parents had intended her Christian name to serve as a model for her behaviour, it was clear Virtue had other ideas. What followed was swift but pleasurable. They didn't get as far as the bedroom. The rest of the heap of unwashed linen served their purpose.

Walking back past St. Andrews, Robert could see groups of children leaving Sunday School in the charge of mothers or siblings. The Blomfields were amongst them. Robert hurried on by, not wishing to look them in the eye.

The guilty feeling lasted all of ten minutes. By that time he was feeling quite 'Jack the lad,' flattered that such a chance should come his way. The dry dusty earth of the Suffolk lanes muffled sound, so he didn't hear the clop of hooves from behind him until the figure on horseback was level with him.

"Are you the one they call Saunders?"

Robert was wary, The mounted figure looked familiar, but he wasn't too sure where he'd heard that voice before. He should have done. It was none other than Nathaniel Mayhew, one of the Overseers to whom he had pleaded poverty. Mayhew, known generally as 'Hum', managed lands in both Cotton and Bacton. He had an idea on his mind.

"They say you can supply things, or if you can't, you'll know someone who can."

"'T'all depends," said Robert, "on what t'is you want supplied."

"The Overseers want to have one parish dinner for harvest. Invite all the paupers. In October." Mayhew spoke in short sharp ejaculations, as if the words were being forced out of him. "Farmers'll supply most of it. Need to be sure we've got plenty. I'm told you'll slaughter us a beast."

Robert wasn't certain whether Mayhew expected this to be a gift, or if he would be paid for it. The way he said it, you'd have thought he believed Robert had a whole herd just waiting to be butchered. Then he made himself clearer.

"We've been promised most of what we need. We'll pay you a guinea, and lend you another half a guinea for the winter. Can't say fairer."

"Excusing me sir, but will I get that in advance?" Robert had no idea how he was going to lay hands on a bullock for October, but it was worthwhile investigating legal ways first.

"Not a hope. Bring the carcass - fresh, mind - to my barn off the Broad Road. First week in October."

It was clear that Nathaniel Mayhew, another in the mould of William Diggins and out to make a name for himself, preferred not to know the source of this purchase, just so long as he got it cheap.

If Robert had stopped to consider, he might have been more concerned that a virtual stranger knew of his reputation as a handler of illicit goods.

Like many other labourers, Robert often fattened a pig for the summer, but that was to keep them in meat for the early part of the winter. Pigs were cheap and easily come by. Sheep likewise. But a bullock was a different matter. He would have to plan this one. He'd talk about it the next time he saw Wimble.

* * * * * * * * * * * * * *

The last week in June, children living round The Lodge began to fall ill. It was known to be serious by some mothers' reluctance to leave their bedsides, though there was plenty of money to be earned in the fields. Anne had heard mention of rashes and fevers but assumed that Elizabeth, Annie, Mary and little Sarah would be safe by virtue of their isolation. It wasn't to be. Mary was the first to go down with it. She complained of a headache during the night, and within hours was running a temperature and vomiting. By the light of the morning, you could see first red pinpricks appearing on her neck and chest. Eerily, her lips and lower face remained unnaturally pale. As the fever began to take hold, Anne was lost as to how to treat her. Concerned as much for the safety of her unborn child as for Mary, she left the nursing to Elizabeth and kept the other two children well away from their sick sister.

After another day's fever and diarrhoea, Anne was resigned to the worst, especially as Sarah was now showing many of the same symptoms. She too was consigned to Elizabeth's care. Still only twelve, Elizabeth demonstrated maturity well beyond her years. Unsure of what to do for the best, she spoke to old Sophie. Though feeble and house-bound, confined to the Parish poor houses, old Sophie told Elizabeth what to look for and how to treat the fever.

"Look at their tongues and tell me what you see," said the old lady. "Meantime let 'em suck on a wet cloth - a clean one, mind. No solid food, but plenty of cold water. And a bit of broth," she advised.

Elizabeth looked at Mary's tongue. It looked like it had white fur

54

on it. Sarah's was almost as bad. She reported her observations.

"It's as I thought - Scarlatina. At least it'll only be the children as get it. Now did you put cold flannel on the head, and warm on the belly?"

"Yes," Elizabeth answered, "and I found the roots you said to boil and gave them a spoon or two of it."

"You're not feeling poorly yourself?"

"No." Elizabeth was surprised by the question. It hadn't occurred to her that she might catch the disease.

"Let me see your tongue," said old Sophie. "Good - that's fine. Now, you do like I said - drink ale, not water, and certainly not milk. How are the others up The Lodge?"

"There are six families gone down with it - nearly all children. Two have died."

"I know, luvvie, I heard the bells."

Sophie was sitting, as she did most days now outside the front door of her portion of the Parish house. It was a long old building, clay lump and wheat-straw thatch, divided into four separate units for the elderly and infirm. Mostly, relatives came daily to feed them, though those like Sophie who had outlived their children relied on the kindness of folks like the Gaffers round the corner. Now she could no longer minister to the sick herself, there were plenty in the village who had good reason to be grateful for her wisdom and attention in the past, and she didn't go short.

Elizabeth came a number of times to take advice, but only when she could see it was safe to leave her patients for an hour or so. It was now her fourth visit. As the old midwife sat in her chair, looking out towards St. Andrew's church, on hearing Elizabeth's latest report as to the progress of the disease, Sophie said something that the young girl thought rather odd.

"You done well," she began. "It do sound like the worst might be over. Your other sister di'n't get it?"

"No, we thought perhaps she di'n't play where the other two caught it."

"Maybe so, maybe not. Sometimes the Lord give some people the power to ward off danger. Like with yourself. Maybe He's

55

got more important things in mind for you. That's what I want you to consider. Them folks as can't afford the surgeon need old Sophie from time to time. Only old Sophie can't do it no more, so someone else gotter."

"Do you think I could?" Elizabeth was feeling justly proud of her nursing skills.

"Maybe you could, maybe you couldn't, but at least we can give it a try - you're only a young'un yet, but if you're gonna git a hold of all I can larn you afore the Lord hears my bell ringing, you'd best get started."

Elizabeth was intrigued. What should she learn first?

"Now lookie here luvvie - take yourself off to Hill Cottages and tell Margaret I sent you. She'll show you how to birth babies. You want to be a woman what does for folks as is sick, then you've gotta be able to get 'em living in the first place. And then there's the other side to it, getting 'em ready for the burying - that's part of it too. Meantime, I'll tell you what herbs to gather and how to prepare 'em."

Excitedly, Elizabeth took her leave, and later that week, when her sisters were on the mend, received her first instruction in nursing and treatment of the sick. For her there were to be no examinations, no certificates, no book learning, no formal anatomy lectures; just a lifetime of being there for those who could afford little, but deserved more.

One of the first lessons she had to learn was, however good she might become, death could be cruel and inevitable. Flushed with success from her sister's recovery, Elizabeth still believed there was nothing she could not do, no miracle she couldn't work.

Margaret, the midwife, who was to be her other tutor, called for Elizabeth when the time had come for the birth of Verity Underwood's first child. It was a long labour and the child was stillborn. Elizabeth in tears could not understand why more effort was not put into breathing life into the child. Margaret took her outside and explained the harsh reality.

"Look at the mite - it's underweight and born too soon. The mother has no husband and it's better for all like this; God made it happen this way - who are you to say it shouldn't be?"

Two days later when Verity haemorrhaged and died in minutes, Margaret reminded Elizabeth how bleak the future would have been for a baby with no parents.

"What would you do if it had lived? Give it to some drunken sot of a wet nurse - they all die, them what's gets wet-nursed anyway." Gritting her teeth and blinking back the tears, Elizabeth still tried to tell herself that when she was the midwife, things would be different.

Robert came in late after work one day. He had no explanation, but Anne, who had been suffering pains, had asked Sarah Diggins to send word she needed him. He, unfortunately, had taken what seemed like a God-sent opportunity to renew acquaintances with Wimble Blomfield's eldest daughter. She had indicated, rather obviously, Robert felt, that she intended to be at the church, returning the newly laundered vestments at just the time when he would be free to join her.

To his disappointment, what he had perceived as a possible tryst in the vestry had proved to be the opportunity for her to drop a bombshell.

"I hen't had my woman's time this month."

"Don't mean nothin' - could still happen." He hoped.

"I'm always regular, like the seasons. I reckon you got me expectin' - if I go to the parish, they'll make you pay."

"Who says it's mine?" He was grasping at straws.

"I 'in't been with nobody else. You're the only one what come round ours. It gotta be you."

The way she explained it, he could see them at the Overseers believing her. All he could think at that moment was how he was going to explain it to Anne.

"What is it they say on their bits o' paper?" she taunted. "...Robbie Saunders, the reputed father."

Yes, that was exactly what it would say. He couldn't marry her even if he wanted to, so there would be a bastardy order and he'd have to find any amount of money he hadn't got to support her child. Then he remembered the sovereigns.

"Don't say nuthin' - I've got some money put by. I'll see you right if you keep quiet about it."

"Are you sure?" she asked suspiciously. "You 'in't just sayin' that to stop me talkin'?"

"No, I got money. Trust me. When our son is born, I'll give you twenty shillin' - no, forty shillin'." Somehow, he had no doubt this would be a boy.

"Well - you make it sixty shillin' and I might just keep my mouth shut."

As regards what he'd hoped for when he had sneaked into the side door of the church unseen, he had to settle for a kiss and a fierce but brief embrace before she tore herself away and skipped off home, satisfied. Which was more than Robert was.

But they had been inside the church after all.

Even if Robert had been at home when Anne's pains came, it is unlikely it would have made a great deal of difference. This was womens' business and by definition, he was excluded. Elizabeth and Sarah Diggins attended to Anne as best they could, but by the time Robert finally made his entrance, there was a bowl of blood and a foetus to bury, something he'd almost become used to. But this time it was different. The infant her body had rejected, tiny though it was, was perfect in every detail. And it was a boy.

Chapter 7

October 1795

Nothing in life had prepared Robert for the desolation he was to feel in those next few hours. He knew he had wanted a son, but never realised just how much. And to come so close! Anne was quite inconsolable. She was convinced she would never carry a boy infant to full term. On top of that, there had been the accusing looks and disparaging remarks.

"Where were you? We couldn't find you," Anne cried over and over again, never thinking for a moment that it was worse than she had imagined. Sarah Diggins was again cast in the role of her comforter though the loss of the child had struck her every bit as hard as it had Anne.

"Why didn't you say where you were?"

"Most men come straight home when their wife's expecting." He couldn't find it in himself to stave off their condemnation. He couldn't find the answers in the truth and he'd lost the taste for lying. Meanwhile the problem of Virtue Blomfield wasn't going to go away. He hoped she was wrong. Maybe, she was lying. Either way he resolved that he'd not touch her again, and eventually time would tell.

Anne spent the summer healing her wounds and coming to terms with the fact their family might be complete and she should be grateful for her four lovely daughters. But a little of the fire and the sparkle had left her, and she and Robert found that a distance had grown between them.

It had taken a whole fortnight before Robert had been back to the Blomfields' cottage. Wimble had been round to help with his garden on a couple of occasions but Robert was poor company at that time, and anyway, they'd both been working long hours during the day.

Robert had played the attentive husband for a while, but as

Anne buried herself deeper in her despondency, his patience, never his strong suit, wore thin.

He did wonder how he would feel meeting Virtue again and whether his promise to himself to have no more secret liaisons would hold good. Fortunately, he discovered she had been offered a position as a maid at the Rectory. This she had accepted and he was able to avoid her for much of the summer.

Which left the problem of Nathaniel Mayhew and the meat for the Harvest Supper.

"The way I see it, old Hum's sayin' go steal a bullock from some other parish and we'll all keep quiet about it," said Wimble.

It was fast approaching the time appointed and a clear plan had yet to emerge.

"They've got some over at Wickham Abbey," suggested Robert.

"Oh aye and they've got guns and dawgs, and I di'n't like that combination when we come up agin 'em before," said Wimble, prepared to speak his mind for once.

"There's loads on'em - they 'un't miss one."

"But look where they are - miles from a road... what you gonna do - walk it home with no bugger noticing - or slaughter it over there and carry it home on your back - don't be so sorft!" said Wimble.

"Alright - old man Frere's got a herd right next to the Rickinghall road. We borrow the miller's cart, go up there two in the morning, kill it there and bring home the beef, so to speak."
It wasn't much of a plan, but it was better than anything else either of them could offer.

"We'll not be a lotta good for work arter a night like that," said Wimble.

"So we make it Saturday night, early hours o' Sunday morning. Can you get the cart?"

"Better not get blood on it."

"We can give it a good scrub down afterwards."

"Alright," said Wimble, less than convinced. "I only hope it's as easy as what you say."

This conversation had been started on the way back from the Cock Inn and completed in Wimble's front room while his wife was putting the children to bed. When she came down, Robert was surprised to see Virtue was with her.

"Oh good, you're back early," said Hannah Blomfield. "The kids'll appreciate your sayin' goodnight."

Turning to Robert, she explained, "They don't see a lot of their father on account of how he work all the hours God send and when he 'in't a-workin', he's orf alonga you."

She didn't mean it rudely, but she was a blunt woman and it was clear something about their friendship worried her. She accompanied him upstairs. Virtue, now in the livery of a chambermaid, called out, "I'll be off back to the Reverend." But she didn't go immediately. Robert eyed her up and down, more from curiosity than desire. She didn't look particularly pregnant, but then neither had Anne with first two - not until a good five months. She knew what he was thinking.

"I'm still expectin'. It 'un't be a secret much longer. I'll have to tell the Rector an' he'll send me home."

"I told you - I'd see to it."

"Sixty shillings, you said."

"And it will be. Jus' so long as you don't tell no-one it's mine."

"Of course," she grinned, coming closer, "...if you could see your way to making it a bit more, well... you can't make another baby when there be one up there already."

Did she mean what he thought she meant. If so, the transition from innocent temptress to scheming harlot seemed to have coincided with a season spent in the house of the Rector. It didn't bear thinking about. Then, all at once, there were feet coming down creaking stairs and with a flick of her dark hair, she was out the door and down the front path before he had time to decide whether she had been serious or not.

There was no choice. Rainy skies or not, the first weekend in October had to be the time. At least it would be dark. Still unsure of how to trap and kill such a large beast, let alone transport it back,

Robert and Wimble, nevertheless, set off in high spirits. Protecting themselves as best as they could from the elements, they began their journey. The old mill cart made slow progress up the lane to the Broad Road, pulled by a willing but undersized mill pony. Smaller horses were used around the mill due to their manoeuvrability. They were not usually required to pull heavy loads over long distances. Tonight would prove a severe test for the unfortunate animal.

Some time around midnight, passing an inn, they noticed with some satisfaction, bright lamps were no longer visible and only rush lights now burned. They would not be observed. It had only been raining a few hours and fording the stream in Finningham Street was no problem. Things were going their way.

They had already established the fact that a concealed track ran beside the field that served as pasture for Frere's bullocks. Trees masked it from both sides and unless a particularly observant traveller should happen that way just at the wrong moment, the pony and the old mill cart would remain well hidden from view.

An assortment of blades and forks had been brought aboard the cart without any real notion how they might achieve the required result. Their combined limited experience of the slaughter of livestock had made them blasé about the task they were about to embark upon. No animal willingly offers itself up to be slaughtered. But the promise of a guinea and the loan of half as much again was more than enough, on this most inclement of nights, to spur them on.

The roughly-made road had a wide verge on both sides. The bullocks were confined to an enclosed part of what had once been a broad green. A straggly section of hedge separated the verge from the field. Just inside the field was thoroughly wet corner. At times, it dried up completely, but often, as now, by October a sizeable pond had developed, with deep clinging clay edges that could be quite treacherous to both man and beast.

The plan was, if any plan had been devised at all, to separate any animal they could from the rest and drive it in the direction of the road, making a swift kill. Then, they hoped to begin the butchery to the extent that pieces of a size that could be carried would be manhandled to the cart and they could make their escape long before light became a problem.

Ill-equipped for such a venture, they were reduced to chasing shadows in the dark, blundering from one beast to another with little light to guide them and less sense of direction. Pitchforks in their hands, they merely spooked the startled animals and some of the sounds they put up made Robert and Wimble stop to consider how long this could go unnoticed. They were both soaked through all layers of their clothing and so much clay clung to their boots, every step was like a dozen.

Exhausted, demoralised and cold beyond description, Wimble knew when he'd had enough, even if Robert didn't.

"That 'in't no good. They're too quick for us. Give up bo' - 't'in't worth it."

"I don't see as how we can go back without one," said Robert still reluctant to abandon their mission. The lure of so much money was still strong, but these wretched moving mountains of beef weren't going to offer themselves up for slaughter just because some Overseer with more money than sense wanted a beast to roast for Harvest. Or were they?

The little light that existed on such a night gave Robert cause for hope. As he looked back across the pasture towards the road, he became aware of a trapped animal frantically trying to free itself from the treacherous mud at the edge of the watery corner. Now a substantial pond, its waters were being further churned by one stray bullock that had blundered there, fleeing the two flailing pitchforks.

The lucky break, for it had to be perceived as such, gave them new cause for hope. And whether hope springs eternal or not, it proved enough to galvanise them into action. Blades to the ready, they approached the trapped animal with a measure of caution, if not to say respect.

"Slit its throat, go on," said Robert.

But Wimble, who usually left the wringing of necks of capons to Hannah, had no stomach for this part of the venture.

"You want its throat slit - you do it yourself. I 'in't doing it, no ways!"

It wasn't a pleasurable experience, but there was the money to be reckoned on. Robert, steel in hand, floundered into the pool margins, desperately trying to stay on his feet and not to allow himself to become as much a prisoner as the desperate animal.

In later years when he was more prepared to discuss it, he was wont to say, "I never believed an animal had so much blood in it." The bullock died quickly but messily. The blood covered the surface of the pool and much of Robert too. By the time the pair of them had hacked at the carcass with knives and axes and cleavers, they, the ground around them, and the track to the cart bore evidence of their grisly adventure.

The patient pony, troubled by the scent of killing was nervous and they were afraid it might bolt. But side by side, and with such reserves of energy as they never knew they possessed, Robert and Wimble loaded the cart. Oblivious to the evidence they were leaving behind and with the rain still sheeting down, they coaxed the game little pony back towards Cotton and a measure of safety.

As luck would have it, the rain didn't ease for forty-eight hours. The blood in the pond and on the field overflowed into ditches and subsequently into streams, so by daylight, it was diluted. All evidence there might have been at the scene of their escapade had been conveniently washed away, leaving Mr Frere's husbandman to contemplate two days later how one of his best bullocks had come to disappear.

Nathaniel Mayhew discovered what he wanted in his barn on Monday morning, and though it may have been an unimpressive piece of butchery, it would serve his purpose just fine.

It was still dark when Wimble backed the empty cart into his yard. The tools that had served as weapons, washed clean by the rain went back into an outhouse. The cart, they decided, would not need much work. It would wait until later.

The pony had to be dried and bedded down. It was wet and tired, but none the worse for the expedition. Robert walked home, with it still raining and the smell of the killing still about him.

He stripped naked outside the door to his cottage and dried off on some newly washed linen that Anne had hung over the fireplace. Pulling the warm textiles around him, he lay down on the rug in front of the vaguely glowing embers and slipped instantly off to sleep. It had been quite a night.

Of course, he had not told Anne precisely what he had been up to. He never did. She preferred not to know. She did, however, hear him come in and slipped downstairs to see he was all right. It was just turning light. He lay in front of the hearth. He didn't even wake when she built up the fire and held him till he stopped shivering. It was good to have him home. She had this terrible fear that one of these nights, he wouldn't come back, but be arrested like Harry Thurlow or end up dead like Pikey. He looked so vulnerable just lying there.

She felt a real glow of love pass through her. He wasn't a bad man to have for a husband. He provided as best he could; he cared for her and the children. And he wasn't like some women's husbands, out and about with other girls. No she could have done a lot worse; a whole lot worse.

Chapter 8

November 1795

John Eade had a problem. As Rector of the parish of Cotton for little more than two years, he was still cautious about treading carefully. His predecessor had been there a long time and besides had known the parish and its people long before that. As a newcomer, Eade was ever aware of those who eyed him with suspicion and made no secret of the fact they found him wanting. He continued to feel like an outsider and wondered whether he would ever be truly accepted by his flock.

A small clique of tradesmen, tenants and stewards seemed to administer the finances of the parish quite efficiently. Tithes were collected, poor rates levied and money spent fairly and expeditiously. He could find no fault with the parish council elders apart from the way, like the guilds of old, the panel of Overseers seemed to use their position to enhance their own status in the community. But even that was much the same in any parish in England.

Attendance at church was not the problem. They may not have been the most devout and dedicated congregation, but at least they turned up, and there was little sign of the divisive factions that he had observed in other places.

No, the problem was far closer to home; within his own house, in fact. He had no wish to upset any of his parishioners; he certainly wanted to be accepted, though it might take some time. The matter was, however, one requiring the utmost tact and sensitivity, and he wished he had someone with whom he could discuss it.

John Eade was a widow, and therefore it placed him in a position of some vulnerability to notice that a young servant girl in his employ, whom he knew to be unmarried, was growing around the waist. Being Rector of the parish, his position alone should have placed him above suspicion. But as he had been aware of harbouring more than occasional lustful thoughts towards the girl in question, he wondered whether others might have noticed the way he must have looked at her, and come to a wholly improper conclusion. Feeling insecure in his own position, he settled for taking advice from someone who might lend a sympathetic ear, whilst possessing the ability to keep a secret.

Anne Saunders was tidying up in the Corner House when the Rector rode into the yard. He had been to The Lodge twice that week already, and it did occur to Anne that maybe he was looking for another wife and had noticed Sarah.

"I'll tell Miss Diggins you're here. Come you in and make yourself comfy," Anne said. She directed him to John Hart's front room in the Corner House that served as a kind of farm office, before walking across the cobbles to the big house where Sarah was having tea with her sister-in-law. Rather than keep people waiting, she knocked at the front door. She should have gone round the back. They wouldn't like it, but it was the better of two evils. The Lodge wasn't that much of a grand house and Mr. William Diggins wasn't Lord of the Manor, even if he thought he should be. A maid in similar costume to her own answered the door.

"Please can you tell Miss Diggins, the Rector's here - again." she said, not meaning to sound disapproving. Then, having passed on the message, she went back to offer the Reverend Eade tea and cakes.

There wasn't much more privacy in the Corner house than there was in her own. The old stud walls and partitioning weren't designed to mask people's conversations. It wasn't that Anne was nosy, but she was intrigued to see if her suspicions were correct. In that respect, she was to be disappointed.

"I have a matter of the gravest delicacy," she could hear the Rector begin. "And as I value your judgement, I wonder if I might seek a little of your advice."

Oh dear, it didn't sound as though romance was in the air today. On the other hand, matters of the gravest delicacy were usually only discussed by people who had established at least a measure of intimacy.

"I come to you," he continued, "because not only do I regard

67

you as a friend and confidante, but I know you will treat this as a matter of the utmost confidentiality."

It wasn't the kind of conversation Anne had hoped to hear, but it certainly was worth listening to. She busied herself with the tea cups, keeping as quiet as possible, lest they realise her proximity and drop their voices still further.

"I have in my employ, a young girl by the name of Virtue Blomfield," the Rector said in hushed tones. "A delightful and industrious girl. I have no complaint about her work. It is, you understand, her condition I am concerned about. She is, I believe, as the Bible would say, 'with child,' though who the father is, I have no idea."

"You are sure about this?" Sarah Diggins said.

"Quite sure - she grows by the day. She has not mentioned anything about it, but I can't just ignore it. People might talk. The problem is, she shows no evidence of a young man pursuing her. You understand my predicament. Sometimes people make such wild accusations."

"Is she accommodated in your house?" asked Sarah.

"Yes, but only recently has that been the case - certainly not at the time when she..." His voice fell away.

"Quite." Sarah gave it some silent consideration. Then she called out. "Anne, forget the tea! I'm going out."
Turning to the Rector, she said, "You rode over, I presume? Then we'll both ride back and see what can be done."

As Anne appeared in the room to clarify what was next on the agenda, Sarah instructed her. "Please tell your husband to saddle Midas. I shall be riding to the Rectory immediately."

Later that night, when Robert came home, after the younger children were asleep, and only Anne and Elizabeth sat sewing, Anne who was less discrete than Sarah Diggins, couldn't wait to repeat what she'd heard.

"And don't you go mentioning any of this or you'll get me in trouble," said Anne to her eldest daughter. "I only heard what was said in confidence."

"With your ear pressed up against the wall," chuckled Robert, trying to make light of what was making him feel distinctly uncomfortable.

"Shut up you," laughed Anne, pushing him. "And I mean it," she added to Elizabeth.

"S'alright, everyone knows she's growin' one. Old Sophie say she done it in the vestry with some old fella. She'd a' known who it was, 'cept he crept out with a hat pulled down over his head."

"I wonder what Sarah and the Rector said to her," said Anne. "Or if they found out whose it was."

"That 'in't that special," said Robert. "Most girls has babies 'afore they get wed. That way they know they can."

"You had me before you was married, di'n't you?" said Elizabeth.

"Don't mean thass the right way to do it," said Anne. "An' if it's some old bloke, then it's prob'ly someone else's husband and that definitely 'in't right."

"No," thought Robert to himself. "That that 'in't!"

*   *   *   *   *   *   *   *   *   *   *   *   *   *

Sarah Diggins found she had a great deal of time to kill these days. Though in name she was housekeeper to her brother, his wife saw to the management of most things; and their son, now the Parish Constable had married and moved out. To get her teeth into something - anything - was preferable to being the lady of leisure she had never pretended to be.

Once there, and invigorated by a brisk ride, Sarah was prepared to employ none of the delicacy of the Reverend Eade, none of the circumnavigation of the problem. No, it was Sarah's style to get straight to the point.

"You realise," she began as soon as Virtue had accepted their coats, "that you can't possibly remain here in your condition."
As if she considered denying it, then thought better of it, Virtue stopped in her tracks, before bursting into tears. Sarah had a tender side and immediately, it was this that came to the fore.

"Come on, you tell the Rector who the father is and we'll work out when the wedding should be."

At that the girl howled all the more.

"I can't be weddin' him, 'e's wed already," she sobbed.

"Then we'll put it to the parish and he'll be ordered to pay for the infant's keep," said Sarah.

Slowly the story emerged. As she told it, Virtue gave the impression of an innocent girl corrupted by an older man who had, nevertheless, promised to provide for her. She made a convincing victim, but for all their persuasion would not own up to the father's name.

"Very well, Virtue," decided Sarah. "You must go home now until the end of your lying-in. If everything goes well and you are properly cared for, then all well and good, but should the father try to wriggle out of his responsibility - and I'm afraid to say, they often do - then you must name him and allow the parish to fight your case. You promise me you will?"

"Yes ma'am."

"Good, now dry your tears, and if after all this is over, you still want to work here, then I'm sure the Rector will be glad to have you back, though you clearly won't be able to live-in any more."

As Virtue left, Sarah remarked to the Reverend Eade, "I only hope her father shows the consideration toward her that you have."

"I feel I owe you an enormous debt of gratitude," the Rector said to Sarah. "It's so difficult being a man on one's own. It's at times like this I really miss not having a wife around."

Sarah wasn't quite sure how to take this. It almost sounded like a proposal. She wasn't clear whether she should feel pleased or not. However, she did accept his offer to ride back with her.

It was a harsh winter for all concerned. Even with the few shillings of poor relief that came his way, Robert found it hard to find for his family. Anne was being employed less, and with a layer of snow over the ground, there was little work to be had for anyone. That meant more leisure for most of the men - more time to spend the few pence they could muster in the Cock or the back room of the butcher's.

Intending to return for the sovereigns he had secreted all that

70

time ago, Robert had been waiting for a couple of days clear when he might walk the eight miles to the far end of Stowupland. He felt enough time had lapsed since the fated robbery to face any awkward questions that might be thrown his way. He'd already decided to invent an inheritance. Having a host of relatives dotted around the district, it could almost be plausible, were it not for the fact that everyone knew they were all as poor as he was. Still, it had been nearly six years since he had buried the gold and he had been living in a different parish then.

Planning this mission with more than the usual precision, Robert discounted involving Wimble. He'd rather no-one knew the source of Virtue's sixty shillings when she finally received the money. So far, good as her word, Virtue had refused to reveal her lover's identity. She, of course, was relying on Robert to keep his side of the bargain. He'd not been round to see Wimble more than was strictly necessary in the last six weeks, knowing Virtue would be there, growing ever larger with his child. As far as explaining his absence to his own family, he'd use the excuse of visiting relatives. It was just after Christmas and there was little chance of any paid work till the freeze was over. In anticipation, he waxed his boots and sewed pockets inside his coat to conceal the trowel he intended to take with him and the treasures he expected to bring back.

Then Anne dropped a bombshell. The strong winds that had carried the snow to that part of Suffolk had felled a tree in the churchyard. The Rector, who had been a regular visitor to the Lodge, had come pleading for a work-party to cut up the tree and make good the damage it had caused. Of course Anne volunteered his help. In the end, a team of them went from cottages all over the parish with two-handed saws, ropes and block-and-tackle. The women went too, to regale the workers with warm drinks, and all in all, there was quite a party atmosphere. Robert might have enjoyed it more had he not felt he might be more gainfully employed elsewhere. However, impatient though he now was, after six years wait, the sovereigns could stay there a little longer.

71

The tree was a mature beech. Successive graves had been placed beneath its canopy and the roots hacked out to such an extent that a good gale had been enough to uproot it. Ancient bones were exposed where once there had been flat turf. Fortunately, there were no gravestones in that part of the churchyard. Taller than most, the tree had clipped one corner of the chancel, exposing roof timbers and plasterwork to the elements. This could be remedied easily enough, and the bones re-interred, but the tree was a giant and it took the efforts of two dozen men a full day to log it and leave the largest parts safe.

As darkness fell and exhaustion overtook them, the workers and their wives were invited back to the Rectory where Sarah Diggins and Anne had produced broth and bread to fill their starving bellies, washed down with small beer. It was warm in the drawing room of the Rectory and the labourers, unused to such luxurious surroundings, were in no hurry to head back for their cold, damp cottages.

Gradually, however, they drifted away, encouraged by the invitation to carry home as many logs as their aching arms would hold. Anne was always going to be the last to leave. Robert could see there was no point in thinking any further about the sovereigns that day, so he was content to wait for her.

The Rector, encouraged by the help he had received, endlessly repeated words of gratitude as couples left to walk the bitterly cold road home. "This has been a momentous day," he said as Anne finally donned her coat. "So many hands working together in praise of the Lord!"

"Thass not finished yet, Reverend," Robert reminded him, "but that ol' trunk'll stop there till spring now."

"Does the damage to the church matter much?" asked Anne.

"I feel we have done enough to prevent the worst of the weather, but I am afraid that in due course, a sum of money will need to be forthcoming to repair it properly," said the Reverend John Eade, uneasily.

"Still," he remarked, "the Lord will provide."

"You need some rich gentleman to leave you a sum o' money,"

said Robert.

They all knew how unlikely that was. Cotton was a parish of tenant farmers, stewards and labourers. The landowners all lived at a distance. They were committed to the parishes where their family seats lay. There would be no great foundations, no endowments, no bequests as there had been in richer parishes.

"But I s'pose in the end, it's down to thee and me, Rector," said Robert. "Tell you what..." He fished in his pocket, finding a farthing he knew was there. "I'll start you off. I'n't much, but 't's more than you had afore."

"Like the widow's mite," said the Rector, smiling. He paused before adding, "No, we could do with a divine act, like at Stowmarket."

"Wass that Rector?"

"Oh didn't you hear - it was reported in the Journal - I have it here somewhere." He looked to see he had the attention of Anne and Sarah as well as Robert, before continuing.

"It appears that a tenant farmer at Stowupland was out in a thunderstorm when a bolt of lightning was seen to strike this ruined cottage. What remained of the thatch was set ablaze, but the rain soon quenched the flames. On further investigation, the farmer discovered a hole had been exposed in the floor where rusty metal had lain. And do you know, that bolt of lightning had turned some of that base metal to gold."

"No!" Anne was amazed.

"An act of God," Sarah replied.

"Indeed a miracle of the greatest kind. And you know what that farmer did," said Eade. "Recognising it for the heaven-sent gift it was, he gave that gold to the church in Stowmarket for its improvement and maintenance."

To Robert it would not be enough to say this came as a surprise. It shook him with the selfsame force that had shaken Cotton Church. He felt like asking for his farthing back, little use though it would be, when sixty shillings stood between him and everything he valued dear.

*   *   *   *   *   *   *   *   *   *   *   *   *

February 1796

If life had been hard for Robert and Anne through those years of the nineties, it would undoubtedly have been so much worse without Elizabeth to rely on. If anyone was a mother to Annie, Mary and little Sarah, it was Lizzie, who fed and dressed them but was still enough of a child to play their games and to teach them hers. At the time, she was growing up fast, both physically and emotionally. She looked a good two years older than other children of the same age. Already fast approaching her mother's height, it was hard to remember she hadn't yet celebrated her thirteenth birthday. Most remarkable was the way she had been accepted by 'the women that did for people.'

Under old Sophie's tuition, she learned about herbal remedies, treatments long since abandoned by surgeons and other trained medical practitioners and a whole folk-lore based on centuries of caring. Margaret, the village midwife treated her almost as an equal, recognising in Lizzie that special quality that Sophie too had seen. Those other ladies of the surrounding district who were generally present at birth, death and the onset of sickness came to rely on Lizzie for her caring nature, her keenness to learn and her plain good sense.

Another thing that endeared her to them was her willingness to undertake even the most unpleasant of tasks. She knew this wasn't a clean business. From the young wives who died in child-birth, to the children who coughed out their lives with consumption; from the oozing bedsores of the elderly, to the desperation of the bereaved. Elizabeth had taken to her apprenticeship with aptitude and zeal, and was as content to aid the final preparation of the dead as to ease the discomfort of the living.

Thus, as Virtue Blomfield drew near her time, preparations were made for informing Margaret and her ladies when they should be needed. Elizabeth, blissfully unaware that she was about to witness the birth of her own half-brother, was also awaiting that same call.

Robert had learned of the discovery of the gold - his gold - with disbelief. If only he had gone sooner! How could he now explain to Virtue that her sixty shillings were being spent on new pews for Stowmarket church? His answer was to avoid all contact with her whatsoever. Since the day of the tree, he had hardly been out of his house. Work had absorbed some of his time and energy. As for the rest, he stayed at home until Anne, who wasn't used to such an attentive husband, wished she could coax him out for at least a few hours. Wimble had called, as had one or two other friends, but had soon lost interest on discovering how uncommunicative he had become. It was a long way to walk to Meadow Cottage and he was poor company.

Anne and Robert found they had little to say to one another. Sarah Diggins had been spending a good deal of time with the Rector of late, and Anne's main source of local gossip had dried up. Robert's working day was normally concerned with the horses, but with the bad spell of weather, they had been little used, and he had been put to work clearing ditches, a job he hated.

Anne went daily to the Corner House, where John Hart continued to reside and to take on more of the running of the farm. He was a dour man who believed his servants should be invisible. No-one knew what to make of the man. He had been there for over a year, and few could remember having a conversation with him. Give him his due, he wasn't afraid to lead by example. He'd wield a scythe or a flail with the best of them, calm a distracted horse or help round up sheep that had escaped. But he'd never offer a word of compliment or kindness. Anne found him civil enough, but cold and distant. It was as if nobody knew quite why he was there. To begin with, William Diggins and his wife Martha wondered whether the Heighams had sent him to spy on them, but he hadn't even appeared to communicate much with them.

As Diggins began to enjoy his elevated status within the parish, his ambition took hold. Leaving more of the day-to-day running of the farm to his deputy, he was free to use his position to advantage. He bought a small tenement on the Broad Road and let it. Once an owner of property, he began to act the part. He and his wife had taken time away mixing with 'polite' members of society at Bury St. Edmunds. Contacts were developed and the social graces observed. It was plain to all who knew William Diggins, mere stewardship of another man's land would not hold him for long.

One bleak night in the middle of a bleaker month, Virtue Blomfield's pains began. Concerned by Robert's continued absence, she was terrified by the prospect of childbirth. It was at least a fortnight early and her mother, in desperation, sent Wimble in search of Margaret, who duly arrived.

The midwife could see it would be some time before the child would be born, so was in no hurry to enlist further help. She sent Virtue's agitated parents to bed, promising to wake her mother, Hannah, when she was needed. Then she concentrated on calming the frightened girl, a none too easy task.

By daylight, little had changed. Wimble was delegated to fetch the rest of Margaret's helpers, including Elizabeth. They sat, all dressed in black, like crows at a funeral. Wimble took himself off to work. He was already late.

The day dragged on. Hannah Blomfield struggled to feed the hungry gaggle that had descended upon her. Virtue had been made as comfortable as possible on a makeshift bed in the front room where a good fire burned. There was much talk of good omens and the like, but they all knew it was old women's prattle, and a child born premature after a long labour had poor chance of survival.

With still no baby when darkness fell, Virtue's labours eased and one by one, the 'comforters' drifted off home, promising to return the next morning. Eventually, even Margaret lost patience and concerned for her own family, left word with Elizabeth to send for her should the pains start again in earnest.

Finding herself alone with company nearer her own age, Virtue began to relax, even to joke about her situation.

"I shall be truly glad to be back a proper shape agin," she laughed. She was tired, but warm and comfortable.

"Are you wantin' a boy or a girl," Lizzie asked her?

"I don't really mind. My man - he say on one occasion he

76

want a boy, but I say 'ti'n't none o' his business as it's me what's gotta have it."

Lizzie didn't like to ask outright who the father actually was, but thought it wouldn't be a bad idea to ask the odd leading question.

"Do he know you be 'aving this baby right now?"

"Oh I 'spect he'll know soon enough," Virtue said. Then she added, "He say he'll look after me - he say he'll give me sixty shillings."

"He must be some whully rich gentl'man," said Lizzie, impressed."

But Virtue, realising she had said enough, clammed up.

Then, she clenched her hand round Lizzie's wrist.

"Ooh, what's happening - I'm all wet."

"Your waters' broke - I'd better fetch Margaret."

"No, don't leave me!" shouted Virtue. Then, she screamed as a contraction, stronger than any before, began to bite.

"Mrs. Blomfield, Mrs. Blomfield!" yelled Lizzie. "It's Virtue's time, I reckon you'd better get Margaret back."

It took some convincing to persuade Hannah Blomfield there really was a child on the way this time, and Lizzie was beginning to wonder whether it would all be left to her. The pains were coming more frequently and more intensely. Virtue wouldn't let go of her hand.

"Breathe deeply and soon you'll have a baby, then won't your man be pleased," she said, encouragingly.

"Aah!" Virtue screamed. "My man! My Man! Aah! He 'in't my man! He be some other poor bugger's man! Aah!"

"Come on - think how pleased he'll be."

"Pleased? Aah! …Saunders, I hate you! I hate you! Aah!"

"Mrs. Blomfield, I think you'd better come! Quick!" Lizzie called out.

In the end, Wimble was roused from his bed and sent post-haste for the midwife. Before she had returned, Hannah Blomfield, with Lizzie's help had done all that was necessary, and Margaret arrived to find them presenting the baby boy to a tired, relieved mother.

Lizzie assumed she would receive at least a small nod of commendation from the midwife for her part in the birth, but if it was approval she was after, she was to be disappointed.

Outside in the garden, whilst disposing of the afterbirth, Margaret berated her young apprentice.

"What'd you let it live for?" she scolded. "T'in't half a kid; t'in't worth the trouble." She looked at the shock and dismay in Lizzie's eyes.

"I know you want to help everyone - so we all do, but t's kinder to smother a poor little bastard like that. T's mis-shapen, born too soon and it'll die anyway. Then the mother'll get all upset, all over again."

"Had we better baptise it?" Lizzie was tired after forty-eight hours without sleep, and fighting back the tears, but to her credit, was still trying to think like a midwife.

"A bit late to send for the Rector...You're right, we'll do it ourselves and tell him about it in the morning. Then maybe he can put a drop of holy water on it - if it lives that long." She smiled at the young girl. "Get you on home - your mam'll start wonderin' if you 'in't got a fella yourself."

"Don't want one," said Lizzie. But she could see that Margaret was really pleased with her, in spite of the harsh words.

She still had to walk home, after it was all over. And what had all that been about, the yelling and screaming and cursing her father's name. It hadn't even crossed her mind before now that he might be the guilty party, but when she came to think about it, he had spent an awful lot of time over there the previous summer. Nevertheless, she could hardly go to her mother with her suspicions. Not yet!

The Rector came the next day to the Blomfield house. Margaret explained how the child was weak and wouldn't even take to the breast. Virtue, exhausted from her ordeal and upset by the child's refusal to feed, was reluctant to take any part in the proceedings. She wouldn't even so much as discuss a name for the tiny pathetic bundle that lay so lifeless beside her. John Eade opened his note-case, and with pen and ink wrote on a scrap of paper: 'Baptism: Feb. 15th, base-born male child to Virtue Blomfield and…' He stopped. Then he turned to Virtue and said, "Even if we cannot name the child, he should have a father. Won't you at least tell us who he is, so his name can also go in the register?"

The young girl had reached the end of her tether. For all his promises, Robert hadn't yet come up with a penny. She owed him nothing - certainly not her silence.

"The father - I'll tell you who the b'luddy father is. Thass Robert Saunders… and he promised me sixty shillings, so I don't care who knows it."

It was hard to say who was more shocked; the Rector or Margaret. Fortunately, Wimble was at the mill and Hannah had taken the rest of the children out of their way. John Eade completed his entry on the piece of paper: '…and reputed father, Robert Saunders.'

He replaced the cap on the ink-bottle, and after holding the piece of paper in front of the fire to dry, he folded it and slipped it into his pocket for safe-keeping.

The two who had been made party to this information were, fortunately, neither likely to be in any hurry to broadcast it. The nature of both their jobs made discretion an important quality.

John Eade put it to the back of his mind, and it wasn't until later that day that it re-emerged. Sarah Diggins came frequently to the Rectory to help John Eade with his paper work. He was the world's worst when it came to making the monthly returns that had to be submitted to the Bishop, and absolutely hopeless in keeping track of which tenants had paid for the leasing of glebe land.

Though she made him feel a little like a recalcitrant child with her impatience and her scolding, John Eade was glad to have Sarah around, and grateful for her contribution to parish matters. Sarah Diggins scanned the registers covering baptisms, marriages and burials. They were ancient and the bindings were loose, but otherwise, the Cotton records were in remarkably good condition.

"Surely these aren't all of them. Good heavens, you haven't even put down the December ones yet. No wonder the Bishop has been complaining," Sarah said.

"Oh no - I meant to," stammered Eade. "They're here some-where. I did write them down the way you said."

He pulled at his pockets and a pile of folded papers fell to the floor. Writing ran both ways, front and back of the papers.

"You really are hopeless - what would you do if I weren't here to organise you?" Sarah ticked. Then, she softened a little.

"Come on, read them to me, in the right order, if you please. Begin with the baptisms."

He began, but when he reached the dreaded words, 'and the father,' he dropped his voice and was made to repeat the name. On hearing it, the colour drained from Sarah's face. Bastards were common enough. Even the odd wayward husband. But this was too close to home to laugh it off. She could imagine just how Anne would feel. She could imagine how she would feel under the circumstances. And if the parish called Robert for examination to answer why he shouldn't be responsible for the upkeep of the child, what chance would he have to deny it, if it was already there in black and white in the parish register? She knew she couldn't ask John Eade to leave it out. Or could she? A friendship was a friendship and her closeness to Anne, she felt, surpassed everything.

Sarah begged and pleaded to have those words omitted from the book and the paper destroyed, but as Eade said, "not only did God witness it, but Margaret too."

Deep in her heart, Sarah knew he was right, but for the first time a barrier had come down between them. He resented her asking him and she resented his inflexibility and reluctance to consider other people's feelings.

As Sarah rode back alone, she knew Anne would have to know and that, unfortunately, it would come better from her.

Anne found him in the stables. William & Martha Diggins had ridden with the hunt, and their horses needed his attention.

Anne hadn't wanted to believe it at first, but when Sarah said the evidence was in the parish book, she thought about it and it made sense - like when Lizzie had mentioned Virtue had met 'some old bloke' at the church. What hurt most was that it must have been happening when she was losing her son - their son! It all fell into place, even the day of her miscarriage when Robert couldn't be found.

He was standing in the corner of the stables, breeches lowered, relieving himself.

"It's a pity that 'in't all you been using it for?" Anne yelled. She had gathered up the few clothes he possessed and wasn't already wearing and had packed them indiscriminately into a bag. She glared at him.

"What?" He was briefly taken aback.

"Virtue Blomfield - Thass what! She waggles her tits at you and you can't keep it under wraps. Well you can bed down here from now on. I'll not have you in the house."

"But... who told you?"

"Sarah did. I didn't want to believe her, but Lizzie said it was true, and your mate Wimble's been over. He's almost as sick of you as I am. You can lay with the horses - they'll give you more comfort than them as knows you."

"It was only..." He couldn't find the words to explain.

"And where were you gonna get sixty shillings? Lying to a young kid like that! What you gonna do when the justices say you got another child to keep? They'll say you gotta pay her a shilling or more to show you're some kind of father to that kid of hers. Where we gonna find another shilling a week just 'cause you 'in't got no sense regardin' what's below your waist?"

Throwing the bag of clothes at him, tears clouding her vision and anger and disappointment smothering her future, Anne turned her back on him and left him to his regret.

For two weeks, he spent his nights cold and alone and his days looking for things to do. At first, nobody knew he was there, though it wouldn't have surprised anybody. After all, who wants a husband like that?

Annie and Mary would come from time to time with food for him. They didn't say Anne had sent them, though he supposed she had. They kept it to themselves as instructed, but more often than not, the supplies came from an unlikely source.

Nothing much escaped the observant eyes of John Hart. He could see no profit in his workers starving or freezing to death. That was what he told himself. Spotting one of the children from time to time, and warning them to keep it a secret, he sent blankets and such food as wouldn't be missed. Robert did wonder once or twice where Anne was laying hands on fine meats and even fish in the middle of winter, but assumed Sarah Diggins had played a part. Nothing could be further from the truth. Sarah's anger towards Robert had been at least as extreme as Anne's, and to begin with, she didn't care whether he lived or died.

But gradually, her attitude softened, until around the beginning of March, she noticed something that intrigued and mystified her. John Hart, the cold man who never had a word for anyone, kind or otherwise, was talking to two of Robert and Anne's children, quite animatedly. She watched him hand over a small bag, then checking he was, he believed, unseen, carried on about his business. Now was clearly the time to speak to him.

Sarah Diggins crossed the yard to the causeway that bridged the moat. "This can't go on," she said.

"Too right it can't," he answered, knowing exactly what she meant. "It's costing me a fortune."

Good Heavens! Sarah would have sworn there was even the trace of a smile.

"Then, I think you need to speak to his wife," she suggested.

"Me? You're her friend. You know me - I'm a man of few words. Why me?"

"I can't suggest she takes him back after all she's been through. She might at least listen to you."

John Hart had no answer to this and against his better judgement found himself, Sarah at his shoulder, in Anne's kitchen at Meadow Cottage. Unprepared for such a deputation, Anne flustered about, trying to remember what she had in the house to offer by way of food and drink. John Hart could wait no longer.

"There is a man in one of my barns. He cannot remain there. I do not let tied cottages to people who choose not to live in them."

Then, without waiting for an answer, the man of few words left the tiny dwelling to trudge back across the pasture. In his head he was cursing Sarah for forcing this upon him. Now as far as he could see, he had probably only made matters worse. But Sarah, who followed him back at a distance, with tears in her eyes, knew different.

A day later, Virtue's child died. It was no real surprise. It was a miracle it had lived that long. When he heard the news, Robert should have been relieved, but far from it. It had, after all, been a boy.

Annie, Mary and little Sarah came after that, not to bring food, but tell him, "Mum do say you better come on back."
He returned, much chastened, and life was restored to something like normal.

Virtue went into service in another parish, and the child was laid to rest in an unmarked corner of the graveyard. For the second time, Robert's name appeared beside Virtue's in the parish register. It was in the book of burials, March the third, 1796.

Chapter 9

October 1797

Four children, one of them hardly a child any more, were stacking turnips as two riders approached at speed. One was a tall black-jacketed figure; the other a military man sporting the impressive red jacket of Captain of the Essex Regiment. The smallest child stopped her work, impressed by the elegant display and aristocratic bearing of the fine gentlemen, but was chivvied back to her task by her older sister. Lizzie knew what had to be done and how few hours there were before darkness fell. Nevertheless, when Henry Heigham dismounted and stepped her way, she found a moment to attend to him.

"Could you direct me to Mr William Diggins. I have very little time before I sup with the Bishop."

Lizzie left the others working and directed him along the rutted track to The Lodge. She had enough manners and grace to smile and attempt a curtsey. Heigham barely acknowledged her, before he and his colleague cantered off. Having only recently inherited his father's estate, he was attempting to put things in order as quickly as possible.

It couldn't have come at a worse time. He was due to present the quarterly returns for his parish as well as to lead prayers with his father's old regiment. Management of a large family estate was proving tiresome, and there were so many small farms to supervise, which was why he had come to Lodge Farm with an idea in mind: an idea which he hoped would simplify the management of his Cotton lands, to the benefit of all concerned.

Henry Heigham, the middle brother of three now found himself the only surviving son of Pell Heigham, a difficult and domineering father who had left Henry ill-prepared for such responsibility. Henry had buried two brothers in as many years, and was glad of the support of his old school friend, Philip Bennett on this occasion.

For his own part, Captain Bennett was glad of the exercise as he was expecting to be called to war in France at any time.

To say William Diggins was caught by surprise was an understatement. He knew, of course, that he had a new master, but he ran an efficient business and had assumed that rectorial duties at Hunston would occupy Henry Heigham's attention for some time to come. On first recognition of the visitors, the house was at sixes and sevens. Robert appeared, to take charge of the horses as the Reverend Heigham and his friend dismounted. Servants hurried themselves and William Diggins and his wife Martha were roused from their afternoon snooze.

John Hart was nowhere to be found, but this was not really surprising. He was bound to be out in the fields, preferring to make the most of the mild weather before winter struck.

Anne Saunders was dispatched to the kitchen, and under the instructions of Sarah Diggins, made ready the best china. This was not just some chance visit. Something was afoot.

Henry Heigham and Captain Bennett made an impressive pair of figures. Heigham looked every inch his father's heir and had he been anything but the second son, would almost certainly have become an army officer himself instead of the country parson he was resigned to being. Since his brother's untimely death, the inheritance had proved something of an inconvenience, but being a disciplined man, he was determined to start what he regarded as the necessary re-organisation of his estate.

"I must say, you have made a fine farm of The Lodge. Some new ideas coming in too?"

"Those are mostly of John Hart's doing," said Diggins, clearly showing his distaste for the changes. "He wants less livestock and more arable; some new crops in too. But I can't see the sense in growing root crops for feeding cattle if you intend getting rid of your cattle."

"You can sell them on to other farmers - and what's this I hear about cutting out cheese making?" asked Heigham.

"Oh he says you can't make good butter as well as good cheese, though we seem to have done well enough in the past," said

85

Diggins.

"Do I sense a problem here?"

"Oh no, sir, we have our differences, but things run smooth enough, so to speak."

Heigham could tell the time was right to announce his plan.

"I'm away to see the bishop, after which I have business that takes me outside the county, but my people will see to the details…You know the other land we have in Cotton? I'm minded to lease it. Of course it doesn't come with as grand a house as this and it's only a hundred and fifty acres, but if you want it, it's yours. The acreage is a bit scattered, but at least you'd be your own man, not just my Steward. And there may be an option to purchase, in the fullness of time."

He looked across at Diggins. He clearly expected an instant decision. To Diggins, who hated to be beholden to anyone there was no decision to make. Next to being owner, tenant farmer was the most respected position possible. He knew the lands that were being discussed. They were indeed scattered, some fields lying behind the tenements along the Broad Road, others as far apart as Dandy Corner to the North, and close to the Hundred Lane to the South. But it was good land, rich pasture much of it; and above all it would be his to manage as he saw fit.

"I think you know my answer, sir," he replied, unable to conceal his delight. Martha, sitting apart as the men discussed details, glowed with pride at what she saw as her newly elevated status. Sarah Diggins, concealed in the hallway was feeling rather less enthusiastic. Apart from the prospect of leaving The Lodge, she wasn't entirely sure where this left her.

Word then came by way of one of the labourers that John Hart had been located and was on his way. Once Heigham and Diggins had settled such matters as could be discussed there and then, the Reverend and his colleague took themselves off to the Corner House where it was assumed that Heigham would promote John Hart to the position of Steward.

It was no more than Hart deserved. For some time, he had been in effective control of The Lodge and most of the more successful innovations had been down to him. Yet there was one aspect of this rather private discussion that was to have profound consequences on all of those who worked and dwelt around Lodge Farm.

"My father was no fool," said Heigham. "When he put you here, he knew you would be the real force in this enterprise. Now is your chance to really prove yourself. From Easter, I want you to take over. Diggins will be away before then to see his own ploughing and sowing are in order. After that, it'll be up to you to increase the income here. You must cover the tithe and the poor-rate. And by the time I return, I want to see what you can do with this place. If you've any sense, you'll grow crops that look after themselves and keep livestock that need fewer labourers. Keep down your wage bill and there's more profit. Fewer tied cottages to maintain and less idle so-and-so's to try your patience."

John Hart had listened to this without saying a word. He could see the benefit of no longer having to go cap in hand to William Diggins who had long been as resistant to change as a block of granite.

"Oh, and by the way," said Heigham, getting to his feet, as if the one-sided conversation had come to an end, "...get yourself a wife. I don't find my Stewards function half as well without one."

Then, without waiting for an answer, he and the Captain strode out of the door and each in turn ascended the mounting block outside, in anticipation of Robert bringing the freshly watered horses to them. As they moved effortlessly along the lane away from The Lodge they encouraged their mounts to quicken from a trot into a canter. Lizzie and her sisters barely broke rhythm from their turnip-stacking to watch them turn and head to the west.

"What you reckon to them? That there Cap'n Heigham be a whully fine gent," said Anne to Robert that night. "He may be a vicar but he ride a horse like a true soldier."

"Maybe I'd look like him if I took the shilling," said Robert.

"Fat chance o' tha'. They don't take old'uns like you no more."

"They do - if they got skills - like proper horseman."

Anne laughed. "If you was a blacksmith, then they might jus' look at you. But you 'in't, so they 'un't."

"You allus know how to make a bloke feel wanted," Robert laughed and pulled her closer to him.

"Well I don't want you off arter them Frenchy girls - anyway you might come back with a few bits missing." Anne responded eagerly, kissing him, then pulling away with apparent distaste.

"You go git yarself a shave afore you come crawling on me," she grinned and went back to preparing the daily meal.

It was a rare moment of privacy in a house that usually rang with the voices of children. Lizzie had taken Annie, Mary and Sarah with her to visit old Sophie, who was growing feebler by the day. For all that, the old midwife enjoyed seeing the youngsters. And Lizzie, at fourteen, was sensitive enough to recognise it was good for her parents to have a few moments to themselves.

It had taken the best part of a year for Anne to come to terms with Robert's dalliance with Virtue Blomfield. Every time he had gone out for a few beers, she had wondered where he really was and though she knew from local gossip that Virtue was now living over at Westhorpe and courting a young farmer, it had severely knocked her confidence.

Robert, to begin with, had tried almost too hard. When he was extra attentive, Anne wondered what secret he was trying to conceal. When he sat around the house, she wished he would go out. For a whole summer, they had the best tended garden plot in the parish. But gradually, they had both relaxed and Anne was pleased to reflect on how things were probably better now than they had ever been. He wasn't a bad man really. He was weak, and sometimes worried her the way he flouted the law, but at least he never hit her like so many did, and he did still find her desirable, though she'd now make two of the young bride that had walked down the aisle at Wetheringsett ten years earlier.

It had been a precious two hours before Mary burst in. She had run down the lane to Meadow Cottage so as to be the first to relay the news.

"Look what ol' Sophie give me." She held out a small hand-carved wooden doll. "She say it's to bring luck."

"Then you must look after it proper well," said her mother. "How is she? How is old Sophie?"

"She got a terrible cough, but she say we make her feel whully good. She say we can go agin tomorrow."

"Well, maybe you can - we'll have to see," Anne replied, unsure how often such a frail old lady should be pestered by a roomful of lively girls. By this time, the others were there, each clutching a gift and equally excited. At least, the younger ones were. As for Elizabeth, she had heard that rattle of a cough before, and it told her there would not be many more such visits.

Old Sophie died the following day and though it was of course, a pauper's funeral, a good crowd turned out to send her off. She had acted as midwife for long enough to have been at the birth of most of the adults below middle-age. As they filed out for the interment, Anne was reminded of less happy times. The Blomfields were out in force; Virtue too, home for a day for the funeral. The corner of the chancel, damaged by the fallen tree, had never seen more than what was intended as a temporary repair. Anne turned to Margaret, anxious to forget the past and move on.

"I see things are about to change up at The Lodge," said Margaret. News travelled fast.

"Yes, Mr Hart will be our master now," said Anne.

"So what'll happen with Miss Diggins?"

"I don't rightly know," replied Anne. "I don't see as she'll be too happy about moving with her brother."

"Who knows - maybe it's time the Rector made an honest woman of her." Anne resented the implication.

"I'm sure Sarah's the most honest woman I know," she said, "but it would be nice if he were to propose."

The Reverend John Eade had other things on his mind at that moment. He was the father of two sons, both of whom, like himself, had read Divinity at Cambridge. Hoping to acquire for both of them an appropriate living, Eade had worked tirelessly to insinuate himself into the right society in the district. The elder son

Peter was already established in an adjacent parish, which just left Charles, who had recently graduated with some aplomb. For the time being, it had been agreed by the Church Council that Charles should serve as Curate to his father at Cotton. As well as giving the young man the necessary apprenticeship, it would enable his father to spend more time cultivating relationships with potential patrons.

As a result of these family distractions, John Eade had found little time for Sarah Diggins during the past few weeks. It wasn't that he had grown tired of her, but his priorities lay elsewhere at that time, and he saw little reward in paying undue attention to a woman one could so easily take for granted.

On leaving the church, Sarah found herself mounting her horse beside the new Steward of Cotton Lodge. John Hart had no real reason for attending old Sophie's funeral. She had never been a part of his life in the way she had touched so many others in the village. However, it was a rare opportunity on the ride home to speak to Miss Diggins about a matter that had been troubling him for three days.

They were a furlong or two from the church when he chose to speak. He kept it short and to the point. "Miss Diggins, I wonder if I could persuade you to become my wife."

To say Sarah was surprised would have been an understatement. Here was a man who, whilst always being perfectly civil towards her, had never shown the slightest interest of a romantic nature. Nor had even the least trivial form of intimacy occurred between them. So why was she straining to stop herself from grabbing the reins of his horse and dragging him back to the church before he had time to change his mind?

Instead, with the nearest to reckless abandon she had ever shown in her life she replied, "Yes, Mr. Hart, I think you could."

"Married!" cried Anne. "Married - to Mr. Hart, Oh, when will it be?"

"In the New Year, as soon as possible, and I'd like little Sarah to be my bridesmaid."

Sarah Diggins positively glowed. Regardless of the distance there still seemed to be between her and her husband to be, she couldn't hide her delight.

"Have you told the Rector yet?" Anne could foresee problems.

"John and I intend to see him this afternoon."
Already she was referring to him by his Christian name, though she had yet to use it in his presence.

John Hart was a difficult man to get close to, but Sarah knew that given time, she would. She had, over the last twenty-four hours begun to notice so much she liked about this quietly self-assured man. She had no doubt that respect would lead to love. Immediately, however, explaining the situation to John Eade was not something she was looking forward to.

"What did your brother say when you told him?" Anne wondered.

"John did it all properly; he spoke to William and asked him for my hand in marriage. William was right commonly pleased - offered to make over the deeds of his cottage on the Broad Road as a wedding present."

Anne could believe it. William Diggins had no great desire to supply a home to his spinster sister for evermore. Also, as the couple were both turned forty, it was unlikely there would be any offspring to inherit such gifts as might be given.

Though winter came early and brought a bleakness even greater than usual, it stood as a backdrop to scenes of merriment throughout the Christmas period. Anne, clever with her hands, aided by Elizabeth, sewed the fine fabrics that had been purchased for the occasion. Robert found it hard to see what all the fuss was about, but he became drawn into it, as were the rest of the family.

John Eade, the Rector, had tried to be happy for them, but struggled to see it as anything less than a lost opportunity on his part. Eventually, in late December, he called the couple to meet him at the church. They assumed it was to run through the service, which had been planned for January 5th. They arrived to find not John Eade, but his son Peter.

"I am afraid," he informed them, "that my father has had to go

91

away for a month on urgent business. If you have no objection, I shall conduct the service at your wedding: my brother Charles will assist." Peter Eade was a companionable young man with all the charm and charisma that his father lacked. If John Hart felt slightly irritated by the obvious snub, Sarah Diggins, for her part, was greatly relieved.

It had been below freezing for days. The wedding was still a week away. There was little work to be done around the farm, other than basic animal husbandry. It had rained heavily before the freeze and the meadow below the Saunders' cottage had flooded. Now ice covered half an acre of field. It was a temptation to all the children around The Lodge and safer than skating on the moat which was eight feet deep in places. Some of the children cut willow withies and ran them under their boots, tying them above as makeshift skates. Others more fortunate had steel bands forged by the village blacksmith tapped onto their soles. It was a great time to be a child. Elizabeth took her younger sisters, making sure there was a good fire made up to warm themselves by on their return.

This left Robert and Anne alone; she was sewing, he was repairing a bundle of old gin traps he had been given.

"What y' goin' to wear for this here wedding?" Robert asked. "I don't reckon you'll fit into that posh frock she's given you."

"Oh I'll let it out a bit," smiled Anne. "It's just as well the wedding's when it is." She paused before delivering her news. "'Cos I reckon I've got a bit more growin' to do in the next few months."

"You mean..." Robert was thrilled. It had been over four years since Sarah had been born and he did so want a son. "You sure?"

"I've missed two months. I reckon I'll be having it just afore harvest."

"So you're not certain?" "Pretty certain."

"Kids'll be out for a couple of hours - we could always make certain." And like a couple of newlyweds, they ran giggling upstairs.

Chapter 10

Spring 1798

The changes came, and within a short space of time, it was as if that was how things had always been. An uncomfortable number had not been re-appointed, and new faces appeared around the farm after John Hart attended the Easter Hiring-Fair at Stoke Ash. It was at that point that Anne was most glad of her past friendship with Sarah Hart. It at least ensured security of tenure.

Not that their friendship seemed to amount to much any more. Now mistress of the house, Sarah kept her distance. She rarely wandered down to Meadow Cottage and, perhaps on the advice of her husband, hardly spoke to Anne, treating her as just another one of the servants.

The wedding had been as grand an affair as had been seen in Cotton for many a long day. Several wealthy relatives had emerged from around the county from both sides of the family. Gifts abounded. Robert had taken the opportunity to get drunker than he had done in years, something that was now becoming a habit again. Money was tighter than ever and Anne began to wonder how they were to cope with another mouth to feed. As Anne had begun to swell, she had grown more tired. For once, Elizabeth was not much help. She clearly resented what she saw as another baby for her to manage and was seeking better paid employment.

Though still too young to be taken seriously as a midwife, her skills were, nevertheless, in demand. Her potions and poultices, her child-minding, her last rites, commanded more than her mother could earn as a house-maid and, but for her duties at home, would have enabled her to be fully self-sufficient. Anne knew, surely after aiding at the birth of her son, Lizzie would not remain with them much longer.

Strangely, both Anne and Robert had no doubt this was a boy that she had carried for over five months already. It felt different from the way she had felt when pregnant with the girls. As time went on, the child moved more, she felt sick more often; she had back-ache like never before. All the signs were, it was different, and that meant a boy. They had agreed; he should be called Robert.

Lined up, outside the farm office, Robert Saunders waited for his wages. He owed money for rent, but that was separate. It would wait. They had all owed back rent to Diggins. Now Hart was Steward, it shouldn't make any difference, should it? As the line shuffled forward, he moved out of the brightness of the spring sunshine into the darkness of the office, which was compounded by smoke emanating from the clay pipe John Hart tended to smoke. Robert held out his hand to receive his due. He acknowledged the pitiful amount by making his mark on the account book.

"You'll be owing for rent." Hart had removed the pipe and was staring up at him.

"I can't find it this week - missus is off work soon and there's no money to spare."

"Then you'll have to drink less or beg off the parish like you usually do."

Unlike William Diggins, John Hart found it hard to accept that the wages he paid needed to be supplemented from the poor-rate. He knew only too well that Robert had been to the parish five times in the last year.

"You'll owe two guineas rent by the time your wife's finished her lying in. I don't see you making that up with overtime."

Was it that much? How on earth would he find that much? He wasn't averse to a little thieving, a bit of poaching; but two guineas!

Come to think of it, there were all kinds of problems coming about as a result of this baby. It was due just as the harvest would begin. He would be working all hours; Anne would too if she hadn't been pregnant. The very time of year when you might put a bit by, they'd be struggling to survive. They didn't even have clothes for boys, though that wouldn't matter yet, and some of the girls' dresses would alter to make breeches. Robert gulped. He wanted this baby, he really did, but it didn't half make life difficult.

Two guineas! What would the overseers say this time - it was his fault for drinking half of what he earned? There were those like Garnham and Canler who back in July had looked down their noses at him as if to say, 'there you old sod, take your three and sixpence and bugger off and don't come back for many a long day.'

He knew what he'd do. He'd send Anne. She could plead a case better than he could. And they'd know if they gave her the money, it'd be spent on what was intended. As he trekked across Home Meadow, he pocketed what he would need for the night ahead. Anne could have the rest, and maybe she could be persuaded to beg for the money to pay the debt.

"Two guineas! Where does he expect the likes of us to find two guineas?" Anne was even more enraged than he had been. "He expects us to pay him two guineas for the privilege of living in this muck-hole?" She spat out the words.

"I'll speak to Sarah. I'll ask her if she knows what her high-and-mighty husband is doing to thems as is unfortunate enough to work for him."

But they both knew it was all so much bluster. Anne had barely passed half a dozen words with Sarah Hart since the wedding and Sarah was hardly going to take Anne's side against her husband.

"Mr. Hart say you oughter git you on down to the parish and see if they'll pay it." It wasn't exactly how Hart had worded it, but Anne could see it made sense.

I suppose I could pad myself up a bit, so as to make it look a bit more of a baby than what it do right now. Robert was glad to hear she was taking the idea seriously.

"I'll put him off a week or three so as your time'll be a bit nearer. You can go see 'em around the time of Whit Sunday and say as how Mr. Hart is threatening to put us all out."

It wasn't a bad suggestion. The overseers would sooner pay one bill for back rent than face being landed with a whole family to house and feed for the forthcoming winter.

"Meantime, I'm off down the Cock," said Robert. "One or two on'us got a bit of business over at Thornham Wood." He reached for the sack of traps that hung from a hook beside the fire. He was in high spirits. The rent would be paid and soon, he would have a son that he could teach to trap pheasants and catch carp. But right now, it was to Thornham: land belonging to John Henniker, Baronet. It was funny how the more respectable and important the landowner was, the greater the pleasure that could be had from stealing from him.

Three months into his marriage, John Hart had no doubt he had done the right thing. Sarah offered him the three things he valued most. She showed a good measure of respect for him, accepting his decisions without question. She was a good organiser and though not the most proficient at committing things to paper, had a fine memory and ran the house with a military precision that would have impressed their overlords. Thirdly she was warm and tender, though undemanding.

Until Henry Heigham had suggested it, the thought of marriage hadn't even occurred to Hart. But even a marriage of expediency requires a willing partner, and he felt lucky that with his lack of experience in such matters, he still knew he had made the right choice.

It had become something of a habit for the two of them to take afternoon tea together and though it was more in the form of a business lunch than a comfortable soirée, they both looked forward to that time of day. Planting was well underway and the younger, fitter work force was ahead of even the most optimistic predictions. For once then, John and Sarah found little to discuss and could enjoy the luxury of a more intimate conversation.

"I thought we might decorate the old servants' attic room." said John. "Then if anyone came to stay, they could do so in comfort. It's one of the largest rooms in the house and it seems a pity to leave it empty."

"Not just lime-washed walls, though," suggested Sarah. "If we're going to do it, couldn't we take a trip to Norwich and buy paper or fabric to cover the walls."

"Norwich would take three or four days - perhaps we'll try Bury instead. But it's a good idea. It may not be our house, but it's our home and I don't see why we shouldn't take a pride in it."

"You don't think…" began Sarah.

"Think what?"

"You don't think… we might have a child and need the room for a nursery?" John Hart paused. Theirs had been a marriage of convenience, not one borne of passion.

"I think," he began, choosing his words with care, "…I would like that very much. But, I think we would need to know one another rather better."

"We are both forty four years old. I don't think we have time to wait."

John Hart looked with some tenderness at the wife he had barely begun to know, and realised with some surprise that he was experiencing feelings of desire.

"Finish your tea. I'll see you when you're ready," she said as coyly as a forty-four year old woman could.

Then, she made her way up the western staircase to his bedroom. John Hart gave her just enough time before joining her. He never did finish his tea.

From that day on, his bedroom became their bedroom, and electing to stop for 'afternoon tea' became their very own euphemism.

Anne knew that things had changed between John and Sarah. You noticed things like that when you were a housemaid. You also noticed when your husband was getting in too deep. He spent many a night laying traps and coming home with a belly full of beer and a sack full of other men's game. Anne was worried while he had been night-adventuring with Wimble, but it had mostly been harmless thieving - the odd capon or pheasant for the pot. Now it was sacks full, filched from coverts and thickets of the gentry, which he sold openly round Cotton and Mendlesham. How long must it be before a Constable appeared at the door to search the house again? And what might he find this time?

One night in June, he didn't come home at all. Anne was worried to distraction. By now approaching the end of her pregnancy, she felt bloated and uncomfortable. At least the problem over the payment of rent had been solved. She had been to see the Overseers. Robert's advice had been to dress to look as pathetic as possible. That hadn't been necessary. She looked awful anyway. This pregnancy seemed as if it had been going on forever. All remaining energy had ebbed away as if the child inside her was draining her of even her personality. Ambrose Canler had taken one look at her and recommended the bill should be paid. Robert had responded by leaving a pheasant on the doorstep of each of the Overseers. He said that was the way things were done. Anne couldn't see it was strictly necessary, but there were no complaints.

The night he didn't come home, his dog did. That May, he had acquired a dog - a mongrel with a fair bit of terrier in it that he said he could train to catch hares. In truth, it was a useless beast, scared of its own shadow and was just another mouth to be fed.

Around four hours after dawn, two men that Anne had never seen before, helped Robert into his kitchen. She had already been at work for two hours at The Lodge and had come back to see if he had appeared yet and to attend to her own children. Robert could hardly walk, was clearly in great pain, and blood stained his breeches and ran down his legs.

"B'luddy keepers got guns," he grunted. Anne cleared the table.

"Here, lay him on here, - then you can just bugger off!"

There were no thanks for the two who had propped, walked and carried him the five miles from the scene of the shooting. Struggling to get close enough to the table because of the lump in front of her, Anne freed his breeches and ignoring his yells of pain, bared his peppered rear quarters. Then, leaving him still whimpering, and now aided by Elizabeth, began to wash the area with hot water. It was not a pretty sight. With blades sterilised over a flame, they dug out forty eight pieces of shot from his thighs, bottom and lower back, and whilst Elizabeth went to gather herbs for a poultice, the other girls laughed themselves silly at their wailing father and scolding mother.

"Oh it's easy dodging the keepers, is it? I tell you, that stupid hound's got more sense than you - at least it knew when to run away." Anne was not amused.

"It's a miracle this baby 'in't choosing to come right now, though what kind of shock it would get being born into this room I can't imagine."

"Leave me alone and let me die." Robert pleaded.

The little girls shrieked and giggled.

"You 'in't gonna die, you stupid old sod, but I whully hope when Lizzie get back with them 'erbs, they sting like buggery. Then perhaps you'll stick to workin' for a livin' 'stead of thievin'."

"I 'in't never goin' to do it agin. I promise Anne, I 'un't go poachin' no more."

"I'll remind you you said that, mark my wuds I will," said Anne. And she meant it.

Sarah had not been to Meadow Cottage for months. Though it only lay half a furlong to the South of the Lodge, there was something about her new position that seemed to set her apart from the work force. Also there was the fact that she didn't seem to need Anne's friendship quite as much as she had in the past. Growing ever closer to John, she was less her own person, more a part of what they had become.

Nevertheless, she had news to share, and couldn't keep it to herself any longer.

"You're going to have what?" Anne was amazed.

"A baby - in the new year. I was afraid I'd be too old, but I'm sure it's right."

"Lizzie will have to come and see to you. She's well used to the birthing of babies."

"I think John will send for the Surgeon, when it's time," ventured Sarah.

"A man - you can't have a man at a birth - it's unnatural."

"John says all the best families have a male doctor to deliver

99

their babies.   One or two of the medical men in Bury do nothing else."

"Oh Margaret and Lizzie'll be delivering my little Robbie," said Anne, unconvinced.

"You're still sure it's a boy this time?"

"I tell you, when you've carried the number I have, you know these things.   If you have a little boy, they can play together." Sarah, who had already discussed boarding school education with her husband, didn't have the heart to make it clear that any child of theirs would not be playing with the sons of servants.

Towards the end of July when, in spite of the weeds, every labourer was being diverted from hoeing and mowing to attend to the harvesting of the barley, Anne knew the birth was imminent. Lizzie and the other girls had been gathering the cut pease down on the field they called Little Champions.   Leaving Anne to mind little Sarah, Lizzie sent Mary after the midwife and prepared as she had seen Margaret do countless times.

"You do know what you be at, don' you?" called Anne, unusually anxious for one who had seen it all before.   Of course she did.   Elizabeth knew how to treat sores with root of comfrey: how to prepare elder and peppermint for stomach upsets.   She knew that crowfoot juice helped to remove warts and that feverfew relieved migraine.   She knew a few tricks of her own too, like chewing dandelion leaves for arthritis and even that juniper berries could induce abortion, if that was the aim.   But above all, she knew about delivering babies.   She and Margaret had become a team to be reckoned with and she had every confidence that the son her mother and father so desired would be delivered safe and well.

Margaret arrived, hot foot from the fields.   It was a time when all hands were needed, not just the men, but women and children too could earn a little extra to see them through the lean months that were to come.

For once, they weren't hampered by the old gossips, who tended to arrive for such events.   Meadow Cottage was about as isolated and inaccessible a place as existed in that part of Suffolk, and even the elderly could earn a few pence in the fields in July.

Long hours of daylight and good weather meant long hours working. There was no hurry to send news to Robert. He'd be back at sundown, and with any luck it would all be over by then.

Indeed it was. By the time Annie came home with the two younger ones, they could see the tiny face, swathed in linen, lying in the crib Robert had woven from osiers he had cut himself.

"What yer gonna call 'im?" Mary asked.

"T'in't a him, 's a her," replied Lizzie.

"But I thought mam say we was goin' to have a brother."

"She got it wrong, di'n' she," Lizzie retorted. "All we ever gets is girls in this house," she continued. "I reckon it'll be down to me to make boys."

"You'll need a husban' first," answered little Sarah.

"I'll need a man, but that don' mean I 'ave to marry he," said Lizzie contemptuously.

"Elizabeth!" snapped her mother from her bedroom above. "I heard that! You'd just not better let your father hear it. That's all."

"Alright then what yer gonna call 'er?" Mary continued.

"Mum say she'll call her Lydia. Can't think why. T'in't as if anyone in the family got called that afore."

Elizabeth had been surprised. Her mother didn't seem half as disappointed as she'd expected, with it not being a boy. It was as if all along, she'd been convincing herself it would be for her father's sake.

The same couldn't be said for Robert. He took one look at the child, then without speaking to Anne went off mumbling, "Lydia - what kind of b'luddy name is tha'?"

He came home in the early hours, reeking of beer and horses. It was a hot night and he stripped off in the moonlight, before lying naked beside her.

"Why'd you choose Lydia?"

"Twas sommat the Curate said. About a beautiful country called Greece. An' how Lydia was a special place and anyone called Lydia was special. D'you mind?"

He put a sweaty arm around her and hugged her.

"Of course I don't mind. We're getting a bit old for all this and I reckon the Lord don' want us havin' boys, but another girl's the next best thing."

"An' can she be Lydia?"

"You know what I done this evening? I hoofed off out of here and I di'n't stop till I got to the turnpike at Stonham. There's this crowd of gentry taking a coach stop for the night, so after a jug or two I tells one on'em about li'l Lydia. An' 'e say... *"Lap me in soft Lydian airs..."* Thass poetry - a bloke called Milton writ it. An' it struck me, if it's arright for a fine gent like that, who am I to object?"

Then, as an afterthought, he added, "An' with parents like us she oughter be a darn sight prettier than anything the grand Mr. and Mrs. Hart give birth to."

"Come here you stupid old sod," said Anne ignoring the tenderness of her breasts and hugging him.

"The Curate reckon she's special, and your fine gentleman reckon she's poetry. An' now she's even got her father's blessing. Thass not a bad start in life, even if we do be as poor as church mice."

PART TWO

Chapter 11

Summer 1800

Robert's promise to give up poaching lasted the best part of six months. After that, he was drawn back into it by a combination of the thrill and the necessity. A long cold winter and a wet summer meant wages were at an all-time low, and almost monthly, dozens of Cotton's labourers supplemented their meagre income by going to the parish. John Hart, now himself an Overseer, could well understand that things could not continue like this. It was a viciously tightening circle. Poor rates and tithes meant that he could not afford to raise wages, especially as the prices received for the crops, meat and dairy products they produced had slumped. Hart was now the father of a fine son who shared his name and, he hoped, would eventually be Steward after him. It was in everybody's best interest that he ran Lodge Farm prudently and efficiently.

Sarah Hart had taken to motherhood with a passion. Of course, a woman in her position expected to employ a nurse to be responsible for the day-to-day care of the child. But it had been weeks after her churching before she had felt able to entrust young Jack to a stranger. Which is probably why she chose someone who was not a complete stranger.

Elizabeth Saunders was ideally qualified for the job and quite happy to live in at The Lodge. She requested that she might still attend on child-births if required, but had proved to be conscientious as well as both presentable and intelligent. After their initial concerns, Sarah and John Hart now had no fears about leaving Jack in Lizzie's capable hands.

Sarah remembered, with some distaste, the last time she had been to Meadow Cottage to see Anne. It had been back in the autumn when the house had been cramped and crowded and smelt of damp and decay and poverty. Anne had been pregnant again and

Robert had been drinking heavily. It was an unpleasant experience she wasn't in a hurry to repeat. She almost felt they had rescued Elizabeth from an unpleasant and unsuitable environment. As Jack's nurse, she would be clothed, fed and accommodated, as well as less put-upon. The mantle of carer for the young ones had now fallen to Annie, who at twelve years of age was next in line.

Robert and Anne's new child, again a daughter, was named Maria and she seemed to thrive, in spite of her environment, which was more than could be said for Lydia. Anne's 'special' child was a poor little thing who seemed to catch everything that was going. But for Elizabeth's concoctions, she would surely have faded away long since. Light as air, she spent much of the day strapped to her mother's back. She had been late learning to walk, and even at two still cried when she was put down. She made little that could be recognised as speech, though Annie acted as a kind of interpreter, explaining what her cries and grunts meant.

In her new post of responsibility, Elizabeth could see the difference between Jack, some six months younger, and Lydia. Nothing in her experience could help her explain her sister's problem, but Elizabeth was sure something was wrong. She came to Meadow Cottage as often as possible, but her employers expected her full time attendance on their son, and often days went by without her seeing her family. She was under firm instructions not to take young Jack into any of the labourers' cottages. Where he was concerned, Elizabeth's medical knowledge was not trusted. At any sign of illness, the doctor would be summoned, and paid accordingly.

Since his shotgun peppering, Robert had found riding uncomfortable and moved more onto land work. This was less regular than the ostlery he had been used to, but throughout the summer months, it suited him well enough. At times, the whole family would work together in the fields; like on the cabbage planting in April. The land was ploughed up into ridges and Robert and others would dibble holes into which young plants would be dropped and firmed in by women and children.

In May there was hand-hoeing of carrots and potatoes, and livestock to be brought out onto sectioned parts of the pasture. In June, the hay and lucerne were mowed and even the youngest children were employed in carrying and stooking.

As summer came on apace, crops ripened almost too quickly to gather in and whole families were needed to attend to the thousand and one jobs that had to be done on a mixed farm. Of an evening, if they weren't already exhausted, men would see to their own gardens or plots of land, and traditionally women and children would glean whatever was left behind after a field was cleared.

But these were blighted times, and what had been seen traditionally as a right, now the landowners asserted was a privilege they had as much right to withdraw. Turnip tops, plough-split potatoes, ears of buck-wheat and forgotten pods of pease, whilst regarded by labourers as their lifeline rather than purely a perk, could also nourish livestock. Hogs, in particular, were adept at turning what had formerly been abandoned, into fat meat.

A flock of black-shawled harridans busied themselves as dusk fell one summer evening.

"I don't know what you people think you're doing but you're to leave this field alone." John Hart was adamant.

"But we've always been allowed the gleaning," protested Bridget Filby.

"Not any more. Besides these are hog beans - they're not fit to eat."

"They'll make a pottage," called Rachel Last. And then under her breath, "...for the likes of us, if not for your household."

"There'll be no more gleaning, I tell you," Hart thundered. "Why, half of you don't even belong here. Get home with you or I'll turn the bull onto this field and that'll see you off sharpish."

It was only the first of a number of such incidents in the district and though few came to court, Constables supported the farmers in depriving many of what they had come to rely on. Robert, for his part, made sure his night-time excursions included pulling a few carrots or cutting a cabbage on the way home. It all helped to flavour the pot, and it was his way of evening up the score.

However, his mission to part the rich from their wealth in the pursuit of feeding his family led Robert to develop a friendship with one as inventive as Robert was committed.

Obadiah Short certainly demonstrated plenty of imagination when it came to thieving. He devised traps of devilish ingenuity and enjoyed no small measure of success. Reluctant to expose himself to the danger of keepers with guns and man-traps, he had the sense to avoid the best policed places and instead, to plunder the lands of the more careless members of the gentry.

His latest plan was to net fish from the deserted moats spread around the district. Who knew what past history had led to their creation, but in Bacton and Cotton alone there were six such abandoned sites in isolated spots all within a moonlit stroll. Robert and Obadiah had slaved over the construction of the net for weeks. They had plaited fibres lifted from the Mendlesham hemp pools, and by trial and error worked out a system of knots that would serve their purpose. A fishwife from the coast would have turned her nose up at their clumsy efforts, but as it grew, they became more adept and they were well pleased with the result.

Their first attempts to use it had been, even by their own admission, a failure. Throwing and dragging the net had enabled their quarry to swim away with impunity, and they returned home tired and soaked through from retrieving the net after accidentally letting it go. Then Obie had an idea. He was never short of ideas, but this one, they felt, should work.

The nearest unoccupied moat was off the Stonham Road, barely half a mile away. It was a wide rectangular shape enclosing half an acre of scrub and trees. There wasn't even a trace of masonry to show what might once have been there. However, only yards away, one of a host of drainage ditches ran. After weeks of dry weather, it was almost empty and at a level below the moat. Obie had contrived the plan of digging a channel between the moat and the ditch that would allow water to drain from one to the other. If, he surmised, they placed their net across such a channel, then the carp they were after would be bound to find the net. It was Tyrell land but well away from farms and cottages. There was no fear of being caught.

This time then, armed with picks and shovels, as well as the precious net and sacks to carry home the fish, they were ready to try again.

It wasn't quite as easy as they had expected. It was dark and the nettles were high and uncomfortable. Also, the gap they had to dig looked far greater than they remembered it, and it became clear that one night's digging wouldn't be enough.

"I'm right done for," sighed Robert. "We 'in't gonna do this tonight."

"Thass a bit of a bugger," said Obadiah, anxious to complete the scheme. But he could see Robert was right. They were bare-ly half way and by now thoroughly exhausted. They both had to be at work in a few hours.

"There's nawthin' for it but we cover it up." Robert suggested. So they pulled at nettles and ivy and suchlike to spread over their digging, in the hope that no one would pay it close enough attention until they could return and finish the job. Somewhat dispirited, they trudged back to grab what sleep was left to them. Neither man was much use to his employer that day.

Early in the summer, Robert had, after persistent requests from the girls, built them a play-house. An old senescent pollarded oak stood as a marker at the corner of Home Meadow. Annie and Mary could climb to what was a kind of natural platform, and once they had hung a knotted rope from one of its branches, Sarah could join them, Robert built a floor and tied bundles of rushes above as a makeshift roof. While Lizzie had been in charge of them, they had rarely been allowed to indulge in such games. But Annie was still only twelve, and closer in age to her sisters. When they weren't needed in the fields, the girls would play in their tree.

Gradually, Lydia began to be more a part of their games, but unable to climb, she would sit at the bottom and look up. She showed no desire to join them and no frustration at being left behind as they ascended.   Maria, Anne's latest child accompanied her mother to the fields where she lay in the shade and could be breast-fed on demand.

One particular evening, after their meal, Annie and Mary with Lydia holding hands between them, and Sarah running alongside, scampered on down to their tree. Lydia half ran, half swung as her older sisters raised their arms, and she giggled.   For once, she seemed cheerful and enjoying life.

Either by climbing the branches, or by holding onto the knotted rope, one by one, the girls reached the platform.   It wasn't the only entertainment that the tree had to offer.   One long sturdy branch stuck out into the field at right angles to the trunk.   You could stretch out and lower yourself so you were dangling by your arms from what the girls had come to call 'the swinging branch.' Already, the bark was worn smooth from usage and the grass beneath flattened from successive swingers jumping down. It wasn't a big drop and the three older ones were well practised.

This time, Lydia was not content to just watch.   She whined and bickered until Annie could bear it no longer.

"Look, shut your minging, babby!" she cried from above.

"Thwing, thwing, Liddy thwing."

It was about as clear a communication as they had ever heard from her.

"We could pull her up - see if she likes it," suggested Mary.

"I'll help lift her," called Sarah who, having finished her swing, had jumped down and was in the process of picking up her sister. Lydia stopped whining, and giggled as Sarah attempted to put her hands underarm to lift her.   Lydia reached up and the two on the platform pulled one hand each until the tiny child was beside them. Once up there, Lydia wanted more.

"Liddy thwing."

"No you can't, you're too little."

"Liddy thwing." Two-year olds are nothing if not persistent.

"Liddy thwing, Liddy thwing!"

"Look you can't," said Mary. "You'll hurt yourself."

"Liddy thwing!" The volume was rising.

"I s'pose we could put her on there, so long as someone's underneath to catch her," suggested Sarah.

Against her better judgement, but for a bit of peace, Annie consented. At that moment, Mary was having her turn. She swung a couple of times, then jumped nimbly to the flattened ground beneath.

Instead of climbing up again, she stayed put as the other two carefully manoeuvred Lydia so she was hanging from the swinging branch. She seemed to like it and showed no fear. Mary reached up and swung her legs a couple of times, then she held out her hands to allow Lydia to drop gently, taking her weight as she fell.

If they thought this would satisfy Lydia, they were mistaken. Oblivious to turn-taking and of the opinion that her sisters existed simply to engineer such entertainment, again she whinged and fretted until she got her way. Each time she seemed to do more for herself, attempting to climb, pull, edge out along the branch and finally to swing unaided. More reckless and oblivious of danger than the rest, she swung her tiny body with such vigour, she was one moment looking at the sky, the next looking at the meadow. She had seen the others let go and drop, so why shouldn't she? Unfortunately they always chose a moment when they were vertical to the ground. Lydia, unversed in such matters, literally flew from the branch whilst horizontal, hitting the ground with frightening force on the back of her head.

The other girls, not prepared for this, waited for the inevitable shrieks. They didn't come. Lydia lay, exactly where she had fallen. She didn't move. She didn't cry.

Mary who had been intending to catch her was the first to her. The others scrambled down to join their sister.

"Oh, you don't think she's dead do you?"

"I thought you was goin' to catch her."

"I di'n't know she was goin' to let go then, did I?"

"Best get mum."

"No, get Lizzie, she'll know what's best to do."

Sarah ran across the meadow to The Lodge in search of her eldest sister, tears blinding her as she ran, and within minutes, the limp body of the injured toddler was being carried back to Meadow Cottage.

That night, Elizabeth, Anne and even Robert took it in turns to sit with Lydia. She was alive but showed no response, nor any inclination to come to. Robert had intended to finish netting the fish from the moat, but somehow all that seemed rather unimportant. Obadiah turned up to inquire why he'd failed to 'report for duty' as he called it, then left to finish the job alone.

"I'll leave a small cut-through till last," he said, "then I'll peg the net across the channel. I'll bring you your share, I hope the kid's all right."

For the hours they sat in silence, each thought his or her own private thoughts. Elizabeth trawled through her knowledge of the healing arts but could come up with no answer. Robert wished for Anne's sake that the child would survive. But he was not optimistic. He had known so many families that had buried infants. And many of them had seemed so much stronger than this pathetic little bundle beside him. Was she really breathing? Elizabeth said she was, but how could you tell? You couldn't really blame the other girls. They'd gone to bed wreathed in tears, and sobbed themselves to sleep. It was too much of a responsibility to lay at their door. It was Anne, their Mother, who shouldered the blame, feeling that she should have been there, caring for a child who was, after all, little more than a baby. But she refused to give up hope. Still convinced that Lydia was her 'special' child, as she prayed in the silence of that blighted house, she nevertheless felt this was a problem that would resolve itself. Never for a moment did she waver in the belief that Lydia would recover and that this would show itself to be an event that had a purpose in the overall way of things.

At a time around dawn, there was a knocking at the back door and a distraught Sal Short burst in.

"Is Robert here? Have you heard? They got Obie."

"I'm here," called Robert. He turned up the lamp. "What you mean they got 'im? Who's got 'im?"

"Tyrell's men. They found where you'd dug and they waited

two nights until Obie come back. How come you wun't there too?" He told her about the poorly child and how he'd not been able to go with Obadiah after all.

"Constable's got 'im now, manacled to the end o' his bed, they say - they're goin' to take 'im to the gaol tomorrow morning."

They all fell silent but for Sal's sobs until another, higher register sound reached their ears. It was from Lydia's cot. Then the child sat up in the lamplight, and they could see a broad grin across her face as she remembered.

"Liddy thwing," she informed them.

Sal Short went home where she had left her own two children. She needn't have panicked. Obie used all his ingenuity that night. By the time the Constable awoke, he found his prisoner had devised a way to release himself from his chains. Obadiah Short had had time to gather up his wife and children, 'borrow' two horses and make for the coast where it was assumed they had used money from the sale of the animals to pay their passage to somewhere where they might make a new life. But of course, that was all hearsay and the truth may well have been far less comforting.

By the time the Short family reappeared twenty years later, there were few around that remembered what had driven them away and they preferred to keep their story to themselves.

Whatever that blow on the head had done to Lydia, it certainly didn't seem to have done her any harm. From that day on, she was a changed child. She blossomed and grew strong and tall and lithe. Her father said the bang on the head had knocked some cheer into her. And her mother was more convinced than ever that she was indeed special.

Chapter 12

February 1804

Anne could always tell when Lydia was up to something. Like the fine lady at Banbury Cross, she made music wherever she went. If she wasn't singing, she was drawing out a tune on the flute her father had fashioned for her out of a piece of elder. Robert taught her songs too; some he had known as a child, others he had learned at work from the ostlers in the stables or the women hoeing. She learnt the words and tunes as easily as he sang them to her. He only had to repeat a song once or twice, and a few days later there she would be, singing it, word-perfect or picking out the melody on her flute. If there was no music to be heard, Lydia wasn't there. That was how Anne knew she had slipped out without so much as asking. She abandoned her upstairs tidying and looked across the meadow.

It seemed safe enough; Lydia's elder sisters weren't around; they had taken little Maria into the village. Gypsies were camped on the green and they had gone to look at the tents and the ponies. Annie had taken her lucky coin to see if she could have her fortune told. The cold weather had abated and Anne, their mother, had been only too pleased to see them outside in the fresh air. Lydia hadn't wanted to go: she had a new song to practice, she said. Probably it was one of the bawdy ones her father brought back from the beer-house from time to time. In a way, Anne was glad she'd stayed: she felt so much more protective towards Lydia than to any of her other children. Robert was the same. Since she had so nearly died falling from the tree, they tended to watch over her far more than was strictly necessary, for their own piece of mind. Coming downstairs, Anne opened the front door and called across the meadow, "Stay away from them ponds and don't be too long."

At nearly six years of age Lydia was still young enough to enjoy her parents' protectiveness and not to feel swamped by it.

She hummed a familiar melody, and pulling the flute from a pocket specially constructed to hold it, attempted to finger the notes. Finding a flatter, drier patch of grass, she danced in time to the tune in her head as melody and rhythm mingled. Then, she became aware of a small boy, about her own size, watching her from behind a hedgerow. She knew who he was of course. He was the boy they called Jack. The one that her sister Elizabeth used to look after; only now he had a governess instead. He wasn't allowed to mix with the likes of her, she had been told. Not that she wanted him to, particularly. She thought he must be rather stupid. Didn't he know that you couldn't hide behind an elm hedge in winter? Her parents said that the Harts were very grand, but this boy didn't look very grand. They'd only just stopped dressing him in girls' clothes. Lydia could understand that if a child wore only hand-me-downs, but Jack Hart had obviously never worn a hand-me-down in his whole short life. Lydia thought he looked lonely, not grand at all. And what was the point in being grand if it meant you were lonely.

"I'm an old country traveller,
No nobleman am I," she sang, loud enough for him to hear.
"I whistle and sing from morn till night
And trouble I'll defy;
I've one to share my company,
Of work she does her share
It's not me wife, upon me life,
But me rattling old grey mare."
She raised her voice still louder as she reached the chorus:
"Round go the wheels, fiddly, diddly dee,
Jogging along, together me boys, the old grey mare and me."

She continued for three more verses, sometimes walking, sometimes dancing, as she made her way up the meadow. The boy followed, still separated from her by the hedgerow. But by the last chorus, Lydia was aware of another voice joining her…
"Round go the wheels, fiddly, diddly dee
Jogging along, together me boys, the old grey mare and me."

"You sing very well," he called; then slipping into a gap between the branches, he was through and beside her.

"My dad larn me that 'un," she told him proudly.

"Do you know any more?"

"I know hundreds, and some on'em I can play on my flute, but I can't sing and play at the same time." She sounded disappointed.

"Could you teach me a song?" he asked.

Lydia, flattered beyond words, ran her mind over her vast repertoire.

"My dad lunt me one last week - one he git down the pub."

"What is it called?"

"I don't know, he never say, but thass another one about an ol' mare."

Jack Hart stood, open-mouthed, waiting for Lydia's next performance.

Irritatingly and with all the stagecraft of a veteran who knows she has her audience hooked, Lydia slowly prepared herself. She coughed as if to clear her throat, then ran a trill of notes through her flute, before launching into the song.

"When I was just a little 'ol gal
My mother often said
Don't let a boy get 'is 'and on yer joy
Till he take yer to the church to wed
   And now I'm a little bit older
   And I know what things is what,
   I've got me a mare, and the lads all stare
   When I show 'em what a mare I've got
   Now some lads stroke her top knot
   And tickle her under the chin
   And that's when I sigh and I say, 'oh my!'
   And I ask them to do it agin,
   And agin and agin and agin and agin,
   And agin and agin and agin.
   And agin and agin and agin and agin,
   And agin and agin and agin."

116

Doubtless, the true sentiment behind the words was as much a mystery to young Jack as it had been to Lydia, but it was a good song and he encouraged her to sing it 'agin and agin.'

He gradually joined in with more and more, until after about the fourth time he was word perfect. He was well pleased with the song, which is more than could be said for his scandalised governess to whom he repeated it later in the day. Even at the tender age of five, however, he had enough nous to recognise, from her reaction, he should not acknowledge the source of 'that dreadful song.'

Elizabeth Saunders had not been sorry when her employers decided young Jack should have a governess rather than a nurse. Their demands on her were such that they expected far more of her than she was prepared to give, and the time had come for her to move on.

Her only regret about leaving was she had grown very fond of the boy in her charge. He had shown every indication that he would possess a warmth and sensitivity that now seemed foreign to both of his parents. They, for their part, had made her job more difficult than it ever should have been. Typical, perhaps of older parents, they were smotheringly protective, to the extent that the boy had few friends, nor was ever likely to make any.

Elizabeth could only compare Jack Hart with her sister, Lydia. That child could charm a nation! To see all the sisters together, it was clear which one had the personality and gregarious nature. Elizabeth recognised herself as being cold and aloof by comparison. She had plenty of admirers, but offered them little encouragement.

The next of the sisters, Annie, now in service at Wickham Skeith, was a competent and diligent girl who would make a reliable wife and mother. Mary, who had grown up almost her twin, was already anxious to leave the family home and to follow her sister.

The odd one out was Sarah. Quiet and totally lacking in the self-esteem the others all seemed to possess, she was a plain child. Now nearly twelve, it was hard to imagine her as a woman with family and responsibilities. How would she ever cope?

The last of the brood, Maria was a cheerful and healthy infant, who, as her mother so often said, 'rounded off the family nicely.'

But it was Lydia who was special, and it wasn't only her mother that said as much any more. Lydia, with her effervescence, her talent, her joi-de-vivre was indeed special. Even Elizabeth had to admit that.

Nobody referred to Elizabeth as Lizzie any more, not even her mother. She was too much a part of the community for diminutives. She had been offered a tiny cottage in Back Street in Mendlesham. The row of houses had not so long ago, been a hive of activity. Women had worked long hours, wool combing, but now the wool and the linen trade had declined and moved away north. Many of the cottages had lain empty for some time and when Isaac Stannard, a distant relative on her mother's side, indicated a willingness to rent one to her, Elizabeth was delighted.

From this base, she was able to fulfil the role she had craved; a nurse to small children, producer of herbal remedies, midwife and layer-out of the dead. These were only a few of her many roles. Already, Elizabeth's talents were recognised in Cotton; now she found she could widen her horizons and could offer the poor of a number of villages the benefits of her skills.

With two of their children in service, and able to send home a little money, Robert and Anne found things easier than they had been for many a long year. They didn't need to go to the parish. Neither did they need to rely on Robert's night-time contributions. But old habits die hard, and besides, a new scheme had come into his head.

It all came about one night, when a group of them had attended a quoits game between Cotton and Stonham. The two teams had ended up beside the turnpike in the round-the-back-bar of a large coaching inn. After a jug or two, whilst seeking to relieve himself, Robert noticed that coaches were parked to the rear, out of sight of the road and even of the inn itself.

They weren't carrying only passengers. Any amount of boxes stood unguarded on racks and roofs. Robert could only surmise what they might hold, but suffice it to say, his curiosity and his greed were aroused. If coachmen were delegated to guard such freight, the drink had got the better of them, and to Robert, this seemed like a bounty sent from God.

So it came about, that one icy night late in February, without the distraction of a quoits game, Robert walked by the shortest route he knew to that selfsame inn with a sack tied around his waist for the bagging of the booty, so to speak.

He had informed no-one as to his intentions. Only Lydia had been promised something special if she was a 'good girl.' Robert began the visit with a tankard of ale. Partly it was Dutch courage, but also it was to bend an ear in the direction of the carriers who drank and caroused and let it be well known where they were bound and who they were working for.

The bar at the rear of the Pie Inn was convivial enough, though less comfortable than the large front room where the wealthier travellers gathered. Ale was brought through in jugs and jars and drunk from practically anything that would hold liquid. Spirits were available but rarely ordered there.

"Whup there, bo'!"
A basic and customary welcome from an assortment of carters and horsemen and labourers like himself.

"'In't seen you since the quoits," remarked one of the drinking crowd. "Come back for another thrashin' 'ave yer?"

"Just you wait bo' - we'll 'ave you when it's on our patch." Robert answered with some jollity.

"Yew still wuckin' at Lodge Farm?" Robert nodded.

"Wass 'e like, that master o' yars?"

"A bit too high and mighty, but 'in't they all?" Robert replied.

"Yew oughter git you on down to the hirin' at Eye this Easter," suggested one old boy in the corner. He was supping a pint and clutching a small wooden box. "Folks is all a-movin away up North. Do yew could git a good job up towards Narfolk."

"I wouldn't mind workin' with horses agin," Robert mused.

"Well bo', we git plenty o' farmers call in here and wasn't one sayin' jus' the other day how as you couldn't git good horsemen even if you was to offer a small fortune."

This wasn't what Robert had come to hear, but it was worth remembering. Perhaps he'd give the hiring a look. He was sure he could do better than spend the rest of his life in Cotton.

He still wore his working smock, so the sack, wound around his chest was well hidden. Walking there, it was none too warm and he was glad of the extra layer. Inside the inn, however, it was a lot warmer and he began to sweat. It gave him a thirst. He could hardly go ferreting among the wagons and coaches yet. No, he'd better get a quart or two down him first.

Of course, once well established with good company and a belly full of ale, there seemed even less urgency to complete his quest. The old boy he had just spoken to produced a box of dominoes and began to set them up on a table at the side of the room. Robert and one or two others joined him. A number of games later, the dominoes and their owner departed, several shillings the richer.

Periodically, in twos and threes they would wander out to empty their bursting bladders against a board that diverted copious quantities of urine into a stinking ditch behind the stables.

It was after one such visit that Robert did not return to the bar room with the others. Instead, he made his excuses as if he was intending to stagger away home. In reality, he'd drunk a few pints but was nowhere near the staggering stage. Confident the others had returned to their drinking, he crept along beside the stables to where an assortment of wagons, carts and coaches stood. As he had noticed before, boxes and trunks sat unguarded, awaiting his attention.

It seemed clear to Robert that anything of real value was unlikely to be left without so much as a lock to protect it. His attention, then, was drawn to a large coffer attached to the rear of one of the grander coaches. Two padlocks held it shut, but the fastenings they protected were each held by just three rusty screws.

Robert cursed himself for forgetting to bring so much as a crowbar with him and had to search around in the dark for a lump of metal that would serve the same purpose. A farrier's shed stood beside the stables. All manner of pieces of iron littered the ground. It didn't take a lot of searching to find one piece suited to the task. There were roars and guffaws coming from inside the inn. Someone was singing. Horses moved about restlessly inside the stables. There was no-one to take much notice of the sound of wood splintering as Robert levered away the padlocked brackets that supplied poor protection for the contents of the coffer.

To be frank, what he found, proved to be something of a disappointment. Even by the limited light of his shadowy surroundings, there was nothing to set his pulses racing. He found two hat boxes. He considered taking one, remembering his promise to Lydia. She would love dressing up in such finery. But it was big and bulky and there was little or no profit in it. There was a lady's vanity case. Anne would love it, but she'd want to know how he came by it. He removed a perfume bottle from the case. He could easily pocket that. There were books and papers in leather pouches. Unable to read, he had no idea as to their value. Some of the documents had seals attached. Would they have any worth except to their owners? One piece of paper he did recognise. It was a promissory note from a local Bank. He had never had one himself, but he knew what they represented. Folks said that they were as good as money. All you had to do was present them and the Bank paid you the amount on the note. He may not have been much good at reading, but he could recognise the symbols for five pounds. That was a piece of luck. Maybe this hadn't been such a bad idea after all.

Having removed all visible objects from the trunk, Robert noticed something else. He muttered under his breath.

"This don't seem so deep on the inside as what it looks on the outside."

Of course, the box had a false bottom, which presumably meant the real valuables were hidden underneath. He felt around for the metal strip that had served him so well before, and wedging it into the corner of the bottom of the box, attempted to force up the wood. Small slivers broke free, but short of poking and prodding, there was no easy way to prise up the floor of the box. Gradually, as more came free, he told himself, he could see the glint of what could only be precious metal beneath.

Once or twice, inebriated men reeled out of one or other of the inn's doorways to answer a call of nature. Then, Robert would crouch down still and silent, hardly daring to breathe until they had finished and caroused their drunken way back inside for more of the same.

Robert was growing ever more bold, striking at the barrier with loud but effective blows. Soon, he would have a hole large enough to accommodate his hand and he would know what lay beneath.

Tantalisingly, his first clutches betrayed what was under there, without allowing the space to withdraw it. Clearly, most of what had been valuable enough to hide in such a way was metal - possibly silver. It was cold to the touch and heavy enough to make for an uncomfortable walk home.

There were more voices, emerging from the front room this time; gentlemen's voices, scything through the frosty air.

"Not a bad drop of ale," called one.

"The ale's good enough, but it runs right through you," returned another as he urinated against the stable wall.

They were some time passing water and readjusting their clothing.

"Should we check the coaches?"

"No, they'll have stable lads employed to keep watch over them. Never you fear."

"Some hope," thought Robert, then he waited till they had departed back indoors, before setting to his task with a will.

Clearly, he couldn't take everything, nor did he wish to. Some of the items in that trunk were just too grand or too heavy to consider lugging back along the frozen tracks to Cotton. He couldn't resist the candlesticks, though. They even carried candles, which was just as well because he had never owned candles that size. They were like the ones they burned on the altar at St. Andrew's on feast days. A silver bowl, simpler in design than the rest, and with no obvious monogram, also went into his sack.

An assortment of items of clothing had been used to pack the silver into the trunk, and Robert saw some advantage in using them for the self-same purpose. There were gowns and lace scarves, even a pair of high shoes and gloves. Thinking of the house full of ladies at home, Robert packed the sack full enough to be an inconvenience and slunk off laden into the night.

The hardest part of the whole project would be explaining to Anne how he had come by such treasures. On the way back he concocted his story: not the most convincing account, but a valiant attempt that had elements of the truth about it.

It wasn't long after midnight when he found himself climbing the stairs to the room he and Anne had shared for the last fourteen years. He didn't need to avoid the creaking stair, three from the top. She was awake anyway. She always was.

"So what's that you just laid down in the corner?"

She was, by nature, suspicious.

"Had a bit a' luck di'n't I?" he replied.

He had rehearsed this all the way home.

"Played dominoes with this farmer - right gent he was. More money than sense. An' guess who won?"

"I reckon you're goin' to tell me you did."

There was still an edge to her voice as if she was waiting to find the fault in his story.

"An' when he runned out a' money, he give us this stuff out a' his fancy carriage."

"What sort of stuff?"

"Oh like you never saw - metal stuff, an' fancy clothes and - this." He produced the perfume bottle from his pocket.

"Wass that?"

"Thass that there scent stuff. You put it on you and it do make me want to have my way with'ee."

"I hen't noticed you needin' fancy perfume for that," she giggled. But she still put some on. Just to see if it worked. And it did.

In the cold light of day, Robert's story seemed considerably less plausible, especially when Anne surveyed the contents of the sack. She wanted to trust her husband. She really did. But just for safety's sake, she thought she would tuck away the spoils of the supposed dominoes game and suggest Robert got rid of it all just as soon as possible.

Lydia, always the most observant of the brood, watched as her mother examined first the silver, then the rest of the contents of the sack. She couldn't understand why all the pretty things had to go away out of sight. And where was the present her father had promised her? Presumably it was somewhere in the cupboard her mother had insisted on filling with what her father had brought home with him. Lydia could picture herself dressed in the fine gowns, wearing the high shoes and elegant gloves. She loved the look of the shiny candlesticks and longed to light the magnificent pearl-like candles.

Robert found time from his work to call in, mid-morning. Anne was not expected at The Lodge until later in the day, as the Harts were away for a few days.

There was news to deliver. "I got me some time off." Robert announced. "Spoke to the Foreman. Some fellow say at the inn last night, how as you can get better wages if you go up the hiring fair at Eye."

"But our home is here. We live here."

"Only while Mr. Hart do say we do. An' we both have to work all the hours God sends to never quite make ends meet."
She couldn't disagree with that.

"No, my mind's made up. I'm going off up the turnpike, and mark my words, I'll come back with a right good job an' you wun't have to wuck like what you do."

There was no arguing with him. His mind was set, though Anne could well see him coming back a few days later with a capful of excuses why the jobs on offer weren't to his liking. It was no good telling him he was forty-four with a family in tow and little to recommend him over younger, fitter men. As so often before, Anne shrugged her shoulders and waited for him to come to his senses. In the meantime, someone had to get on with the day-to-day things of life.

Chapter 13

April 1804

Footsore and discouraged, Robert's spirits nevertheless began to rise as he entered the final approach to Meadow Cottage. Oh well, if people didn't want to offer him a job at double his normal wages, he would just have to stay put. Things could be worse. There were worse places than Meadow Cottage - It was a bit isolated and you had to walk a hundred yards to fetch water, but they'd made it their home and that was probably how it was meant to be. He was sure he'd be coming home to a kettle on the hearth and children's voices in the garden. There was no reason to believe anything would be any different from when he had left four days earlier.

He remembered packing a minimum of belongings into a shoulder bag. He had casually unfolded the bank note, still in his pocket. Perhaps there might be a Bank in the small town of Eye where he was going. But he knew so little about such things. Could you take a note to any Bank, or were they only redeemable at the one where they were issued? What name of Bank was on the top of the note? He had wished, not for the first time, that he'd taken the trouble to learn to read. He had looked at his shabby clothes and realised he was in no position to pass himself off as the true owner of the note. With a sign of regret, he had then lifted the straw mattress Anne and he shared and laid it underneath. He'd give it more thought when he returned. In the meantime, he resolved to find the few odd shillings they had put by and to take them to pay for his food and lodging in Eye. It would drain them dry but he had chosen to regard it as a kind of investment.

Unfortunately, the cruel truth was that any job on offer was no better paid and the conditions a good sight worse than what he had already. On his return, no one seemed to be on the lookout for his coming, so Robert was at the door and inside before anyone knew he was home. Elizabeth was there. She had the four children seated round the table and was feeding them. They seemed unusually subdued. "Where's your mum?" Robert asked.

"You mean you still don't know?" Elizabeth sounded surprised.

"They took Mummy away," called Lydia, "and locked her up." Robert stared, open-mouthed. "But - why?"

"As if you didn't know," Elizabeth rasped. "They said she was in charge of stolen property and we can all guess who stole it."

"They took away all the pretty things," cried Mary.

"And my candlesticks," said Lydia. She sounded more upset about the candlesticks than about the absence of her mother.

So then, sending them all out to play, Elizabeth sat her father down and explained how a sequence of bad luck had led to her mother being apprehended and taken before the local justices. She had pleaded guilty, presumably to save Robert's hide and was already a day into a month's sentence at the Bridewell in Ipswich. It had been as if all the good fortune Robert had called upon in his life to keep him out of trouble had accumulated and now it was pay-back time.

Gradually, the story unravelled, and a sorry tale it was too. A distant relative, meaning to call on John Hart had mistakenly taken the lane to Meadow Cottage. Anxious to correct his mistake, the traveller had knocked, to be met by an apparition at the door. Anne at the time was out at work and the girls were alone. Lydia had taken the opportunity to liberate the objects she had seen her mother conceal. As a result, the unwary visitor was treated to the sight of Lydia dressed in an exquisitely tailored ball gown, high shoes and long calf skin gloves. She was clutching the most incongruous object of all, a massive moulded silver candlestick complete with lighted candle. Quite an articulate child, she ascertained what he wanted and directed him to The Lodge where he recounted the episode to John Hart.

"You must pay your labourers well," the man had remarked, and when questioned why, had described the items which he had observed serving as props for a child's game.

126

John Hart had long held doubts as to Robert's honesty, but without evidence, had been unable or unprepared to act on the rumours. This time, a word in the ear of the village Constable had led to a search of the cottage, and the discovery of the spoils of Robert's most recent campaign - even the five-pound note secreted under the mattress.

Further investigation at the inn on the turnpike revealed that Robert had been there but, in the words of witnesses, he had drunk and played dominoes all evening. The supposition was that while he drank, Anne had carried out the theft or at least been an accomplice to taking possession of the stolen property. Anne, for her part, could see that one of them would be tried for receiving and like the dutiful wife she was, confessed. Once again, there were plenty prepared to point the finger at Robert, but suspicion was one thing; legal proof was another, and at least the justices had one guilty party to send down for a month to contemplate her mistake.

Robert, whilst feeling twinges of guilt felt also a certain relief in the knowledge that had he been caught instead, he would almost certainly now be serving at least a year's hard labour.

"You really are a stupid old sod!" Elizabeth was contemptuous.

"Here, steady on, have a bit a' respect. I am your father."

"And what did you think you were going to do with a pair of silver candlesticks?"

"I di'n't think…"

"No you di'n't. Now look where it's got us. Well you needn't think I'm stayin' around to do your motherin' for you. You'll have to be a mother to this lot for a month. And I hope for their sake you make a better job of it than you do bein' a father."

With that, Elizabeth abandoned him to his lot, taking herself back down the lane to Mendlesham, whilst her father was left to rue the fateful day when the luck ran out.

Anne's absence was less of a hindrance than it might have been. Young Mary was well used to minding the younger three, only now she was expected to keep house too. The episode served to make her all the more determined to follow her sister Annie into service just as soon as she could.

Robert turned up for work the next morning as though nothing had changed. If only that had been so. If only the world didn't know his wife was in the Ipswich Bridewell, serving time for his crime. If only he had found himself a job over at Eye where such misdemeanours were, in all likelihood unknown. If only, on that blustery April morning, John Hart had not sent Sarah to deliver the next crushing body blow.

"You'll have heard by now what is common knowledge?" she said. "I thought I might go see 'er," he replied limply.

"They'll not let you see her. Men are not admitted to the women's prison. I shall, of course visit her; take her some food, and console her with the knowledge things are under control at home." "I am doin' my best…"

"Regardless of what is really happening," Sarah interrupted, "she needs to feel the children are being properly cared for and she will have a family to come home to."

She stared at Robert, glad to see he clearly felt as uncomfortable as she had wished him to. "What I shall not inform her, of course, is the fact that you, she and your family will no longer be employed or housed at Lodge Farm."

"But - we bin here for half our lives," Robert protested.

"Then you must learn to live and work somewhere else. My husband and I are in complete agreement over this. We have no real complaints regarding your work; especially not Anne's, but we cannot employ a convicted criminal."

"But it wun't Anne's fault."

"I know that only too well. I also know whose fault it really was. This time one of you was caught. I suppose you will view it as making up for all the times you weren't."

"But… how long have we got?"

"When Anne is released from prison, I will send a carriage for her," began Sarah. "The parish paid to take her there. They'll not pay to bring her back. After that, you have a week. Many would say we've been overly fair."

"So you're throwin' us out?" The full impact was dawning on Robert.

"We live in a small and close community out here. If we can't trust those in our midst, then they must go." Sarah spoke with chilling finality.

"But we 'in't never took nuthin' from our friends," Robert protested.

Sarah Hart stared back coldly. "How do we know?" she replied, before turning her back on him and heading towards The Lodge where she intended to berate her husband for always leaving her to deal with the least pleasant tasks.

The future looked bleak. Robert had no idea where they would go when Anne was released. He worked harder than ever to please the Harts in the forlorn hope they might just change their minds. Some hope!

Robert had been reasonably honest with the children regarding their mother's absence. They seemed to take it in good heart. They knew she would soon be back. But he did not tell them they would have to move from Meadow Cottage, the only home they had known.

One breathtakingly beautiful spring Sunday, Robert and the children were attending church. They had been rather more regular visitors to church since Anne's enforced departure, which was rather ironic, as it had usually been Robert who had been reluctant to attend. Somehow, since her incarceration, he had become keener to socialise. War was not the only misfortune that drew people to worship.

It had been a long, drawn out service. The Reverend John Eade was beginning to show his age. Since his son, Charles had left to take up his own living, the Rector had been forced to preach more often than he really liked. He was not an inspired speaker. The younger children had been fidgety and restless, especially Lydia, and Mary had struggled to keep them in order.

Leaving the church by the South porch, they were all struck by the power of the sun's rays. It was the first really warm day of the year. A large congregation filed out in family groups, then spread out to take on the truly social part of the Sabbath. Matins completed, Cotton folk chatted. It was a rare occasion when rich and poor conversed together, regardless of social position. They spread across the green of the churchyard in the full glow of an April sun. There was little to impede them. A few stones and a handful of monuments had been erected close to the church on the South and East sides. Some recent graves were marked with flowers or wooden crosses. Most, however, were merely grassy mounds over which folks walked with impunity, almost disrespect.

Robert stopped to join in conversation with a cluster of men while their wives formed their own clique near the churchyard gate. Children played games of chase, in and out of the trees around the edge.

John and Sarah Hart were speaking to William and Martha Diggins. Checking young Jack was safely engaged in a game of five-stones on the path, they could divert their attention to catching up on the latest village gossip. Theirs was, after all, a somewhat lonely existence. Young Jack, spotting the girl who had once sung for him, gravitated towards her. She saw him coming.

"You want me sing another song?" Lydia said.

"Would you? I'd like that," Jack answered.

"No point in me singin' you a song if you 'in't allowed to sing it yourself," she teased. She had somehow heard that he had been punished for repeating the last one she had taught him.

"I don't mind. I can always sing it where they can't hear," he replied boldly.

"Ha' you bin down the water splash?" Lydia asked, changing the subject entirely.

"What is a water splash?" asked Jack.

"Come wi' me an' I'll show yer."

Jack wasn't too sure he should be following this girl who had led him into trouble before, but a glance across the churchyard showed him that his parents and governess were engrossed in conversation and were likely to be so for some time. It really was a wonderful morning.

Just down from the church was a crossing of two tracks. Two

of the ways led to the village alehouses, but the third ran down to a stream, still swollen from spring rains and more like a river. It ran right across the road. Lydia kicked off her shoes and splashed about in the cool sparkling water, lifting up her skirt as she did so.

Jack Hart needed no further encouragement. He unlaced his boots and removed both breeches and hose. The two danced about for all they were worth. Just small children enjoying watery play and the first flush of spring, they forgot that anyone might become anxious about their absence.

In the churchyard, families had begun to drift away home. Robert was concerned. All of his other children were there. It was like a roll-call. Mary, Sarah, Lydia, Maria: except this time there was no Lydia.

The Harts were equally worried. They only had one to find, and it was now clear he too wasn't there. They asked one or two children still playing round the churchyard gate.

"I see two on'em hook off down by the water splash," suggested a larger child. That had both sets of parents worried. The water was known to be deeper than usual and more powerful.

Best Sunday clothes were never designed for quick progress along rutted lanes, but Robert Saunders and his three daughters, John and Sarah Hart, and the governess with no-one to govern, did their best.

They needn't have worried. From a distance, the shrieks of delight, the splashing, the flute-blown tunes and the sight of the two wet dancing children should have been enough to allay their worst fears.

Robert's worst fear was that Anne's 'special child,' Lydia, might have drowned. The Harts however, came to observe something far worse - their precious son reduced to his underclothes dancing in the midst of a stream with a most unsuitable companion, who clearly didn't possess any.

Oblivious to the world, eyes tight shut, Lydia held her bunched skirt high with one hand, whilst tootling on her flute with the other. Her father couldn't have been more relieved; which is more than could be said for John and Sarah Hart.

Chapter 14

July 1810

Those were, for the Saunders family, the wandering years. No sooner did they appear to find themselves established in a village or on an estate, than the brief period of hiring ended, and they were like gypsies again. Not that there was a shortage of work. Too many young men had taken the King's shilling and gone to serve on land or at sea. Other families were caught in the surge towards the towns, to Ipswich or to Norwich or even further afield. But Robert and Anne were past the age when a complete change to their way of life had any appeal and they drifted, hopelessly and aimlessly.

No parish would let them outstay their welcome. Recognised as paupers, they never settled long enough to become accepted as belonging to another place. There was no escaping the fact that sooner or later they would have to return to Cotton.

Lydia proved the most able to cope with the insecurity of it all. She made friends wherever she went, bewitching young and old alike with her charm and her sociability, and of course, her music. The rest of the family looked upon her as their good luck charm and as she grew in stature and confidence, often as not it was Lydia who won them a job and a place to lay their heads.

The family had started to shrink. Anne was past childbearing and was beginning to part with her daughters. Mary was now in service and being courted by a Cotton farmer. Annie had married Will Oldridge two years previously, though sadness had visited their union on the death of their firstborn, a girl named Marianne.

Elizabeth continued to ply her trade as nurse and midwife, added to which she now wet-nursed babies. When she had announced she was pregnant and that her second cousin Isaac Stannard was the father, Robert had been of the mind to give him a good thrashing. In the cold light of day it became clear that it was no accident as far as Elizabeth was concerned. Stannard paid for the upkeep of the child and Elizabeth was able to make an additional living as a wet-nurse. Added to which, she made it quite clear to her father that should her milk begin to dry up, she would have no qualms about following the same course again.

There was no talk of marriage there. In fact, Elizabeth seemed to enjoy the company of a number of men, to the extent that some in the locality were apt to suggest she had widened her job description still further.

By mid July, the barley was browning nicely, and the wheat already on the turn. Lydia was sharing her time between field-work with her mother and a cluster of other women and children, and entertaining. It was the season for fairs and village celebrations and a small group of local musicians would play for weddings and the like. Lydia, still only twelve, was as adept as any in the group on the flute and upon a tiny accordion given to her by one of her father's previous employers. Most of the musicians were travellers of one sort or another, but welcomed the girl into their midst, dressing her to look like a Spanish dancer, recognising that as she grew to fill the blouse, it would benefit them all. She was a comely child and already it was her looks and personality that was winning them attention and a reputation.

It was close to harvest time and in Debenham, as elsewhere, farmers were filling their fields with workers to remove weeds from fields of crops. Another week, and there would be no time for hoeing and stone-picking. It would be a case of all hands turning to reaping and bundling. As the foreman looked on, women and children laboured apace, heads bowed, muttering under their breath as they worked.

"Wass your Robert doin'?" Charlotte Tilney asked Anne.

"He's up tha' field over yonder," said Anne. "He got the hogs what's having the second litter. Them's a-gobblin' on the pease what's bin cut." She sighed.

Lydia, as if reading her mind added, "He say he'm better with horses than hogs, but they already got someone to plough 'tween

133

the taters." She cast her eyes toward the next field where a solitary horseman was walking between the rows of potatoes, hoeing up the weeds and mounding up the plants.

Both Sarah and Maria were also in the field. They hardly broke rhythm as their mother and sister, catching a glance from the foreman, returned to their labours. Each nursed her own thoughts, as she rooted out nettles and thistles and wild oats. Lydia thought of Saturday's entertainment. She and her traveller friends were being paid to make music for a dance at a grand house over at Stonham. She hummed the tunes she would play, and her fingers danced over the weed stems in mime of playing her flute.

Anne thought of Robert and how he missed his time with the horses and how she wished she was back with the friends she had known years before. She thought of her empty belly and how little there would be to fill it. Really, the hogs on the pease field would eat more regally than they would tonight.

Maria, now ten years old, longed for winter to return. Summer was warm, but summer meant work from dawn till dusk, and if you stopped, they shouted at you. Maria wanted to be like her big sister Elizabeth who didn't seem to need to work as hard as the rest of them. She wanted to go and live with Elizabeth and look after her baby for her. She knew she was Elizabeth's favourite of all the sisters. Elizabeth had named her baby after her, Maria. No, she wanted to live an altogether different kind of life from this. Elizabeth didn't have to spend her day bent double under a fierce and unremitting sun; Elizabeth didn't have a foreman sucking on his clay pipe and shouting at them to work harder. Elizabeth spent her days doing what she really wanted to do and earned decent money and respect for doing so.

Sarah's thoughts were altogether more private and personal than the others. In what should have been the full flush of youth, she had yet to find a lover. To tell the truth, Sarah didn't mind the monotony of hand-hoeing. She could feel the release of her own imagination as she chopped at the weeds, and could enjoy a certain satisfaction in clearing the ground, so the crops could thrive. She could dream. She could dream and fantasise about a time when instead of fields to tend there would be a home; and in place of crops, she would have children of her own. She could dream and savour the image of a loving husband - not a rough agricultural labourer, but a man of the world, a scholar, a craftsman, a soldier maybe. Locked inside her dreams, Sarah, of all of them was most content.

Come the end of a long day, home for Robert and Anne and the three girls was a tiny cottage, a full mile from where they had been working. A small lean-to at the back served as a kind of kitchen. The rest of the downstairs was one moderately sized room from which a staircase, little better than a ladder ran to an open space, beyond which lay the single bedroom. It was cramped in the extreme but it had a tiled roof and was probably more weatherproof than most they'd known.

Lydia as ever, practised tunes, as Maria and her mother prepared a meagre meal. Sarah fetched and carried, saying little and communicating less. Robert was out on the garden finding vegetables to add to the last scrapings of a capon Anne had stewed earlier in the week. "'In't you got them carrots yet?"

"Tiddly litt'ol buggers; hardly worth the effort," he called back.

"You said all along, soil 'in't right for carrots."

"Mam - can I go see Elizabeth, Sunday?" asked Maria.

She often did. Since they had moved to Debenham, Elizabeth had been living only up the road in Wetheringsett and Maria made the most of every opportunity to be with her eldest sister, who was more like a second mother to her.

"Just so long as you don' stop her getting on. She's whully busy is Elizabeth right now.   What wi' babies to feed and little Maria to look after, and it's the time for gatherin' herbs."

Secretly, Anne was quite glad to get a day to herself. Lydia would be out with the travellers making music. Sarah was no bother; you hardly knew she was there.   If Maria cared to take herself off for the day, that was fine as far as Anne was concerned.

"There 'in't much more'n a mouthful," complained Robert,

135

handing her what little he had been able to gather from the garden. "Trouble is, when you want it to rain, it be as dry as buggery, an' when it start, you can't b'luddy turn it off."

"They'll have to do," said Anne, taking the excuses for carrots. "Fill up on bread. There's plenty o' that."

"You want to go gleanin' them pease what get left for the hogs," suggested Robert.

"I wouldn't mind if the hogs hen't got at'em first. T'in't much good you sayin' about 'em now," Anne replied.

"Thass what I was comin' to," Robert continued. "There's a whole other field we 'in't put the hogs on yet."

"You can't glean no more; it's 'gainst the law," said Maria.

"Rich buggers' law," said her father.

"They don't lock people up for gleanin'," said Lydia.

"Have to lock up half the country folks if they did," Robert observed. "Anyhow, prison's better'n starving."

"'Specially if the one what goes to gaol 'in't the one what done it." Anne was never going to let him forget that.

Truth to tell, it hadn't been that bad. Ipswich gaol had been a new building and the regime, by the standards of the day, liberal. Anne had spent most of her month in the Bridewell, those six years before, caring for those who found prison impossible to bear. The inmates had been a strange mixture of the old lags, for whom prison was a way of life, the mentally unsound, who didn't even understand the nature of their crimes and young girls encased inside prison walls for their first trivial offence.

It was this last group in particular who looked upon Anne as a kind of mother figure. Many had no living parents and some were little more than Lydia's age. But at least they were fed and housed, and if it had been too cold at night, they had been allowed to bed down together in the infirmary where it was warm. Even the work had not been that bad. Women were not forced to walk the treadmill as the men were. Picking oakum was boring and it made your fingers bleed but Anne had been forced to do worse jobs in her time. No, prison hadn't been that bad for Anne: but she never

136

intended to let Robert forget that she had served time for his crime, and above all, that was the reason for their present predicament.

It was a poor pot to serve five hungry bellies. Nevertheless, they made the most of it before heading off in the direction of the field of cut pease Robert had described.

There was still an hour of daylight, and Anne and the girls joined what looked like a dozen or so who were already there searching for pods left after the picking.

"You and your girls can git you on over there," pointed one old lady that Anne didn't recognise. "…an' he…" she pointed at Robert "…he can keep guard an' see the Bailiff don't get wind of what we're doin'."

"Not that we've got nawthin' to be ashamed of," added another woman with a baby strapped to her back.

"If the Bailiff and his foreman care to remember, they'll think on the time they was a-gleanin' along a'us arter every field what got cut." This was spoken by a toothless woman with two small children in tow.

All together, there were now upwards of twenty old women, plus mothers and children of all ages. In spite of a hard day's work in the fields, they were scrabbing to gather in what they could before the sun dropped. Robert was the only man there. Gleaning was essentially women's work.

What none of them had noticed was the farm Bailiff, from the protection of a dense hedgerow, jotting down the names of all he could recognise amongst the figures at work in the field. Most he did recognise. Others, he would know soon enough. The magistrates would be busy. Drawn from the land-owning community; they were more anxious than most to stamp out unprofitable practices.

In noting the names of the offenders, the Bailiff observed from a distance how one man seemed to be marshalling the trespassers. He recognised the man as Robert Saunders - a rogue whose flagrant disregard for the law was legend. Yet to his knowledge, this man Saunders had never yet been found guilty of any crime. Well, let him try and wriggle out of this one.

137

* * * * * * * * * * * * * *

"Jack, have you checked that all of your clothes are packed - all that you require for the week?"

John Hart encouraged his only son to be as independent as possible. Yes, there were servants to see to such details, but he felt it was best for the lad to take on a measure of responsibility for his own affairs. Sarah Hart was staying out of the way. It had not been her decision to send Jack away to school, but she appreciated he could not remain at home with a governess forever. Neither could he find an appropriate education within easy travelling distance each day. As a result, Jack Hart, at the age of eleven was to be found lodgings in Bury St. Edmunds during the week, returning home each weekend.

Lodge Farm had prospered under the Harts and the big house sported an air of affluence. Sarah knew it was for the best and there was no doubting they could afford it, but she would miss her son dreadfully and her days would become even more lonely than they already were.

The Lodge had always been an isolated place. There were few close neighbours, and she cared for none of them. Since Anne's departure, they had grown, as a family, ever more distant from their employees. John Eade, the Rector, once her close friend, had grown old and frail and rarely went outside the Rectory. About the only friends they saw regularly were the Turners. A powerful farming family with lands in Old Newton and Gipping, they invited the Harts to join them for the occasional day's shooting. They were pleasant enough, but clearly enjoyed lording it over their less influential neighbours. Unlike the Harts, the Turners had married young, and their house rang with the excited chatter of boys and girls. Sarah Hart envied them that. Now, even her Jack was going away to school and the house would be too big, too quiet, too lonely.

Not that there was anything wrong in her relationship with John. If anything, the two had grown closer than ever and in many ways, Sarah was happier now than she had ever been, but if it was their aim to see Jack become Steward of The Lodge after them, why did he need a classical education?

"Come along Jack - the carriage is ready," his father informed the boy.

"You're sure I can't come with you?" Sarah's eyes pleaded.

"You know what we said," her husband frowned back. "He's going away for a few days at a time and must learn to stand on his own two feet."

Jack for his part, went willingly. He looked forward to mixing with boys of his own age and living for part of each week in a town. He would learn Latin and Greek, play games and sports and, he hoped, be taught to make music on an instrument. Split between the affectionate nature of his mother and the aloof stand-offishness of his father, he gave his mother a hug, then ignoring her tears, heaved a sigh of relief and climbed aboard the carriage.

*   *   *   *   *   *   *   *   *   *   *   *   *   *

The ad hoc Magistrates Court at Eye was a poor affair, the building ill-suited to its purpose. Brampton Dillingham examined the papers relating to the next case with obvious distaste. It was bad enough when the defendants numbered three or four, but here there were to be sixteen, nearly all women, doubtless accompanied by children and babes in arms. Even before the court began to fill up, he could imagine the disruption that would be caused by a crowded cluster of labourers' wives and their raucous retinue. It would be a morning punctuated by ignorance and disrespect.

The second Justice, William Carthew Esquire, was less perturbed. He had seen it all before, and being a leading landowner in the district, had little sympathy with those who sought to disrupt the efficient management of food production. He did not expect to suffer the anticipated melée long or lightly.

Rapidly the benches filled. What served as the dock was far from adequate and the gleaners spread out across the benches at the front of the designated courtroom. Children of all ages from the tiniest new-borns to strapping girls as tall as their mothers filled up the limited seated space. A sultry group of men stood at the back. One or two babies began to cry. One mother quietened hers by openly pulling a breast from under her chemise and stuffing it over the child's mouth.

Briefly, the court fell silent as the charges were read out relating to the women. They consisted of 'the theft and removal of produce belonging to one Edward Dove, contrary to the rule of law.'

"Please your worship, your lordship," began Ethel Barritt unsure of the correct address. "We was only a-gleanin' and even them in the Bible got to glean."

"Thass true enough," came a voice from the back and many of the throng murmured their assent. A child began to wail and though its mother rocked it vigorously, the noise continued. It set others going.

"Is it really necessary to bring these children into court?" protested Justice Dillingham.

"We 'in't got nobody to leave 'em with. We got to bring' em," explained a young mother.

"But what do your employers say when you turn up for work with babies?"

"Ooh, we 'in't s'posed to do that. They send us hoom if we do that."

"Precisely. Then why bring them with you today?"

"Cos like we say, we 'in't got nobody to leave 'em with. Everybody be here."

There was a curious logic about it all. William Carthew knew the only answer was to administer swift justice. He looked down at the line of defendants and spotted Robert, a lone male in their midst. He checked his papers.

"What is this man accused of? Surely he was not gleaning with them?" He looked quizzically towards Edward Dove and his Bailiff.

"I watch the man Saunders from a distance, your honour, and in my opinion he were the one what was in charge o' the lot on'em," explained the Bailiff.

"No!" cried Anne. "T'weren't like that at all."

"But you do admit you were all helping yourself to the crop belonging to Mr. Dove?" asked Dillingham.

140

"Only as was our right," explained Ethel Barritt.

"These people," observed Carthew, "take it as their right to help themselves to what remains after the harvest. They believe they can glean with impunity what rightly belongs to their betters."

"Then," replied Dillingham, "they must learn otherwise." The two justices consulted as babies' cries and adults' cat-calls filled the court. Carthew rapped a gavel on the desk.

"There seems to be nothing gained by a severe administration of the law. However, we are of the mind that in releasing you..." The court rang with cheers, especially from the men at the back. William Carthew waited for the noise to subside before continuing. "...it should serve as a warning that you have been brought to this place at all. If any one of you is brought before this bench again for a similar offence, she will at the very least, be sentenced to a period of confinement."

Thinking he had finished, one or two of the women rose to join their menfolk.

"As regards the man..." Carthew consulted his list, "...Robert Saunders. He, it would appear, was the instigator of this crime and thus will serve fourteen days hard labour."

In their delight at their own good fortune, most of the Debenham women made their way, laughing, out of court. Anne sat transfixed, surrounded by her daughters. Only Lydia spoke.

"Are they a-takin' dadda away?"

Anne caught the look of resignation in Robert's face and allowed him to be taken out before she put her face in her hands and wept. He had looked at her as if to say, "Now we're even!"

*   *   *   *   *   *   *   *   *   *   *   *   *   *

Lydia rode in front with the driver and blew tunes all the way from Debenham to Cotton. Anne sat behind with Sarah and Maria, surrounded by the few possessions they could still lay claim to. It was a beautiful day and hard to feel anything other than glad to be alive. She clutched the settlement order with one hand and hung on with the other as the cart seemed to find every bump in the road.

Anne remembered the last time when they had been carted

141

back to their parish of origin. She looked at her children. They hadn't even been born then; yet Anne remembered the shame and the apprehension that came with that piece of paper. She couldn't read it, of course, but she had a pretty good idea what all that legal wording meant. It meant, 'Parishes round here will use your sweat and toil, but stay too long or put a foot out of line, and paupers like you will be on a one-way journey back the way you came.' There were the seals and signatures of the two justices to represent the overseers of the poor of Debenham, all with the intention of sending them packing.

Robert still had a week to serve and as far as Anne could see, no home to come home to. What pity or support could they expect from Cotton, six years after leaving under a cloud.

"I'll be dropping you on the green beside the church," the carter explained as they crossed the turnpike. It was no use feeling angry with him. He'd been more helpful than they had any right to expect, but once he'd executed his duty, the best Anne could hope for was a slave-like existence in the slum they referred to as the 'house of industry.'

"Now all my jolly fellows come listen to my song,
It's only just a ditty and I won't detain you long.
'Tis of a pretty young maid who in Wetheringsett did dwell
Who went a-gatherin' nuts, the young men for to sell.
With me falla-la-lal, rallar-la-lal, fal-de-roll all day
And all the nuts that poor girl had, she strew them all away."

You had to smile. Nothing worried Lydia. Anne's special child certainly had the talent to raise everyone's spirits. Almost before they could stop themselves, they all joined in with her; the carter, Sarah, Maria; even Anne. And they sang every song that Lydia sang, right into the heart of Cotton.

Sarah Hart was on an errand of mercy. Even after all this time, she felt a real warmth for John Eade the Rector. Not so much older than her, he looked haggard and drawn by comparison. The years hung heavily on him and those who knew and cared for him doubted he would see the year out. The surgeon still attended from time to time, but admitted he could do no more. Peter Eade, the Rector's son was spending more time in his father's parish than his own and it was assumed that he would eventually replace his father permanently at Cotton. Sarah quite liked the young man who was clearly grateful for the time and attention she was able to afford his father. John Hart was less impressed. He spoke somewhat disparagingly of Peter Eade as 'that man who married his house-keeper,' until Sarah sternly reminded him he had done much the same.

So it was, on a bright August morning, with the air thick with the dust of harvest and the promise of a hot week ahead, Sarah Hart and Peter Eade were discussing their patient's progress.

"I must admit, I'm worried," said Eade. "We are both doing the best we can, but he is in decline and is now in need of constant attention."

"I come as often as I can, but there is the harvest to consider," Sarah explained.

"Nobody could do more than you have," said Eade. "The problem is the servant girl, Rachel. She means well, but she is young and a simple soul. She doesn't even live in. It would be too much to expect her to cope as my father's health deteriorates."

Suddenly the two were treated to the unlikely spectacle of a cart loaded high with furniture trundling towards them. The patient pair of chestnuts drawing the cart seemed not to notice the fact that the five figures behind them were bellowing out a song as if to waken the souls beneath the sod of the graveyard opposite.

"And the blackbird and the thrush,
They sang out from every bush
Keep you hand upon your little ball of yarn."

From the drive of the Rectory, Sarah Hart and Peter Eade watched as the carter set down his passengers, then unloaded their possessions onto the edge of the green. It had been six years since she had seen Anne Saunders, but Sarah recognised her instantly. As the children caroused, refusing to be dismayed by their situation, Sarah saw her old friend slump down on a rickety chair, still clutching the document she had been given, as if taking on the air of defeat for the whole family.

"They sent you back with this settlement order?" Peter Eade said. It wasn't really a question. "And in all this time, you were never able to stay long enough in one place to become chargeable elsewhere"

"A year and a day, Robbie used to say," explained Anne. "Then you got to belong to a place, only they'd never let you stay that long. Once or twice, we thought we were settled and then it was 'pack your belongings and away with you'"

"And your husband is in Ipswich till next week?" asked Sarah.

"Thass the worst of it, he didn't do nothin'. I know he's not always been the most law abidin', but he 'in't done nothin wrong - not for a long time. We was only gleanin' like how we always use' to. An' he wun't even doin' tha'. He were on'y watchin' an' they say he were the insti... insti..."

"Instigator," completed Peter Eade. "Yes, I can see how they might have chosen to believe that. Well, clearly we must find you somewhere to stay, at least for the time being."

He moved away from the family, drawing Sarah with him.

"I don't suppose you could see your way to..." he began.

"I can't say - not without asking John, but more hands for the harvest would be welcome. I can't be sure where they'd live. It's true Meadow Cottage is still empty, but it's in a wretched state."

As she spoke, the trace of a smile drifted across her face as if an idea had just implanted itself in her brain - a very good idea indeed.

"Just suppose," she began, "my husband is prepared to take them back and to see Meadow Cottage is made fit to live in... Well, it wouldn't be straight away, would it? But the servants' quarters in the Rectory are available and you do need someone to nurse your father."

"...I ... I don't know..." Eade began.

"Anne is the most caring and responsible woman I know," said Sarah. There was fire and a determination in her eyes. "I can't believe you could ever find anyone better."

Peter Eade smiled. "You're a good woman, Sarah Hart. I can see why my father is so fond of you. We'll say nothing about Meadow Cottage until you've spoken to your husband. In the meantime, I suggest we carry their belongings into the tithe barn and I'll see if Rachel can find them a little sustenance. They look as if they've not eaten a decent meal in a long while."

He looked across at Lydia who was standing on a table, tootling out a tune on her flute. "Who knows," he said, "I might even be entertained for my trouble."

Chapter 15

Summer 1813

Making old dresses fête-worthy was the kind of thing the Saunders family did well. Sun-dried flowers, scraps of ribbon twisted into buds and bows, shiny mother-of-pearl buttons found in boxes of bric-a-brac, tiny wreaths of leaves of evergreen: all served to stitch over tears and frayed fabric to almost convince the onlooker those ragged girls were presenting themselves in newly fashioned garments.

They might be poor, but for a day at least, it was to be hoped they might look like princesses. Each summer, the high point for many was the Church outing. Not that they went far. That wasn't necessary. It was, however, an occasion when all the families of the village could come together and feel a sense of belonging.

Carts, wagons and carriages visited all corners of the parish conveying rich and poor alike, with whatever foodstuffs they could muster to the glebe meadow just to the north of the church.

Robert had struggled into his Sunday best: Anne looked at herself and at Robert and felt with a slight heaviness of heart that they must appear old and dowdy. So much effort had gone into the girls' dresses, they had had to take second place. Actually, it was more like fifth and sixth places where their family was concerned. But at least their daughters looked wonderful. At least they could look on as proud as proud parents might.

Mary, home for the day, sat beside her intended at the back of the cart. Thomas Mallows was clearly delighted to accompany the one he was sure was the most beautiful there. Lydia and Maria, like twin flower-fairies, giggled at the village boys who pulled and prodded at the adornments to their dresses. Even Sarah, plain Sarah, looked almost pretty, such efforts had Anne made to help her in her transformation. It didn't matter, thought Anne, that the old 'uns looked - frankly - old. Just so long as their girls looked attractive and exciting and the way she had, not so many years before. They even smelt good. They had bathed in water scented with cloves and rose-petals, and brushed their hair till it shone like the early sun on dew-laden spiders' webs.

Wagons unloaded and trundled off for more. Groups formed, mothers chatted, children chased and fathers edged away in the direction of the Cock. As tradition had it, the old gossips, all in black, stationed themselves along the edge of the moat to Elm Grove Farm. Nobody wanted any unnecessary accidents and the stern looking line of ladies presented a formidable barrier to over-adventurous children.

Lydia and Maria flounced around the green, drawing lascivious looks from males of all ages. But they were like young swans, not quite in their full plumage and putting on a display that was merely a practice for the real thing. Mary was already entwined with her Thomas, as if to say to any other posturing females, 'this one is mine and mine alone.'

Sarah sat hunched, as if her comfortable old dress had some-how been made less well fitting by its pretty adornments. From time to time, men spoke to her, but her answers were monosyllab-ic; not so much coy as hesitant, and they soon went away again, so she sat alone like the last cake on a plate that no-one feels comfort-able taking.

From time to time, the numbers already gathered were swelled by others joining them. Most came by cart, even the ones living close by, for the journey was part of the treat, and this was some treat. Families had brought along food and drink, but it was added to what the parish had provided; a mountain of summer cheer. Peter Eade, the Rector could be seen welcoming each new wagon-load of arrivals. He was becoming a popular figure in his own community and unlike his late father was very much the man for a social gathering. He had a particularly warm greeting for all the Saunders family. He hadn't forgotten how Anne and her daughters had cared for his father for the last six months of his life, allowing him to live out his final weeks with a measure of comfort and dignity.

And when they had returned to Meadow Cottage, it had been Peter Eade's idea that Sarah Saunders should remain at the Rectory as nursemaid to his young family. Now only Lydia and Maria lived at home with their parents, but it didn't make for any quieter a household. No, those two were as lively and mischievous as a pair of young March hares. Peter Eade smiled at the sight of the two youngest Saunders girls, arm in arm, whisking the ground with their skirts as they skipped over the buttercup-laden green, lapping up the attention they received.

Of course, it wasn't long before the music started.

"Come on Liddy, give us a tune."

"Well, you get out your fiddle and maybe I'll look-see where I've hid my flute," she taunted them.

"Where have you hid your flute?" cackled one. "I reckon I can guess where you got it hid."

"You got a disgustin' mind, Jeremiah Baker," laughed Lydia. "My little sister Maria is only fourteen. She don't un'erstan' language like that." But Maria's giggles and blushes made it only too obvious that she did.

It still didn't take long to coax Lydia and a host of others to set a succession of familiar tunes ringing across the green, and with ale and cider to relax the timid, lines of dancing pairs took up the rhythm. Even Sarah was coaxed to dance. A quiet young man named Robert Head who was normally as reticent as she was shy was badgered by the other lads to dance with her. They neither looked comfortable, but entered into the spirit of things, nevertheless.

After an hour or so, Lydia, feeling like a break from the crowds and the excitement of it all, put down her flute and slipped into the shadows of the Elms around Elm Grove. One or two couples had already made off into the undergrowth, but they were otherwise occupied and scarcely noticed her. Having walked a short way, Lydia was aware that someone was following her. He was dodging in and out of the shadows, but she could sense he was there. More amused than afraid, Lydia darted behind a tree, then ducked under some bushes.

He - and she was sure it was a he - was still there, only now he knew he had been seen. What followed then was a strange game of chase cum hide-and-seek, until some way from where the music was, now faintly playing, Lydia stopped and called out.

"I know you're there, so I reckon you ought to stop and show yourself."

There was a pause, then from behind a mature beech, stepped a boy. Lydia recognised him as the boy from The Lodge. He went away to school, so was rarely there. He seemed very young, though she knew he was only about a year younger than her. He also looked quite comical. Encased in his Sunday best, recently bought, one size too large for him, he was hot and uncomfortable. She laughed.

"Don't be frightened," he said. "I'm not going to hurt you."

That amused her even more.

"Fat chance," she said. "You 'in't got a hope."

"You played music to me and taught me a song once. Do you remember?"

"Wuz it a rude song?"

"I think it must have been. They got very upset about it."

"Thass what I'm best at - rude songs."

"You're very pretty," he observed. "You're called Lydia, aren't you? My name's Jack."

"So?"

"Can I kiss you?"

"Why should you want to do that?"

"Then I can tell the boys at school I've kissed a real angel."

"Ooh I 'in't no angel, ask my mam," Lydia replied.

"I think you are. I've watched you sometimes. And I've heard you play in the evening down by Meadow Cottage."

"So?"

"So can I kiss you?" he repeated.

"Wass in it for me?"

"I've been learning music at school. I can play the pianoforte and we have a harpsichord at home."

"So?"

"If I ask my father, he may let you play with me sometimes."

If any bribe could have been designed to extract a kiss from Lydia, this was it. A kiss - yes, he could have his kiss. It meant nothing to kiss a little boy like this. She was used to the looks of desire she received from older lads, even the men, but she enjoyed teasing them. So far, that was as far as it had gone. But such an offer was too good to refuse.

Checking they weren't overlooked, Lydia pulled the boy by the hand into the shade of the trees. Irritatingly, she pulled herself up to her full height, so Jack, shorter by several inches, had to almost climb her to plant the promised kiss. He overbalanced and in trying to steady himself, ran his hand down her, as yet, tiny breasts.

"Here, you, keep your paws to yourself."

"I'm sorry... I didn't mean... I couldn't reach."

"Thass cos you're only a little squit. Come 'ere."

Then just so long as he couldn't doubt she had kissed him properly, Lydia grabbed hold of him in a firm embrace and kissed him as thoroughly as her lack of expertise and practice would allow. And to her surprise, she quite liked it.

Jack Hart was as good as his word. He did have a harpsichord, and for much of the summer he played whilst Lydia accompanied him, finding she could adapt to a totally different kind of music. The adult Harts became used to Lydia's presence and found her to be both charming and talented. They were quite glad Jack had found a companion to spend some spare time with. An unexpected bonus for Lydia came in the discovery that Jack was quite a competent musician, though he hadn't boasted about it. Lydia liked that. She also liked the way he hadn't told anyone else that he'd kissed her. Oh, she knew he would tell his friends at school, but she never expected to meet any of them, so that didn't matter.

However, it didn't go unnoticed the time they were spending together; and when her father started to refer to Jack as 'her young feller,' Lydia was not sorry it was nearly time for Jack Hart to return to school.

They shook hands after a final practice together.

"You can write to me if you like," he said.   It didn't occur to him she couldn't, and she didn't bother to enlighten him.   He would be gone the whole of the Michaelmas Term, and in all probability Lydia would be in service by the time he returned.   For all that, in later years, Lydia always looked back on that as her most happy summer, when everything seemed to be music.

1815 - After Waterloo

There was never a greater sense of national pride than during the summer of Waterloo.   As news of the victory broke, an epidemic of celebration hit every street of every town, and every village and hamlet in the land.   Families looked forward to the return of the soldiers - losses amongst the troops were reputed to be low and hopes were high of a safe return for the three or four that had gone from each of the local villages.   If they were alive, they would return as heroes.   They belonged to a variety of regiments. The East Suffolks, His Majesty's 12th, had spent the whole campaign on the other side of the world in India.   So it had been open season as regards recruitment in Suffolk. Young men, anxious to make a reputation for themselves had joined up, in a fervour of national pride, with any battalion bound for France or Belgium.

Cotton prepared to welcome back its own.   Even the harvest would have to wait a day or two to allow the population to honour Wellington's elite.   It was as if all the celebrations of the past, even those which had marked Nelson's triumph ten years before, had been a mere rehearsal for this, Britain's finest hour.   The fatted calf was just for starters.

Of the three returning to Cotton, one at least looked every inch the scourge of Bonaparte's France that the locals had been led to expect.   Unlike his two colleagues, who slouched in, dirty and smelling of the campaign, John Hubbard, anticipating the welcome he might receive, had taken the trouble to give them what they wanted - a hero worthy of the name.   The people of Cotton lined the crossroads with crudely-fashioned flags to cheer them in.

The families were there of course. John Hubbard's parents, who worked a smallholding on the Broad Road close to the Finningham boundary, had walked the furthest. They had already received word that all three were safe and due back within the hour. They could scarcely contain themselves.

Though all were merely foot-soldiers, the three arrived on horseback, courtesy of the Overseers, and the cheers could surely have been heard in the next county.

Robert and Anne Saunders, glad of a break from the harvest, were there with a good portion of their family. Maria, pretty as charm itself, chattered with her sister Lydia, whom she hadn't seen for a month, on account of the fact Lydia was well established in service over at Westhorpe. Sarah was also enjoying the celebrations, but much less talkative than her sisters. She still worked at the Rectory, but after the deaths of two of the children in her care, had taken it hard and no longer saw herself as being a fit person to mind children. In spite of their grief, the Rector and his wife had been at pains to explain to Sarah that they held her in no way responsible for what was surely the Lord's way of testing their faith. But she remained unconvinced and seemed more lost in her dreams than ever.

The sight of such a splendid figure of a man as John Hubbard: boots spit and polish shiny, and his buttons glistening in the sun, brought a smile even to Sarah's glum features. This surely was the man of her dreams. No mere farm labourer, a man of the world. She was not to know he had seen less action than most, and the nearest he had been to any real military confrontation had been in the mopping up after the battle.

Smiling beside her two sisters, Sarah looked not unattractive, and as the merrymaking progressed and Hubbard discovered the trio of Saunders girls, it was Sarah to whom he seemed to be giving the bulk of his attention.

"He like you," Lydia laughed. "Git you in there afore he run away."

"Perhaps he's really interested in you," suggested Sarah. That was how things usually were.

"But I 'in't interested in him. He be a soldier boy. Them's rum owd folks is soldier boys," cracked Lydia.

She had sung so many songs of soldier boys and the mischief they had caused with unsuspecting maidens, she believed she knew a good deal about them, and what she knew was generally bad.

For once, Sarah found she was not tongue-tied and withdrawn. With the aid of a drink or two of George Cobb's mead, she quite came out of herself; so that by the end of the day, plain old Sarah Saunders, whom many regarded at twenty two as bound for spinsterhood, could be seen arm in arm with Cotton's hero as if they had been going together for years.

John Hubbard came to the house the next day. He was still in uniform, anxious to milk the esteem in which he was presently held to the full. He knew it couldn't last. Lydia, who was owed time off, was still there. Like most of the village, she had a thick head. She couldn't remember what time any of them had returned home the previous night. That had been some party!

"Is Sarah here?" Hubbard asked.

"We're all a bit behind 'asmornin'," Lydia replied.

Her father had dragged himself off to work. Anne had gone to The Lodge. Master Jack was due back from visiting relatives in Cambridge and his room needed preparing. Maria was hanging out the washing that Lydia was mangling outside the kitchen door. Only Sarah was still abed. Unused to strong liquor, she was evidently suffering worse than most. However, hearing John Hubbard's voice, she pulled herself together calling, "I'll be right on down. Jus' give me a few minutes."

Lydia worked on with a will. She didn't intend her mother to come home to this lot. Anne slaved hard enough as it was, and it was beginning to show in the way she was tired so much of the time.

"What time'd you bring our Sarah back las' night?" Lydia asked.

"How should I know?" he replied flippantly. "'In't got no watch."

"Lost it in the battle did you?"

"Could'a had one or two. Plenty took 'em off the bodies after," he explained. "I di'n't like to. Dun't seem right."

Lydia looked at Hubbard. She wasn't sure why, but her suspicions were aroused. He was too good to be true, she thought. But she couldn't tell Sarah that, and doubtless, time would tell. She carried on mangling.

"Where's there more pegs?" asked Maria.

"Try the shed," Lydia suggested.

By this, she meant the walk-in cupboard at the back of the kitchen that was half-pantry, half-storeroom. Maria went in search.

It was a bright day again and it took more than a few moments for her eyes to become accustomed to the dark. Maria did not notice that Hubbard had followed her into the shed.

The first she knew about it was when two hands reached across her chest from behind and began to insinuate themselves inside her blouse. She felt powerless as he pressed himself against her. Village boys had fooled with her in harmless playful ways before, but this was different. He was panting down her neck and thrusting at her in a way that seemed less than decent. It was out of her control and it felt serious and wrong. Wrenching free, Maria rushed from the room, hardly acknowledging Sarah as she brushed past her and ran upstairs.

Stepping out of the shed door, Hubbard met Sarah coming into the kitchen.

"What are yew a-doin' down there?" she smiled.

"Oh, wrong door; so many ways to go and I don't know this place - not yet I don't." Sarah was satisfied. She came close and pushed against him like a cat demanding attention.

Lydia left them to it and followed her younger sister up to the bedroom where she found her in tears.

"What'd he do to you?" asked Lydia.

"Oh it weren't much really, but why'd he do it. He's s'posed to be walkin' out with Sarah. An' I di'n't ask him to, I really di'n't." She lay on the bed and cried still more.

"Look, he broke my button."

The gap in the blouse was obvious. Then as an afterthought, she added, "You won't tell Sarah about it will you? I'm sure she'll say thass all my fault, but it wun't, you know."

"No," said Lydia. "I know it wun't."

But she also knew, there was no way anyone could tell Sarah of this incident. Sarah who had waited so long for someone to take notice of her: and him a hero too. Lydia determined she would now be on her guard. She hoped it was an isolated incident, where a genuinely good man had behaved out of character. But somehow, she doubted it.

Lydia said nothing to her elder sister, but determined to be as protective as she was sure she should, at least during the days before her return to Westhorpe. For two days, she hardly let Maria out of her sight.

Hubbard arrived and departed like a bit-part actor making fleeting appearances. Sarah, besotted, followed him like a disciple. She glowed in a way that was so unlike the way she had ever been, to the extent that Lydia began to wonder if her fears were unfounded and Sarah's soldier was doing her the power of good. She didn't seem to notice that, having now discarded his uniform, he just looked like any son of the soil, rough in his speech and manners, and terminally unkempt. Sarah still saw in her mind's eye the elegant hero that had ridden into Cotton to the cheers of the whole parish.

Lydia was gathering together her few possessions in anticipation of returning to Westhorpe. For once, it was a dull morning and it threatened to rain. The rest of the family had taken to the fields to gather the harvest in before the storm.

"On your own are you?" Those few words were the first indication Hubbard had turned up.

"Sarah 'in't here. She'll be up the top meadow with the women. They don' need her up the Rectory till later."
But she was sure he knew that much already. So why was he there?

"You don' like me a lot, do you?" he asked.

"'In't for me to decide."

155

"You think you're too good for me - that right?"

"If you really want to know, I reckon you 'in't good enough for my sister, Sarah; but she 'in't stupid and she'll come to see that, all in good time."

"You're a right pretty gel, Lydia Saunders," he smirked.

"Well thass right kind o' you to say so, sir," she mocked. "But you try on me what you try on my little sister, Maria, and I'll stick you!" She brandished a kitchen knife.

"You see, I don't believe for a minute, you be the brave soldier you make out. You're all right with a frightened fifteen-year-old or a poor soul who's so in love with you she's blind to what you're really like. But you mess with me and you'll not have a lot left to mess with anyone - and they'll have to pin your b'luddy medal there to cover up what I cut off."

That shook him, but sporting a nervous smile, he continued.

"Them Flemish gels wu'nt like that. Them Flemish gals was proud to show their gratitude to them what fought to save 'em from the Frenchies."

"Get you on home bo'! I'd sooner wiggle my arse for Napoleon than get laid by you. And if Sarah's got half the sense I reckon she have, then she 'un't have nawthin' to do with you neither."

He could see he was getting nowhere with this one. He wasn't even as good as her at trading insults, but he could leave her with something to ponder. "Too late gal, too b'luddy late!" he called as he stomped away up the lane.

In April the following year, Sarah Saunders gave birth to John Hubbard's child. It was a daughter, named Mary Ann. Hubbard denied the child was his, but by then there were few prepared to believe him. A bond was issued on behalf of the parish marking the tarnished hero responsible for the maintenance of the child.

John Hubbard was married two years later. It was not to Sarah Saunders.

Chapter 16

November 1819

It had been several years since Lydia had been inside the Lodge. It had a kind of rustic grandeur, though to all intents and purposes it was hard to appreciate it as the farmyard spilled into the causeway across the moat. Even approaching the house without carrying half the countryside with you was nigh on impossible.

Lydia raised her skirts and stepped between the puddles. She looked up. At each end of the big house, a massive quadruple chimney-stack gave it a solidity that could lead one to believe the building had once been built to withstand a siege. There was no obvious servants' entrance to the rear, but of the two doors opening at the front, one was clearly far grander than the other. The door to the north of the Western front was plain and unobtrusive, whereas adorning the other, a large round wooden window, diamond-panelled with extravagant carvings above marked it as the main entrance. Lydia chose the former and, finding no bell, rapped her knuckles on the panels. John Hart himself opened the door. Having not seen him for six years, she was shocked at how he had aged.

"We're glad you could come. Step this way please."
Lydia removed her bonnet and followed. It was odd; almost, as if he were the servant and she the fine lady. She found herself in a small study room off the hallway. Sarah Hart was already there.

"You'll remember the house, of course?" said Sarah.

"Yes ma'am, but I never noticed much, only the music room," replied Lydia.

"You speak rather differently from the way I remember; I hope you don't mind but as I recall, you had a stronger Suffolk sound to your speech"

"That would be working where I bin - where I have been, that is," Lydia explained. When you spend a lot of time where the people all talk proper, it sort of rubs off, I s'pose."

"And you've been to London?" she was asked.

"Some months each year, the family I've been in service with went to town, and the last two years, they wanted me to go too."

"But now they have no further need of your services?"

"No ma'am." "So you have come to wait on us. This is not a grand house, you understand."

"No ma'am," said Lydia, then wondering if she was meant to agree or not, added, "but grand to the likes of me, ma'am."

"And we shall not be taking you to London for the winter."

"No ma'am, but I was ever happier closer to home."

"And we hope this will be a happier house than the one you left," added John Hart.

"'T'were a dismal place at Westhorpe, after the baby did die," reflected Lydia. "And as it were me what...who... looked after the baby, I reckon I made my Lady be reminded of the tragedy; which is why she did say I should leave." She paused, then added, "But she promised me right good references."

John Hart smiled. "You can rest assured, you come highly recommended. My wife will make you familiar with your duties and show you where you will sleep. I know your family are just across the meadow, but we would prefer you to live in."

"Yes sir," Lydia, unsure of how much formality was expected, curtsied.

"By the way," John Hart added, "Our son Jack will be home before Christmas. He has been travelling abroad. I don't think he has had much time for music in recent years though. Do you still play?"

"Not so much no more. It's not been the sort of place for gay music where I bin working, you understand. But I can still find a tune when I need one."

"I'm sure you can. Well, if we are not here and your duties are complete, feel free to play on the harpsichord. It is used far too little and this house could do with being the sort of place for gay music, as you describe it."

Lydia was shown around the house. There were far more

rooms than she had ever realised and even then, one or two doors remained closed from view.

"You will sleep upstairs in the corner house above the winter dairy," Hart informed her. "You should use the door you entered by today." "Yes sir."

"And whilst we remain less formal than doubtless it was in your former employment, especially when we have visitors, we shall expect you to know how to present yourself."

"Yes sir."

That was as much as to say, 'You may have once been a guest and a friend of our son, but remember your place. You are, after all, just a servant.'

"We expect things to change around here when our son returns from abroad," John Hart continued. "He will take on, increasingly, the running of the farm. My wife will manage the house, which is why we no longer need a housekeeper. However, if we have guests, you will be expected to show a measure of initiative. You will work with the cook, Mrs. Clarke, to ensure things run smoothly. You may employ occasional staff if necessary."

Lydia's mind was in a whirl. She wasn't sure she was ready for such responsibility, but was flattered that others believed she was. "You still have a sister at home?"

"Yes sir, Maria," Lydia replied.

"We would be happy for her to wait on us on such occasions. Just ensure she is clean and well dressed and above all, discreet. Such conversations as might pass in our dining room are not for publication, you understand."

"No sir." The conversation over, Lydia curtsied again.

"And I don't think that will be strictly necessary - not for our benefit anyway." He meant the curtseying.

"I suggest you fetch your belongings to your room and make yourself comfortable. Mrs. Clarke will show you where uniforms are kept. And we will expect you to commence your duties at six tomorrow morning."

"Yes sir." She half bobbed, then remembered just in time she wasn't meant to.

For Lydia, this was a homecoming that was beyond her wildest dreams. She had worked in service for five years as under-maid, nurse and finally as chamber-maid to a wealthy local family with business connections in London. At first, it had been hard work, but a delight, nevertheless. There were times when she had been so tired she could hardly stand up.

But the house had been so full of life that each day had brought new experiences, fresh pleasures and she had thrown her whole being into becoming the best maid-of-all-work her employers could wish for. A wealthy and influential family, they had recognised her value and her diligence by making her nurse to their new baby, a sweet, but sickly child who, despite her loving care, had died in London only eighteen weeks later. To Lydia, whose mother had raised six daughters in poverty, why with all that money and power this privileged infant should not live was a mystery. But then, the Reverend Eade had buried three of his and he had God as well as money on his side.

After the death, Lydia's mistress had fallen into a great period of despondency and depression. Two years had slipped away with mourning behind closed shutters and an end to laughter and pleasure. By the time her employers had heard word of the post at The Lodge, Lydia had already begun to wonder if she, Lydia, was the main cause of her mistress's inability to come to terms with the tragedy.

Moving back to Cotton seemed so right somehow; Lydia was determined to repay the Harts' confidence in her by being to them all they might wish, and more. As she placed her few belongings in the drawers and trunks provided, the coldness of her room could not chill the glow of pleasure she felt about the move.

Towards the end of November, a lavish dinner party was arranged at the Lodge. John Hart had been to a shooting party at Gipping and was returning the favour by inviting Philip Turner and his family to dine at Cotton.

As well as Philip Turner and his wife Mary, three of their children came too, Maria, William and Amelia. Every thing about the Turners seemed designed to accentuate the fact that they were one rung on the social ladder above the Harts. They arrived in a newly purchased carriage drawn by the most elegantly turned out pair of coach-horses that John Hart had ever seen. Lydia's father, Robert, grumbled to himself at the state of their hooves as they drew into the farmyard. He knew it would be his job to wash and comb the feathering before their return.

It was as well clean straw had been laid along the causeway over the moat, as Mary Turner and the girls sported gowns and shoes that were certainly not purchased in Suffolk. Mrs. Turner dripped jewellery wherever it seemed possible to attach it. The Harts, by comparison, were made to feel like the poor relations. Of course, they knew that was exactly how the Turners treated all their neighbours and they were prepared to suffer this minor humiliation in pursuit of a higher aim, so to speak.

"I'm so sorry Jack has not yet returned from the continent," said John Hart, "but you must join us again, all of you, just as soon as he does."

As he uttered the words, "all of you," he glanced in the direction of Maria Turner. She blushed and tittered nervously, trying to pretend she had not noticed what he might be suggesting. She was a silly little thing, really, but presentable enough and she was, of course, a Turner.

"So what has your son been doing these last months?" asked Philip Turner.

"Finishing his education, so he tells me," laughed John Hart. "From what it's cost me, I hope it's working; that's all I can say on the matter. Still, he can begin to earn his keep from now on - take some of the work from me."

"I was glad when my sons were old enough to do the same," said Philip Turner. "And as for Jack's homecoming, I think we shall all look forward to that."

With a complicitous wink, he glanced at his daughter who again looked away and coughed into her napkin in embarrassment.

Lydia and her sister Maria served and carried as the dinner party ran its predictable gamut of polite conversation, coloured with occasional intrigue. They knew it was their place to remain invisible. And even when the Turner children performed on the harpsichord (badly) and sang (worse), Lydia by now could close her ears to such dissonance and rest content in the knowledge that there were at least a few things at which she could better her betters.

In anticipation of Jack Hart's return, a cart was dispatched to Ipswich to meet the London coach. Those who remained at The Lodge set about with a will to prepare for the homecoming. Typical of Jack Hart, he put his luggage on the cart before riding a hired horse, hell for leather, back to The Lodge to catch them all unprepared for his arrival.

Not one to idle while others laboured, he set about learning the business of Stewardship with a will. Like his father before him, he was content to take his turn on the threshing floor or to cart grain sacks to the mill. When not at home learning his father's system of accounts, like as not, Jack Hart would be layering hedges or clearing ditches. With all the energy of youth, he threw himself into a frisson of activity, as if life wasn't long enough to learn all he needed to know.

Then there was the social side. What began as a homecoming party, stretched into weeks of visits and introductions, until Jack Hart declared to his parents once and for all that he didn't mind if he never had to be displayed in front of and behave politely to another member of the landed gentry ever again. Which was why he was not particularly enthused to learn that Philip and Mary Turner had invited them to dine at Netherhall.

"The last I remember of that ghastly household, there seemed to be endless bullies of boys and pudding-faced girls. They seemed to permeate every corner," Jack protested when informed that his presence at just one more dinner party would be greatly appreciated.

"They have been good friends of ours for many years," said his mother. "And besides, your father has a special reason for wanting you there." She did not elaborate and he did not ask her to. He was used to his parents wishing to show off the son of whom they were intensely proud.

Netherhall was much as he remembered it, a barn of a place, full of dogs and daughters, where the talk was mostly of hunting and shooting. The meal seemed interminable; endless courses that were clearly designed to show off copious amounts of silver and porcelain. The two elder Turner sons were there, Philip and Jonathan. They already had effective control of their own portion of their father's estate and had plenty of advice for Jack, knowing he was embarking on the same career.

The youngest daughter, Maria, was there, visibly embarrassed by the comments from both sets of adults stating that she and Jack 'really ought to get to know one another better.'

Several times during the carriage ride back, Jack was asked what he thought of Maria Turner. What could he say? She struck him as a silly little girl who was just eighteen and seemed years younger, forced into a revealing dress when she had little to reveal. In fact, his comments were non-committal and he was glad when the journey was at an end.

Lydia was still up when they returned. She took their coats.

"I've warmed the beds," she announced, hoping she would now be dismissed for the night and could get some sleep. She would still be expected to be up at six to tend the fires.

John and Sarah Hart said their goodnights and took themselves off. Jack poured himself a brandy.

"Did you have a pleasant evening, sir?" asked Lydia.

"I think it fair to say," Jack informed her, "of all the evenings since my return, that must have been without doubt the most dreadful."

"I'm sorry to hear that sir." What more could she say?

"Do you know the youngest Turner girl, Maria?"

"I have waited on her, sir."

"I do believe my parents have it in mind to marry me to her. What do you think about that, eh?"

"Well, if she pleases you, sir," Lydia answered.

"I do think," Jack replied, "she must be quite the most, immature, vacuous, uninteresting little girl I have ever met."

Then, to show that he wasn't entirely without feeling, he added, "and I'm sure she will make somebody else a very good wife."

"Yes, sir."

"But what need have I for a wife right now? I have comfort, a purpose in life and I have you to wait upon my every need. So I am resigned not to marry - not yet - maybe not ever."

He looked at the servant girl who was trying hard to stifle a yawn.

"But here am I keeping you from your hard-earned sleep. I'm far too selfish to be a husband to anyone. Away with you to your bed! I'll not keep you up any longer."

"Thank you, sir."

"Goodnight Lydia," Jack Hart called.

"Goodnight sir."

From time to time, either Reverend Heigham or his son Charles would cast a paternal eye over the way in which his lands were being managed. But as far as Lodge Farm was concerned, it was little more than that. John Hart was trusted implicitly, and if the Reverend did make an appearance, it was in all probability to visit his old University colleague, Peter Eade at the Rectory.

However, there would be the occasional summons for John Hart and his wife to visit Hunston Hall. This was one such call. It was no surprise. John Hart had communicated the fact that he intended his son Jack to take a role in the management of the farm. Whilst there should be no problem, he knew he was required to explain this in detail. Jack would be called to be approved of later.

So it was that about a week before Christmas, John and Sarah Hart found it necessary to make ready for an overnight stay at Hunston. Lydia saw to it that warm yet presentable clothing was packed into a small trunk and that her father was fetched from more onerous duties to drive his employers to visit their 'Lord and Master' as they affectionately described Reverend Heigham.

It was all rather hurried and Lydia was glad to see them depart so she could get on with the task of clearing up all the clothing that had been considered, then hastily discarded.

Jack Hart announced that he would be riding around the

164

pastures to check the fencing. He did not expect to be back in a hurry. Lydia felt a sense of relief. She could restore a measure of order to the house, maybe even find time to walk across the meadow to see her mother. The Lodge was quieter than she had known it for weeks. Barely a breath of wind blew outside and from the upstairs window, to the east the world looked flat and feature-less and empty, save a few cattle and lines of pollarded trees; oak, willow and black poplar.

Steadily, and with no real sense of urgency, Lydia fulfilled the tasks expected of her. As she came back downstairs, she was drawn to the living room where the harpsichord stood. Though John Hart had invited her to play, it had never seemed quite right, and anyway, there was never a time when her work was finished. Now, in this quiet empty house, it seemed like too good an opportunity to miss.

She lifted the lid covering the keys. Unfamiliar with such an instrument, her hands seemed clumsy and she did little more to begin with, than press them gently, then harder, to experience how much pressure was necessary to make the sounds and to discover which keys produced which notes.

Soon, she was at the stage of fingering simple tunes, but with the effortlessness of a natural musician, began to employ both hands to find chords and harmonies. Whilst far from adept, she was surprised to discover how similar it was in many ways to the little accordion she had once played, and she could start to string melodies and accompaniments together that were not altogether displeasing to the ear.

A song from her childhood flashed across her mind, a memory of days past. She began to sing and play slowly.

"A little cock sparrow, he sat in a tree,
A little cock sparrow, he sat in a tree,
A little cock sparrow, he sat in a tree,
He chirruped, he chirruped..."

She stopped, aware of a rich baritone voice joining her.

165

The voice continued…. "as happy can be."

She hadn't heard Jack Hart return. A little embarrassed, she shut the lid and tried to explain.

"Your father he did say if all was out, I could have a play."

"Don't stop for my sake." He lifted the lid and they played side by side as they sang.

"A naughty boy came with his bow and his arrow
A naughty boy came with his bow and his arrow
A naughty boy came with his bow and his arrow
Determined to shoot at that little cock sparrow."

"Your big sister Elizabeth taught me that one, when I was very small," said Jack.

"Me too - its prob'ly the first song I ever knew," replied Lydia. And they continued to the end.

"Have you ever played one of these?" asked Jack.

"Oh no, I only ever played a flute and an accordion," said Lydia. "Thass why I'm all thumbs."

"It took me years to play as well as you do with your 'all thumbs' indeed," Jack smiled at her. "Do you remember when you taught me that rude song?" he asked.

"I do, but that wun't my fault: they never say it were rude when they larned it to me. You don't still remember it, do you?"

"No, but I can remember the other song you sang that day."
His hands searched for the right key.

"Round go the wheels, tiddley, diddley dee
Jogging along, together me boys, the old grey mare and me."
They sang together at the tops of their voices.

"I do remember some o' them tunes we played together when we was about fourteen."

She tried to move her fingers to fit the notes in her head, but it was harder than the simple folk songs, and her fingers wouldn't stretch the way she wanted. His fingers rested on hers and placed

166

them where they were meant to be.   His hand was still cold from outside.   His breath was close to her face.

"Is that all you remember from when we were about fourteen?"

"I remember I were a bit o' a saucy strumpet then," Lydia said.

"I thought you were an angel."

"Is tha' what you tell your fine friends at school?"

"That I'd kissed an angel?   No, I never did.   They wouldn't have believed me.   I'm not sure I could believe it myself."

Lydia's fingers began to find another familiar tune.   Again Jack laid his hand on hers, but this time it was to stop her playing.

"I want to kiss you again, but I'm not going to ask this time." And he didn't.   He didn't ask the next time either, or the next, or the next.   Then he told her to sit down and he played and sang to her, a song of some antiquity and no little beauty.   The words sounded strange, and the tune belonged to a bygone age: but the message cut through her as though she had been kissed again by his song.

"Wilt thou be wulful still?
Wilt thou be wulful still?
Wilt thou be wulful still?
Shem, for they wulful will.
For the lass that I loved well
Did steal my heart and my will.
For the lass that I loved well
Did steal my heart and my will.

There was a bonny young lad
That kept a fair flock o' sheep.
He met wi' a bonny young lass
And waded the waters so deep.
The lass that he loved well
Did steal his heart and his will.
'Have faith,' said the bonny young lad
'My love will rest with you still.'"

167

It was a song that seemed to capture the moment. And she could still hear it repeating inside her head long after he had returned to his fences and she to her household duties.

Chapter 17

Christmas 1819

The harpsichord remained unplayed for the weeks leading up to Christmas. Lydia saw surprisingly little of Jack Hart in that time. Their brief moment of intimacy left Lydia confused. It was as if they were still childhood sweethearts and a shared song or a shared kiss amounted to much the same thing. Really, she felt, nothing had changed since they had been five years old.

Sarah and John Hart had taken a day in the market town of Eye to stock up with gifts and provisions for the New Year. Lydia had been given a set of verbal instructions that would have kept a company of servants busy for a month. Any thoughts she might have had of visiting her family were quickly dispelled. In her disciplined and organised way, she considered her tasks and mentally sorted them into some kind of order of priority. Jack Hart had a habit of wandering the downstairs rooms in mud-laden boots halfway through the day, so starting at the top of the house, Lydia began to clean and tidy, noting as she went what else might need attention. A drape was coming unhemmed. In one of the bedrooms she discovered a discarded pair of shoes that needed cleaning. The sun slanted in through the diamond leaded panes of a window showing every mark.

These were not particularly urgent matters, but neither would they be completely forgotten. Lydia had every intention of having the house in good order on her employers' return.

She heard a door creak and steps on the flagged floor of the hallway. Then the house fell silent again. She liked it like that. It was so easy to take a pride and a pleasure in one's work when there was no-one around to disrupt the effort. She carried on, brushing the north staircase and it was only as she reached the bottom that she felt a pair of hands on her shoulders and realised someone was there.

"Oh, you give me a fright," she said, though she knew who it must be?

"Come here," he said. "I want to show you something."

Jack Hart had removed his boots this time, Lydia was grateful to notice. He led her by the hand to the extreme northern end of the house.

"Have you ever seen the chapel?"

"No sir." What could he mean by 'the chapel?'

There was a door that to her knowledge always remained locked at that end of the house. She had assumed it was a cupboard for valuables or something like that. It would not have occurred to her to ask. It was not the only door in the house that remained locked. Jack Hart produced a key and with a little difficulty, persuaded a reluctant lock mechanism to turn. He opened the door, ushering her in. She stepped inside. It was quite a revelation. The small room was aligned east-west and what little light came into the room from outside came by way of a small stained-glass window, heavily overgrown outside by trees and the ivy smothering that end of the building. Her eyes very slowly adjusted to the darkness and she could just make out a magnificently carved reredos, such as might have once belonged to a grand church. At each end, there were two elegant pillars with smaller ones equidistant between. There was a crucifixion scene, elaborately carved into the centre panel, and a pair of candlesticks on an ancient altar table in front.

Jack Hart, who had disappeared briefly, re-emerged with a lighted taper. He lit the two candles on the altar. Suddenly the place became inundated with light and in spite of the smell of damp and decay, rather special. Flickering flames revealed peeling paint and plaster that once must have been religious wall paintings.

"What is it? I mean what's it here for?"

"Some time back in the past, the family in this house had this as their own private chapel," explained Hart. "Probably when the house was built or soon after."

"But why keep it secret?" To Lydia, this was a treasure that should not stay hidden.

"They do say that the Papists who tried to blow up Parliament met here. It's probably not true of course, but it was certainly not built for our kind of worship. The previous Rector said we should wall it up, like it was an abomination, but even he stopped short of suggesting we destroy it."

"You wouldn't destroy it?" Lydia was appalled.

"You really like this place, don't you?"

"It feels...special... kind of... holy, in a way St. Andrews never does."

"That's how I feel about it. My father insists we keep it locked. But I have the key and I like to come here sometimes."
Lydia shivered. It was damp and bitterly cold.

"Here, you're shivering, and no wonder." Hart stepped back to the altar and snuffed the flames from the candles with his fingers. The fading colours on the walls disappeared from view. Hart led Lydia back into the hallway before securing the door once more.

"I used to think I'd like to be married in there," said Hart, "but of course, that's impossible. It is a papist chapel and probably should remain locked. Unfortunately, it may be that those who live here after us will not value it the way we do."

"No sir."

"So, it must remain our secret."

"Yes sir." Then, after a thought, she added. "But if we should happen on a day like this to be on our own here, I'd be whully grateful to see it again."

"You shall my dear, you shall."
Then as he faced her, Jack Hart planted a kiss on her forehead, a kiss that seemed to say, 'now we have two secrets, you and I, two secrets we shall continue to share.'

*   *   *   *   *   *   *   *   *   *   *   *   *   *

"Lydia!"
This time it was the master calling her. She was used to being at the family's beck and call, but usually her instructions were channelled through Sarah Hart."

"Lydia!" More urgent this time. She hurried from the far corner of the moat where waste water was tipped. There was clear

171

understanding of what could be dumped into the moat, even that far from the house. Water from washing or from the preparation of food was all right. Foul water was committed to the earth at a greater distance. All manner of spoil was discarded beneath the waters of the moat - bottles, broken crockery, unreclaimable metal. But care was taken not to taint the waters. Even the water from the far side of the moat would find its way to the front of the house eventually, and it smelt bad enough in summer anyway.

"Yes sir." Out of breath and clutching a wooden pail, Lydia tried to make it clear she had hurried to answer his call.
Evidently, John Hart had come in from riding. He still wore mud-splattered boots and held a riding crop in his left hand.

"I've been to see the man Eade." He meant the Rector. "And he has this idea that Christmas is a time to demean oneself. He wants all the landowners, bailiffs and stewards, himself included, to serve a dinner for their employees after church on Christmas morning. He has this notion that for this one day, we should wait upon those who normally serve us. And that we should even go so far as to make a generous gift to our labourers upon their departure."

He stopped, to allow her time to answer, but as Lydia had not yet perceived a question, she remained silent. He continued.

"If we make ready the ground floor of the dairy, light fires to warm it, then with fowl culled from around the moat and a cask of strong ale from the Bacton malt-house, it should be possible to see the wretched man gets his way."

"Yes sir." Lydia wasn't quite sure where this placed her. She wasn't strictly a labourer, but neither was she a part of the family. She was soon to learn.

"My wife and I and Jack will serve, but we can hardly be in church and cook for twenty or more. You and Mrs Clarke will attend the first service of Communion - one of us will drive you there. That way, you will be free to prepare the feast whilst the rest of the village attend the midday service."

This came as something of a disappointment to Lydia. The Christmas service at St. Andrews was a highlight of the year. The church was always packed to bursting, athrong with voices

172

and light. Early communion was only for the hardy and the most religious. Spoken rather than sung and devoid of any seasonal cheer, it was a poor substitute for the real thing, Lydia felt.

"I know this is not the way you would wish it, but I suggest you may enlist your mother and even a sister or two in the preparations. And whilst the servers will expect no presents that day, when you receive your half yearly pay next month, account will be taken of how well you satisfy me in this matter."

It had its compensations after all. Lydia excused herself and with her mind still abuzz, took herself off to the kitchen to discover how much Mrs Clarke, the cook knew of these instructions.

Early morning communion was, as expected, a cold and bleak and cheerless affair. It had been a wrench to move out from the warm kitchen she had already occupied for three hours, into the unforgiving December cold of first the outside world, then the church. However, the service was mercifully short, and within an hour of leaving the Lodge, Lydia was back warming her hands in front of the range giggling with her sister Maria, who was raising her skirts to direct the heat at her backside.

There was much to do, and for hours the preparations went ahead apace. They were vaguely aware of horses and carriages departing and were only just beginning to feel on top of things when voices told them the proof of their labours was about to be put to the test.

Even then, the work was not over. The Harts, for all their moans entered into the spirit of things, carving duck and goose and pouring copious quantities of strong ale laced with gin.

But it needed the kitchen staff too to busy themselves to attend to the demands of an ever more inebriated band of customers. It was only too clear there would be no break for Lydia and the others that day.

Carrying a platter bearing little more than bones, Lydia hurried through to deposit it in a small side room. Jack Hart stood there, bottle and glasses in hand.

"Here, try this. My father's favourite wine. I think we deserve a little something for all our hard work."

The bottle was half empty.   Clearly, he had already had quite a little something.

"But I'm needed back in there."

A glass was placed into her hand and promptly filled.   A kiss was planted under her ear.   She needed no further bidding.   She downed the glass, allowed it to be refilled and upended that too. Then she pecked him on the cheek and with a cry of "Happy Christmas," flounced out to answer the calls of "Lydia, more ale!" that issued forth from the assembled throng.

Lydia, who had eaten less than most that day, felt quite light headed from the wine and enjoyed the ribaldry that followed such a feast.

"You can come and sit on my lap, Lydia, have a suck on my wish-bone."

"Jeremiah Baker, what must your wife think?"   Lydia laughed, then turning to his wife, Mary, she said, "I don't know what you do to encourage him but I reckon you ought to take him on home an' give him his Christmas present."

"What you bin a-doin' out there, gal?"

"She got a feller shut out there in the cupboard, thass what she got."   Then all laughed.   Lydia chuckled back.   "Thass for me to know and you to dream about."

"Give us a song and a dance gel, and show 'ee a bit 'a leg for Christmas."

So of course, she did just that, though she showed them a good bit less leg than most would have liked.   Then, after John Hart had made a good show of making a gift of sixpence to each of his labourers and three pence to the boys, as the ale ran dry, they drifted off back to their separate cottages.   Lydia watched her parents depart, then cast her eyes over the debris that had been the feast.

"Mrs Clarke, you've been wonderful - a magnificent meal. You have worked yourself to a standstill.   But enough is enough," said Jack Hart.   "Lydia and I will finish clearing up here.   Mother, father, you look exhausted - if you make for your drawing room,

Maria will bring you a pot of tea. Then she can return home."

Maria looked relieved. There was still any amount of clearing-up to be done.

Jack was right about his parents. The efforts of the day had had their effect on them. All of a sudden, they looked old and tired. For her part, Lydia was surprised how fresh she felt. An hour or so before, she had dreaded the thought of what had to be done after the noisy crowd had departed. Now, she seemed to have gained a second wind. Perhaps it was the two glasses of wine, or maybe it was because something suggested to her that Jack Hart had engineered this all simply to be alone with her.

"You'll have to tell me what is to be done."

Lydia surveyed the scene. She was aware that Jack Hart was awaiting her instructions.

"I don't mind helping where necessary, but you'll have to tell me what to do."

It was as if he was the servant ready to do her bidding.

"Well, the bones can go into the pot for stock. There's plenty of hot water, so we can clean what needs cleaning. The pigs will have such scraps as can't be made into a pottage, but that'll not be a lot."

She moved around the old dairy room with a grace and assurance that clearly impressed the Steward's son.

"There's not a lot of waste, is there?"

"When you have grown up in a house that has had to survive twenty winters, you learn to waste nothing. My father, he say you oughter grind up the bones after you've boiled 'em and put 'em back into the ground for the goodness thass still in 'em."

Gradually, order was created from chaos. Maria carried tea to Jack Hart's parents before taking her leave. By this time, the dairy was clear and spotlessly clean.

"You really are an amazing girl Lydia," said Jack, coming closer and resting his firm, but manicured hands on her shoulders. "Amazing and talented and very beautiful."

Then, he kissed her. Not a stolen, boast-about-to-the-boys-at-school kiss. Not a conspiratorial, 'let's grab the moment' kiss. Not

175

a chaste, brother and sister, lifelong-friends kiss.   Not even a 'carried away in the heat of the moment' kiss.   No, this was a kiss they had both anticipated and waited for to savour, with all the passion that the two of them didn't believe they possessed.   Not until that moment.   And content they would not be interrupted, they continued to kiss and caress and so much more, until it seemed the most natural thing in the world to be making the completest love on the vast kitchen table that had served for the feast only hours before.

It was stupid - servant girl and her master's son, a gulf of class and status.   It was not stupid; from earliest times they had grown together so that this was only a blossoming of a long growing desire, and what was now binding them transcended any differences in their backgrounds.

It was careless - they both knew only too well where such affairs led: to unfulfilled expectations and unwanted bastards.   It was not careless, it was as if they had both been building up to this moment and it would live in both of their memories for the rest of their lives.

It was wanton - on this the most holy feast day of the year to abandon all sense of decency with his parents only yards away.   It was not wanton: just a natural expression of a closeness that had grown since childhood and merely served to demonstrate that childhood was at an end.

It was deplorable - the seduction of a young and innocent servant by a worldly man taking advantage of wealth and privilege. It was not deplorable, for at that moment, Jack Hart felt a love and a passion that defied reason, and was oblivious to rational thought. And Lydia was not so innocent - Lydia, who had danced with gypsies, sung bawdy songs from when she was so young she couldn't understand the words and rebuffed countless advances far less subtle than this.

Yes, it was stupid, it was careless, and wanton and utterly deplorable!   Of course it was. But it was one thing more. It was inevitable.

Since they had played and sung and kept secrets and left their childhood behind together, they knew - they must have known - it would lead to this. He, in the throes of passion, wishing every day could be like this Christmas Day: she, oblivious to any discomfort in her situation, wondering whether she was a slut for wishing it could last forever.

Then, in a moment it was all over and those slightly uncomfortable emotions came to the fore - vulnerability, embarrassment, concern and the thoughts that ran through both their heads as they sought to hide what they had been most free with only moments before.

Was it stupid? Was it careless? Was it wanton or deplorable to behave in such a fashion? Or was it inevitable, and would it be the inevitable start of the story that was to become Jack and Lydia?

Chapter 18

New Year 1820

Elated but exhausted, Lydia retired to her tiny room above the dairy. She could just hear the soft snores of Mrs. Clarke, the cook, sleeping just the other side of the old stud-work walls. Though her mind was abuzz, her tiredness soon got the better of her and she was soon oblivious to the world outside her room.

She woke early, as much from the sense of cold as anything. A full moon shone from a clear sky and crazy frosted patterns on both sides of the leaded window cast hazy shadows across the walls. It was the kind of night that meant all kinds of problems for the menial staff. Water would be frozen in butts and buckets, milk would have the consistency of slush; even the bread and the cheese would be as solid lumps, refusing to be cut.

There was no doubting her first duties. Fires must be coaxed into activity; those that had gone out, re-lit. With a supreme effort of will, she forced herself to emerge from under the covers. They didn't afford much comfort, but she was reluctant to lift them. Feeling the wintry air on her skin made Lydia realise just how cold it had turned and why she, in spite of her tiredness, had woken early.

Throwing on layers of the warmest clothing she possessed, Lydia crept downstairs to check the kitchen fires. It was much warmer down there and it gave her courage to step outside and cross over to The Lodge.

When the family was home, doors were rarely locked, so she was able to slip inside and begin her rounds. There was wood and coal aplenty: no need to fetch more in the dark. Gradually, her toes and fingers, her cheeks and even her nose felt warm. As dawn rose in a magnificence of oranges and purples, the house was ready for its inhabitants to rise to discover the day.

Jack Hart was the first to surface. Not for the first time, he surprised her. His breath was on her neck and his hands cupped her breasts from behind. He kissed the side of her head, nothing more, then as if afraid of being overheard, said, "Good morning Lydia." Just, "Good morning Lydia", as if it was any other morning and the previous night and the last few seconds had never happened.

"Good morning, sir," she replied, presumably for the same audience.

Later that morning, a rider on horseback appeared in the yard. He carried a message - an invitation to the Harts to join their friends the Turners at Old Newton for the New Year. It was still light when later that afternoon a carriage took Jack Hart and his parents those few miles though it seemed to Lydia as if they had departed for a foreign country.

It had its compensations, of course. Provided she prepared the house for their return, Lydia had the prospect of several days during which time she could stay with her parents and visit her sisters. For all that, it was not as she would have wished it.

No firm date or time was arranged for the Steward's return. Lydia would be informed and should have the house warm and the beds aired in anticipation.

With the occupants in residence, the day's work was long at The Lodge. In their absence, life was certainly more relaxed. You didn't need to rise whilst it was still dark and work yourself to a standstill before dropping exhausted into bed at night. You could replenish the spent energies of months. You could sleep at night without the fear you might fail to wake by the time appointed. You could undo the exhaustion that seemed to be a normal part of everyday life for a servant.

There were several times in those few days when Lydia was tempted to reveal the details of her relationship with her employer's son to her own family. But something encouraged her to keep her peace. Even Elizabeth, the most worldly of her family might not have understood, and her mother, she was certain, would have been full of dire predictions.

The most encouraging family news had been from her sister Sarah, who was now courting a fine man by the name of Robert Head and contemplating marriage. Her daughter from her unfortunate liaison with John Hubbard had grown into a delightful infant and Lydia was glad things were looking up for the unlucky Sarah.

It was after a visit to Sarah in Finningham that Lydia had returned on New Year's day. There was no word from her employers, so both she and Mrs. Clarke, the cook, retired to their rooms early.

Something half woke her. It was the sound of horseshoes on flagstones and the whinny of a horse. Drowsily, Lydia snuggled back down beneath her covers, reluctant to wake. The next thing she heard was a door creak and she sensed a body lifting a cover and slipping in beside her.

She started, but a hand closed gently over her mouth and whispered, "Best not wake her next door."

Slowly he removed as few clothes from the two of them as were strictly necessary, then keeping unnaturally quiet, they pressed their bodies together until he at least seemed satisfied. He whispered again as they lay together in the darkness.

"The parents are returning tomorrow. I did the 'dutiful son' act of coming home to make sure the house would be ready and a meal on the table. They think I am being very noble, riding home in the cold and the darkness. I couldn't feel the cold. All I could think of was the warmth of your body and how we could have this night together."

It was as well she had caught up on sleep as they neither had much that night. Just before dawn, Jack Hart slipped away so as not to be observed and Lydia awoke from her short sleep to feel very cold and not a little abandoned.

It was difficult over the next few days to capture any time alone with Jack. His father John seemed ever present and apart from the odd stolen kiss and caress, it was frustrating for both of them to find themselves unable to recapture the closeness of that night.

Soon after that, another messenger appeared at The Lodge. The Reverend Heigham had instructed Jack Hart to join him at Hunston Hall. It was not altogether unexpected. He would soon supersede his father as Steward at Cotton Lodge and would need instruction and approval, not necessarily in that order.

There was much busying to pack appropriate clothing as well as documents. Plans and balance sheets were needed to prove his fitness to assume control of the farm whilst he was still a very young man.

It was with a certain heaviness of heart that Lydia watched her father drive away the man she was quite sure would eventually become her husband. Unbeknown to her, there were those who had other ideas.

No sooner had Jack Hart departed for Hunston, (with never a word for Lydia), than she was summoned to the Master's office.

"You will be expecting your half-yearly pay?" the Steward asked.

"Yes sir."

He was a cold man but on this occasion seemed chillier than usual.

"With a gift for your help at the Christmas feast."

"It was promised, sir."

"And as such, it will be paid, with a small addition for severance."

What did he mean by severance? Had she displeased him?

She looked for a hint of compassion behind his dark eyes but found nothing.

"How far has this matter gone with my son?" Lydia gasped.

"I am not blaming you," he continued, "for appealing to his baser natures, but you understand, this thing cannot continue and as such, the separation must be permanent."

"But he say he love me."

"I'm sure he did, but at this moment the Reverend Heigham is doubtless making him aware of his other duties," John Hart said dismissively.

"He'll tell you, when he return."

Oh dear, with her nervousness, she was slipping back into a dialect she had sought to forget. Now the gulf between her and the Harts was made even clearer.

"Jack will not be back for some considerable time. To prepare him to step into my shoes, he will learn to manage a farm in a parish many miles from here. By the time he does return, you in your turn will have taken your skills and expertise elsewhere."

He paused, then added condescendingly, "I shall of course supply you with a fine reference, on the understanding it is presented several miles from Lodge Farm."

Tears clouded her eyes. At no point had she doubted the sincerity of Jack Hart's embraces. She still felt if she could but speak to him in person, he would quell her fears and reassure her that all was well. But any chance of that had been snatched away and it seemed as though the world was conspiring to separate them.

"Now, I think you should go," the Steward continued. "We shall all be sorry to see you leave, but you will in time come to understand it was necessary. Let me know when you need a testimonial, and I will see it is delivered."

Still he didn't waver in his resolve. There would be no persuading him to change his mind. Any of it!

As Lydia turned to face the task of packing the few belongings that actually belonged to her, she didn't see John Hart wipe a tear from the corner of his eye before reporting to his wife Sarah that he had found the strength to complete this most unpleasant of tasks. He could still hear her parting words.

"I did - I do whully love him, no matter who say it 'in't right."

October 1820

The Overseers met in a back room at the Cock Inn. There was a small amount of stabling for horses beside the road, and space enough for those who had time to attend. It was not a large room and such a meeting meant some discomfort. Normally, only two at any one time served as Overseers of the Poor in Cotton, but matters had come to a head, and on this occasion seven were to be heard voicing their dissatisfaction over the expense to the parish caused by a noticeable moral decline among the working classes. John Hart, himself an Overseer, had chosen to remain at home, having something of an interest in the day's proceedings.

"This is the fifth contested bastardy case in Cotton this year," shouted George Canler. "The parish is already paying for two of them. We're getting as bad as Mendlesham."

"We do have a reputed father; though as usual he denies responsibility," Nathaniel Mayhew informed them.

"And as usual we are supposed to come to a fair and just conclusion on the flimsiest of evidence," complained John Keen.

"This girl Lydia Saunders - what do we know of her?" asked Charles Kemp, the oldest and most level-headed among those present.

"Used to gad about with gypsies; it could be anybody's," suggested George Canler.

"I quite liked the girl," said James Garnham.

"That's the trouble, so did somebody else."

"Where's Hart - couldn't he shed some light on this - she was his servant and it is his son she's saying is the father."

Voices merged in general disapproval of how they would all be better off on their farms attending to the potato harvest than sorting out who paid what to whom for yet another bastard child.

"Problem's that family," said Canler. "Sister Sarah's had one bastard and the older girl Elizabeth's had three over in Mendlesham and still not found a husband."

"Let's all calm down and consider the facts," coaxed Charles Kemp.

"Think about it. Nine months ago, she was living at The Lodge. No one in his right mind would be wandering round there in the dead of winter. I say Jack Hart was the only one it could have been."

"She did seem a clean and respectable girl," added Tiny Waters, "In spite of what we might think of her sisters."

183

"And it's no good comparing here with Mendlesham," said John Keen. "We all know they're an odd lot in Mendlesham and their bastards run to at least a third of all baptisms."

"Old Newton's worse," commented Joseph Canler.

"I say we send it to the Justices with our recommendation," said Charles Kemp.

"Hart won't like it."

"Then Hart'll have to make sure his son keeps his hands off the servants."

"Or employ ugly ones."

There was more laughter and much ribaldry. Other business was less contentious and soon settled.

After the others had departed, Charles Kemp signed the referral document recommending that 'Lydia Saunders, having been delivered of a male child on the fifth of September and it being the opinion of the Overseers of the poor for Cotton that Jack Hart should be accepted as the reputed father, an order might be drawn indemnifying the parish against the cost of supporting the said bastard child, and instructing the reputed father, Jack Hart' to do so instead.

Kemp stopped to consider, then added the word, 'Yeoman' after Jack Hart's name. That should win her a few shillings and probably sixpence a week to see the boy was properly cared for. He had quite liked the girl himself. Pretty, articulate, well turned out; but she'd find it hard to find a husband with somebody else's bastard in tow. The parish was already struggling to care for the deserving poor. No, the father ought to pay and see his son had a reasonable chance in life. Though few of these base-born children amounted to much. Most died in infancy; they were nearly all paupers throughout their short lives. Maybe, just maybe, with this one, things might be different.

Chapter 19

April 1821

Holy Thursday was traditionally the day for Mendlesham Fair. Farmers came to buy cattle to restock after the winter. The common folk came from villages around attracted to stalls, offering all manner of trinkets and trivia.

Tinkers' caravans and peddlars' carts ringed the market place and spilled onto an area of pasture adjacent to it. Travellers bartered with potential customers for ponies and pullets, silks and ribbons and posies. In anticipation of the Easter festival, girls wore bonnets garlanded with spring flowers.

One young lady picked her way between the stalls, a child strapped to her back in the manner of working women of the time. Primroses hung from her bonnet in clusters, framing her pretty face. Newly gathered that morning, they were plentiful along the verges and the roadside between Wickham Skeith and Mendlesham. A single purple orchid crowned the display. As the day went on, the wild flowers would soon start to fade. Even at their best, they still understated her natural beauty.

"Liddy!" A traveller called out from behind his cart. "Now who be that young kiddo sittin' by your shoulder?"

"John," she answered, recognising one of the travellers she had once made music with. "I called him John"

Then, with no further ado, she moved on, examining each stall as she went.

It was a day to cherish, one she could devote entirely to her child. She saw him little enough. He was a big strong lad and a burden to carry, but he would walk soon enough. She would probably miss his first few steps. She was sorry about that, but grateful to those of her family that enabled her to work whilst still maintaining something of a mother's contact.

Old Mrs. Deck, her employer, was very reasonable and understanding. She allowed Lydia the time to visit her sister Mary who now looked after young Johnny. Lydia smiled as she remembered the interview. She had tried to put a gloss on things, to shield her employer from the shame of her plight, never realising the old lady knew the whole story all along and was only too prepared to do her bit to help, in spite of everything.

"You come very highly recommended," Mrs. Deck had said, scanning John Hart's testimonial.

"I always try to be of service," Lydia had replied.

"Then, can you explain," teased Mrs. Deck, "why Mr. Hart chose to part with you, considering I spoke to Sarah, his wife only last week and she was desperate to find a good servant." How could she have been expected to answer that? Fortunately, Mrs. Deck had relented and come to her rescue.

"I understand you have a child, my dear."

"Yes ma'am." Head down; voice faint.

"Speak up, you may have a baby, it doesn't have to render you incomprehensible."

"No ma'am."

"And there is no husband?"

"No ma'am."

"Well, what's done is doubtless God's will and who knows in time, you'll maybe find a father for the child."

"But Johnny, he have a father." She spat out the words, then wished she had kept her peace.

"True, but only in so much as he pays for the child's keep."
So she did know!

"I can see you're going to be ever such a trouble to me. Wanting to run off to see that child of yours every few days."

"No ma'am, my sister, she say so long as I do work here, she will be mother and aunt combined, so to speak. Perhaps I could have one day a month to see my boy. But apart from that, my sister Mary don't mind - she really don't."

"Nevertheless, a child needs to know who its true parents are. Unfortunately, in this case, the mother alone will have to do.

186

Heaven forbid, he's not the only child around here that'll never know his father."

They seemed to have come a long way from the subject of her employment.

"So, do that mean I got the job ma'am?" Lydia struggled to ask.

"My word you are a hasty one. All right, I will take you: Peter Eade speaks very highly of you. But I will insist on one condition." Oh dear, what would that be?

"...You will not leave that child more than four days at a time or the poor boy won't know whether he's coming or going."

Really! She could have hugged the old lady, only it would not have been right and proper to do so.

All that had been just after New Year when she found she could stop feeding him herself and leave the child in Mary's charge. It still took her most of the winter to feel well again. The child seemed to have taken so much of her strength.

As she passed young couples cavorting in the swing-boats, Lydia felt a twinge of sadness. She untied the sling that held the child to her back. She lifted him up to watch the races on the green. At one end, men were throwing horseshoes at an iron peg. They rang as they made contact.

"Hello Lydia." She knew that voice. Yes, it was. Jack Hart stood gravely before her.

"He's a fine boy."

"He look like you. Even my father say he do, but..."

"...But he thinks it is not a recommendation that he should."

"Something like that."

The ice was broken. They both had something to smile about.

"I ought to explain."

"'T'in't necessary I got a good job an' Johnny's well looked after."

"I know all that; I checked that the Mallows' house was a fit place to bring up my child. Give me credit for that at least."

He smiled at her and she felt herself turn to jelly. She had thought she was over all that, but now knew she wasn't.

As they walked, he told her exactly what had happened since he had been sent to the Reverend Heigham. He remembered being ushered into Hunston Hall in the belief he had come to discuss farming. He had been wrong. Instead, Heigham had come right out with it.

"I understand there's a servant girl," he had said with that glare of unfettered disapproval discharged from under massive eyebrows.

"It is nothing," he had lied.

"Such matters have a habit of becoming an unacceptable distraction, and do one no good in the community to which you aim to belong."

"Really," Jack had continued, "it is not a serious matter."

"Your father believes otherwise. He has high hopes of your future which includes making an advantageous marriage in the course of time."

Heigham's steely glare had continued unabated. "If you intend to become Steward of my land you will serve God first, me second, your father third and yourself not at all. I will not be deterred in this matter."

It was made clear there and then that Jack Hart should remain at Hunston until the harvest, working with the Steward of Home Farm, supposedly to learn the principles of farm management. They both knew that was not the main purpose of the arrangement.

Jack Hart knew as soon as he saw Lydia with her primrose bonnet and fine young son, that the sacrifice he had made was almost more than he could bear. Almost!

But his desire to be Steward of The Lodge was so great, even the overwhelming love he still felt for Lydia at that moment would have to remain hidden until for lack of succour it withered like a crop without care or nutrient.

So it was that each in turn politely made light of such feelings; merely explained the convenience of the present situation, then politely parted.

It all sounded so easy - Jack Hart had returned to help with the harvest in July. He had spent a good deal of time at Old

Newton during the summer.   His father said it was to learn good horticulture.   Jack believed it was intended to push him towards Maria Turner who excited no lust and less love in him.   He now knew why.

Lydia too made light of what had been a difficult year. Following her dismissal, she had lived for a time with Elizabeth in Mendlesham.   It had not been easy.   As she had seen her own body grow, she had become more reliant on this older sister whose ways and attitudes were so different from her own.   With three bastard children already, Elizabeth openly consorted with two men, Isaac Stannard who owned the hovel in which she lived in Back Street, and Edward Tye, a shoemaker with shifty eyes and wandering hands.   Even Lydia's condition didn't prevent her from having to fend him off a number of times.

As soon as the child was born and she was fit to move, Lydia had left Elizabeth's house and joined her sister Sarah, who was newly married to Robert Head and living in Finningham.

Her parents had left Meadow Cottage at the end of the summer. Robert Saunders' arthritis was bad, and now unfit to work, he and Anne had been found a place in the Town Estate, a thatched terrace of dwellings reserved rent-free for paupers of the parish.   It was the very house where old Sophie, the midwife had ended her days and Robert and Anne expected to remain there from now on.   Their sons-in-law, had made the place cosy and pleasant.   It was in the centre of the village right opposite the church and for once in their life, they didn't lack for company.   They were probably more comfortable than they had been in years.

Anne had offered to look after little Johnny when Lydia began to look for work.   The first boy born into the family in two generations, he was in their eyes, the son Robert and Anne had never had.   But Lydia could see how frail her parents had become. In their early sixties, they looked much older, and Mary's offer to care for the child had come as a great relief.

Now it seemed as though things were falling into place.   It may not have been the happy ending intended, but there was a satisfaction in service and contentment in motherhood.

The child began to wriggle. She put him down on the grass and played with him, tickling him and hiding her face behind her hands until he smiled and chuckled with delight.

He smelt none too clean, so gathering young Johnny up, she carried him in search of running water. Just past the church and heading for the turnpike, a stream crossed the rutted track that passed for a road. She sat on a dry bank in the sunshine, and removing the clothes that swathed the child's lower quarters, proceeded to wash him. He enjoyed the caress of the cold water and cooed as she cleaned him. She rinsed the soiled cloth, wrung it out and spread it on a nearby hedge, white with blossom. Then finding another piece of cloth in a bag she had brought for the purpose and as if she had had a lifetime's experience of child-care, Lydia expertly secured the clean covering before resting the infant back on the dry ground.

She stared at the contented child unaware that someone was staring at her - staring at both of them. He coughed.

"Oh you give me a start."

"I just wanted to watch you - the two of you, together."

"He'll be tired - all that way here, on my back..."

"He's closed his eyes."

Little Johnny lay like a changeling in the grass, thumb in mouth and softly purring like a kitten.

"Just like his mother," Jack Hart commented.

"So folks do say."

"The face of an angel and best viewed from above."

"Why sir, what can you mean?" Lydia laughed coquettishly.

"Surely not shy? You were never shy with me."

"We shu'n't be here together. My mistress would be much aggrieved."

"No we shouldn't. Others have told us so and doubtless would continue to do so were they to know we were here together."

Lydia made as if to gather her things; the bag, the damp cloth from the hedge and the sleeping child.

"Let me drive you back," he offered.

"No, folks 'ud see and things 'ud be worse for it."

"I meant what I said about caring for you, Lydia. I loved you, I loved our secrets and our times together. You know what - I couldn't bear to enter the chapel again. I threw the key into the moat. Now it's lost and the room will stay locked for as long as I live there. You're a sore temptation Lydia, but I know I can't have you, though I hardly pass an hour without thinking about you."

"I started to play my music again," Lydia announced, desperate to break his melancholy. "The mistress she say she do like it, so I play my flute an' sometimes my accordion."

"You and your music! It reminds me of that first time we met. We were hardly a lot older than this little fellow."

"Do you remember that song what you sung that summer when you play the harpsichord and I play the flute?" Lydia asked.

He began to sing gently.

"Wilt thou be wulful still?
Wilt thou be wulful still?
Wilt thou be wulful still?
Shem, for they wulful will.
For the lass that I loved well
Did steal my heart and my will.
For the lass that I loved well
Did steal my heart and my will."

"You don't forget that sort of thing," Jack Hart continued. Then he came closer and as Lydia gathered the still sleeping child to her, Jack held both of them, wishing with all of his heart he never had to let them go - either of them.

"I got to go. My sister Mary and her husband will be looking to find me."

"You receive the money for his keep?"

"The sixpence a week go to Mary. It's only right, being as she's the one what minds after him. The eight shillings I had when he were newly born - my sister Elizabeth had some and so did Sarah for keeping me and Johnny; but I still have four shillings. I did think I might buy myself a new flute at the fair, but there in't none no better than what I got, so maybe I'll take the money home with me."

Jack Hart faced her, barring her way to hold her there for just a few more precious moments.

"For everything you've ever meant to me, I'll always carry a love for you and Johnny. I promise you, you will have your flute and I'll make him a promise too. He shall have everything that I aspire to and more. More, because he will be his own man, not forced to act as others ordain. Whatever happens to us, rest assured, his future will be secure."

Then, he stood to one side and watched as mother and child walked purposefully back to the fair. It was the last either saw of the other for some considerable time.

A week later, a box was delivered to Wickham Hall. It was addressed to Lydia. It contained a flute and a message that Mrs. Deck read to her which said, "This was only the first of my promises."

"Now, what can he have meant by that?" said the old lady. "What could he have meant by that?"

Chapter 20

June 1823

"Moses Long, you 'in't got what sense you was born with," Lydia scolded.

Moses looked up from his resting-place in the hay, puffing on a pipe filled with a concoction of tobacco and country herbs.

"With the hay this dry, you'll have the whole lot up in smoke if you don't have a care. The only good thing is, it'll probably take you with it."

Incorrigible rogue that he was, Moses was slow to respond even to Lydia's good-natured banter. He was a poor excuse for a labourer, but Mrs. Deck seemed prepared to pay him for the little he achieved, so it wasn't up to Lydia to object to his taking a break. However, if he put the farmyard up in flames, then they would all be out of a job. Moses ticked and tutted, but at least he walked as far as the gate-post to knock out the ashes from his pipe.

"Thass right bo' - you see no sparks get on the dry hay. The next time I catch you, any warning I give'll come in the shape of a bucket o' water." Lydia turned and headed back to the house.

She loved the hay-making. It came with a smell and a satisfaction that was like no other. She looked across to the fields where the latest cutting was being tossed to dry it underneath. Like with the harvest later on, new faces would appear, folks would work for a week or more as though born to be a team, then disappear. Several figures laboured under the June sun. Moses rejoined them.

Robert Head, her brother in law from Finningham was there. So too was Mr. Blomfield who rented a smallholding adjacent to Mrs. Deck's land. He kept a few pigs and liked to think of himself as a farmer, though he employed no one but himself. He was in his late thirties and was a good neighbour to Lydia's mistress, helping out when he could. There were four or five young lads there too. Lydia didn't know most of their names. Mr. Blomfield had rounded them up, explaining they were strong as any men and cheaper to employ.

Every two hours or so, Blomfield would blow on a small horn he carried and stop the team long enough to take a few swigs of ale - even the boys - that Lydia would carry out to them.

Gradually, under the watchful eye of Mrs. Deck, Lydia's confidence and sparkle had returned. She walked tall, carrying the grace and elegance and cheery disposition of happier times. Her joi-de-vivre did not go unnoticed.

"Hey gal," called one fair-haired lad, "Ha' yew got a smile for Edward 'ere; he 'in't yet had a gal and he say he think yar whully pretty." Then as an aside, he commented, "An' I wouldn't mind a squeeze myself."

"You'll do best to mind you keep such thoughts to yourself, master Andrew," replied Blomfield. "Miss Lydia'll be all what's keepin' you from a-dyin' of thirst and I wouldn't be altogether surprised if she dun't pour your share onto the ground."
The lad looked sheepish; Blomfield continued his admonition.

"Jus' yew remember, Miss Lydia 'in't one of your common gels. No she's a lady's companion and that set her above the likes of yew. So let's hear no more on'it."

Lydia noticed the crestfallen look of the lads. She went to the one they called Andrew, a shy, easily embarrassed boy and caressing his neck to lift his long hair whispered in his ear. The boy went scarlet. The rest roared with laughter, Blomfield included.

Only later when questioned, and with much persuasion did he reveal what she had whispered to him.

"She say, 'if I was sixteen agin, I'd take you under the apple trees to lay down and look at the blossom'."

"She di'n't"

"Honest to God, she did."
They thought he'd made it up, but Andrew glowed with pleasure. He knew better.

For all the teasing, and not for lack of asking, Lydia had no young man to call her own. Now in her mid-twenties, most of her friends and certainly her sisters were either married or courting. Though she thought rarely of Jack Hart now, she felt no desire to replace what he had been to her, and as such, seemed resigned to remaining a spinster.

Motherhood on the other hand was the single most important part of Lydia's life and she was grateful to her employer for allowing her the time to see her son as often as she did. He would see her coming and run down the slope from Hill Farm to meet her, chattering about all that had happened since she had last been to see him. Everyone said he had so much of Lydia about him, especially her eyes. With just a tinge of sadness, she felt she could recognise his father in his features, and it would be a painful reminder that would never quite go away.

* * * * * * * * * * * * * *

Lydia rarely envied people their possessions but there was one thing she would have loved to own. Old Mrs. Deck rarely rode these days, but still kept a pedigree hack that had served her well through the years. He was a most pleasant natured of beasts, able to set a steady and comfortable pace and could be relied upon to stay on his feet and rarely to start or to shy.

Freddy Thrower, the stable lad referred to him disparagingly as 'the old roadster,' meaning he was well past his hunting days, but everyone knew and loved the docile creature who had been known to bring back his rider at an even trot despite suffering from calluses and corns.

Those who worked in the house would often take titbits to the stable. They all had their favourites, but Lydia kept her carrot tops and apple cores for Wizard. Mrs. Deck had named him after a winner of the Two Thousand Guineas, but he would never be a racehorse. Standing nearly fifteen hands, his strength was his stamina rather than his speed; his reliability rather than his flair.

One bright June morning, Lydia found Wizard in a lethargic

state. His head hung between his forelegs and he showed no interest in food. He leaned against the wall of his stable instead of coming to meet her. All was not well. She mentioned her concern to the ostler, but as it was hard to pin down the cause of the problem, it was felt things would soon right themselves.

Later that day, Freddy, the stable lad rushed into the house shrieking that the horse had 'gone mad.' Mrs. Deck and Lydia ran to the stable where Wizard was clearly in an agitated state.

He was staring about him, breathing rapidly, every so often darting and dashing himself against rack, manger or wall. After some minutes, Wizard threw himself down, breathless and eyes staring wildly through dilated pupils.

"It's rabies; must be ma'am," suggested the ostler. "I say we poleaxe him. He nearly took my head off with his hind legs."

"No!" cried Lydia. "There must be some way."

"Can't we send for the veterinary?" suggested Mrs. Deck.

"It'll cost a great deal and if it's rabies it'll all come to the same thing in the end," said the ostler.

"We could get Mr. Blomfield," Freddy replied. "He's right good with sick animals."

"Yes," Mrs. Deck answered, "Samuel Blomfield will know what's best." There were tears in her eyes; she already feared the worst.

"I'll go," Lydia called, already halfway up the drive.
She lifted her skirts and ran.

He was not at his tiny cottage, nor with the pigs. Lydia stopped and listened. Nearby, she could hear the sound of chopping. Samuel Blomfield was pollarding a venerable willow that served as a boundary marker between his land and Mrs. Deck's.

"Oh, Mr. Blomfield, can you come please?" Lydia gasped. "Wizard is whully queer and Siddy say thass the rabies and they'll have to poleaxe him."

"Then," Blomfield said, putting down the hook he was using, "we'd best get there afore they do."

Little had changed in the stable yard. The horse, every few

minutes would spring up, kicking forelegs up and lurching from one side to another, panting and perspiring and foaming at the mouth.

"See - thass what I say - rabies - 'in't no cure for rabies."

"Just wait a moment," said Samuel Blomfield. "Have you had any rabid dogs round here?"

"Not as I rightly know," said the ostler. Blomfield edged towards the stable door. He opened it and stepped inside. The animal stirred. Standing to one side he observed as Wizard again underwent a sequence of wild spasmodic movements. Lydia, watching, feared for the man's safety, but the horse seemed oblivious to him and seemed more in danger of harming itself than the smallholder within his stall.

After a few minutes, as the horse settled down again, Samuel Blomfield came back out to join the others.

"I did warn yew - he be dangerous like that," the ostler reminded him.

"You must go to the veterinary," said Samuel Blomfield to the stable lad Freddy, "and purchase a pint of aloes and an eighth of an ounce of Calomel - and be quick!"

"You wun't cure rabies," Siddy continued.

"No, but I might cure the mad staggers."

"Is that what it is?" Mrs. Deck asked. "How can you tell?"

"He had no malice about him in his movements, merely a frenzy. Fear is, the staggers'll rot the brain if we dun't get rid o' the sickness," Blomfield explained.

"Can you cure him?" asked Lydia, pleading with her eyes.

"Maybe, but I'll need help and it wun't be pretty, so I'll not trouble you."

"Please - I don't mind," Lydia begged. "I bin there when my father farrow'd pigs and gelded horses."

"I say as it don't make no difference," said Siddy, reluctant to offer his help. "Rabies or the mad staggers - animal'll be dead by morning anyhow."

"I do think," Blomfield said, "It would be better if just me and

Miss Lydia was left alone to do what's got to be done. When the lad gets back, I'll have the mixture warmed and stirred up, then brought to me, please."

He waited till the others had gone, then rolled up his sleeves and drew a long blade from his belt. He raised a flame using steel, flint and tinder and proceeded to scorch the blade.

"You might prefer to remain here in the yard," he said.

"I'll be where I'm useful," said Lydia and followed him to the stable door.

Together, they watched the pathetic creature staggering and thrashing about, then as it fell into a period of insensibility after a throe, Blomfield acknowledged it was time to move by squeezing Lydia's wrist gently. It was an electric moment.

They eased round to the side of the stricken animal, then as it began to rise once more, to Lydia's horror, Samuel Blomfield measured with his hand against the horse's head and plunged his knife into the jugular vein. Blood sprayed across both of them as the animal continued to thrash around. It seemed as if the horse could have no blood left in him.

Finally, exhausted, Wizard fell gasping back to the blooded straw. Blomfield took a kerchief from round his neck and had Lydia hold it firmly against the wound until the blood flow eased.

Within the hour, the lad Freddy returned with the cathartic mixture, which Samuel Blomfield then administered to the calmed creature. Lydia was caught between a mixture of horror and admiration for the unassuming man. "Will he live?" she asked.

"He'll have a better chance than before."

"What caused it?"

"Some say, bad blood to the brain. You have to release it, then calm the system. It's up to the Lord's work now. I've done all I can."

He wiped his knife on the straw and put it back in his belt.

"I'll look in tonight. I daresay you'll nurse him as well as any. Make sure he get plenty of water. He'll need to make up for what I've shed."

And with that he went.   Back to his tiny cottage and his pigs.
A humble man, but one for whom Lydia felt a deepening warmth
and admiration.

One afternoon that June when most of the hay was in, a young
man could be seen walking the lanes of Wickham clutching a box
and some kind of trestle.

"I am an artist," he announced, "...from Norwich. I am an
interpreter of the countryside."   He set up his easel and then
proceeded to sketch the landscape and the buildings.

Fascinated, Lydia returned to see how his work progressed.
She was most impressed with the way he had captured the sky,
which was forever changing.   It covered a large portion of his
picture.

"You 'in't got no people," she commented as he continued to
paint.

"My aim is to portray a landscape at a given moment in time.
Labourers add nothing to my picture."

"But thass them what made the landscape," she protested.
"Thass them what ploughed the fields and planted the hedges and
minded the sheep and cattle."

"People move about their business.   My picture would be
made to appear static and frozen were I to add people."

"Clouds move about, but you put them in: trees move in the
wind; you painted them: what about them sheep an' pigs; they get
about to graze an' to forage."

The painter smiled.

"Your logic is more perfect than mine," he said.   "For your
sake I will paint in - that man there."   He pointed at a distant
figure feeding a small herd of swine. "Would you say that man
represents the agricultural labourers who have moulded this
landscape?"

"That man's Samuel Blomfield and he'd be whully riled to
be spoken of as an agricultural labourer.   But he'll do.   He be a
good man to be a model for us all, and no one has done more to

fashion this corner than he."

"Sounds like you admire him," the painter observed. "You'd not be sweet on him by any chance?"

"Good Lord - he's old enough to be... well, an older brother at least, and his mind's on raising pigs, not children of his own. Go on with you!"

And with a grin, she slipped away. But she did return later to check he had been as good as his word. Set proudly among the pigs and the managed countryside stood Samuel Blomfield, not seeming to be a labourer; more lord of all he surveyed, examining the evidence of his work and finding it good.

Some days later, when Blomfield appeared at the kitchen door with a ham that had been requested by her mistress, Lydia asked him if he had been shown the picture before the artist left.

"I did see it - but it weren't the countryside as I know it - too neat and tidy by half - I told him and he told me that you made him put me in the picture."

"You di'n't mind?"

"Ho, gel! I di'n't mind. Pictures without people is like farms without livestock. T'in't natural."

Then, and perhaps acting on something else gleaned from the artist, the smallholder smiled and fished inside his jacket. He produced the tiniest piglet Lydia had ever seen.

"'S for you. 'In't much right now, but I'll give him back to his mum till he's weaned, then you can pen him in the kitchen garden an' feed him on scraps. Be worth a bit by spring."

"I don't rightly know what to say. No one ever give me presents afore."

"'S just so's you know I think highly of you Miss Lydia." Then, being irreversibly self-conscious, Samuel Blomfield returned to his pigs and his few acres of land where he at least felt comfortable.

Later that week, Lydia took him a loaf of bread. She had asked the cook to bake one for her but refused to reveal why. Amongst winks from the kitchen staff, she had collected it, still warm, before slipping across the way to Samuel Blomfield's tiny cottage.

"'Tin't right that only you gets to give presents," she said as she gave it to him.

Feeling bolder and more at ease on his own territory, Blomfield cut them both a wedge with the knife he permanently kept in his belt. Lydia didn't like to ask what it might last have been used for. They both tried the bread as if it might be a prelude to trying each other.

"I got a child," Lydia confessed.

"Everyone know that. Don't make no difference."

"Jus' so's you know." She looked at him. "I 'in't sayin' this is no more than me giving you a present 'cos you give me one." She paused. "But so long as you understand I 'in't a maiden, so to speak, and I got a responsibility."

"We all got responsibility, thank the Lord. An' as for maidens, most as say they is, 'in't, so in a way I be gladder to know where I stand."

Then, they kissed, and though Lydia felt none of the passion she had felt for Jack Hart - still did in many ways - she knew here was a good man who would care for her and little Johnny just as he'd care for the piglet he had given her. It may not have been love as such - not yet at any rate - but it was a fair substitute and more than she had any right to expect.

Later that evening, Mrs. Deck found Lydia lost in her own imagination, hemming drapes. Whenever Lydia wanted to think, she sewed. It was something she could do that gave the appearance of being busy but freed her mind from other distractions. Like her mother, she was a natural with a needle and neat tiny stitches strode across the fabric effortlessly.

"Do I hear, my dear, you have a new admirer?"

Could nothing he kept secret in this place?

She thought before she spoke. "If a good man were to find me fair, ma'am, t'were no bad thing?"

"No bad thing at all. You deserve more than life has given you so far. I'll wager God has now seen fit to redress the balance."

"Can I ask you ma'am?"

"Yes…"

"If one were to feel a kind of respect and tenderness for a man, but not be sure it be a love exactly… is that enough?"

"Enough to make a marriage, you mean?"

"Oh we 'in't spoke of marriage yet. But you know how sometimes everything seem right except the one thing - whereas in the past, it were just the one thing that were right and everything else wrong…"

Mrs. Deck laughed.

"My dear, I haven't a clue what you are talking about, but I do know one thing. Few people marry for passion. Those that do often regret it. Respect, admiration, even comfort sound a far firmer basis for a relationship. And anyway there's time - where's your hurry?"

"If I were married, I could bring my boy to be with me all the time. And my man would be a father to him."

"I thought," answered Mrs. Deck, "you told me your son already had a father and had no need of another."

"I were wrong, ma'am."

"Just remember Lydia, let's have things in the right order this time. Any brothers and sisters for your Johnny can wait till their parents are wed."

"Yes ma'am, you can be whully sure of that ma'am. I 'in't havin' no more babies born without there bein' a weddin' first."

That evening, Lydia played firstly on her flute and then on the accordion; a music full of life and love and hope for the future. Mrs. Deck listened with pleasure tempered with a little sadness for she knew she had lost a good servant and a rare companion.

Chapter 21

March 1824

It wasn't the way things were meant to be, but in her short life Lydia had come to realise that, for the likes of her, events were usually beyond her control.

No white wedding! Even if no one had known of her past indiscretions, there was no concealing her present condition. Marrying only two months in advance of the baby's birth, at least they would not suffer to see the words 'base-born' entered in the register beside this child's name, when it was baptised.

It should have been so different. As the summer had drawn to a close and elms and rowans vied with each other to be the first to shed their leaves, Lydia and Samuel had become such an obvious couple, there were those who predicted a wedding before Christmas. Then had come the nightmare that would cast a fearful shadow across their future.

Lydia frequently took small presents from the kitchen to Samuel. Often as not, he could be found attending to his pigs. This time, however he was not alone. A good-looking young man stood beside him. His face was familiar. Lydia felt she recognised him from somewhere. The two men both wore the same expression of fear and alarm. At first, Samuel hardly noticed Lydia. She could see why. Several of the pigs looked distinctly unwell. Their noses were running and they seemed listless and reluctant to come for their food.

"Wass wrong with 'em Sam?" Lydia asked.

"I 'in't rightly sure, though I know what I fear," he replied. Then, remembering his manners, he added, "This is Will Goodrich. He'd a-bin a near neighbour o' yours when you was at Cotton." Of course, now she remembered. His father managed a sizeable acreage in Cotton, and all the village girls had spoken of his handsome looks and fine manners.

"You can make 'em well again?" Lydia asked.

"If thass as I fear - hog cholera, then there's only one fair answer."

"But you're whully good with sick beasts - you cured Wizard, Mrs. Deck's horse."

"Of the mad staggers. This 'in't like that. This is a whole lot wuss. I seen hog cholera. Even when you think they're a-gettin' better, then they turn round an' die on you. Then all the swine in the area get the fever and it's like a plague. An' everyone's blamin' it on the poor sod what got it first an' askin' as why they di'n't just slaughter the lot to begin with. An' I'd be the first to agree with 'em. I 'in't doin' that to folks. If my hogs has got to be culled then I'd sooner do it quick than wait around for the fever to spread."

"You'll sell 'em for meat at least?" Lydia said.

"An' who'll buy 'em? I'll not say they're clean when I know they 'in't, though there's many would."

Will Goodrich entered into the discussion. "If you try to treat 'em, then most'll die anyhow, and farms round about will all catch it. At least if you do for them now, there's a chance others will be spared."

They all knew what that meant. In a month, rent would be payable, and tithes. Everything Blomfield owned would need to be sold to meet his obligations. He could not restock, even if he could afford to. His smallholding may not have amounted to much but it had labelled him a farmer. Now he would be forced to ply his trade as a labourer; just what he had striven to avoid.

Lydia had come that day with more than food from the kitchen. She had brought the news that she expected his child, but could not bring herself to tell him the way things were right at that moment.

"I know it's not how you would have wished it," Will Goodrich uttered, "but you'll always find work with us, and a cottage too."

"Thank you Will."

Lydia had never seen him look so down. He took what she had to offer, then dismissed her.

"'T'in't that I 'in't pleased to see you, but if you leave us we can get on with what needs to be done. If the veterinary say it do be hog cholera, then Will say he'll help with the slaughter. An' for that I be whully grateful."

She could do nothing but leave him to it. After that, it became increasingly difficult to deliver her momentous news. For a while, she found it easy to conceal, letting out her skirts little by little, until Mrs. Deck took a hand.

"You do intend to tell that man he has more to think about than his dead pigs?" the old lady had said, a couple of months into the new year. "I did warn you there was a proper order to things. He'll soon be moved to Cotton and I suppose one day, you intend to frighten the poor fellow by dumping a baby in his lap."

"It just 'in't seemed like the right time," said Lydia.

"I am amazed," retorted Mrs Deck, "that the man is so blind he has not yet noticed."

"He's in a kind of melancholy," said Lydia.

"Then it is high time he snapped out of it! You must go to him at once and appraise him of the situation."

"I suppose we could speak to the Reverend," Lydia mused.

"Go and see Peter Eade at Cotton," suggested Mrs. Deck, "and take Mr. Blomfield with you." The Rector here is a sober enough fellow, but terribly fussy. He'll notice your condition, mark my words, and give you a sermon on the spot." No, Eade is your man, besides, I expect your mother would prefer you were married in Cotton."

"That she would ma'am; that she would!"

Lydia felt cheered that things were out in the open. All she needed now was Samuel's co-operation. But he was a good man and would do the right thing by her.

It seemed, as the winter drew to a close, just what was needed to bring Samuel Blomfield out of his depressed state. He was concerned that Lydia would be a mere labourer's wife, but there was no doubting her delight at the way she now found herself. As she explained it at the time, "there's four good sides to this - I get to marry the man I want, I have his baby (and I don't have to wait), I'll live again in Cotton where my folks and my friends dwell and I get to have my son with me all the time."

Even in his disappointment at his own reduction in fortune, Samuel Blomfield had to admit things were turning for the better.

"So when will this wedding be?" Mrs. Deck asked.

"Not before Mayday ma'am," Lydia replied.

"Mayday! Good heavens, you'll practically give birth in the aisle. That won't do! That won't do at all!"

"The Rector, he say that there must be time for the banns and all the proper arrangements."

"Fiddlesticks! Hasn't he ever heard of a Bishop's licence?"

"They're whully costly ma'am; at least five shillings he think."

"Then let it be my present to you. Don't bother taking your coat off dear - straight back to Mr. Eade and tell him I expect a licence obtained within the week or he'll have me to reckon with!"

So it was that Lydia and Samuel's wedding was a slightly muted affair. Somewhat embarrassed about asking for time off work on a Tuesday afternoon, Samuel Blomfield had arrived late with Will Goodrich and another friend, John Barnham. That, in spite of the fact they had had to do no more than cross the road from Church Farm. Lydia's parents Anne and Robert were there, along with two of her sisters, Mary and Maria. Mrs. Deck came, of course, but apart from those, only the Rector, Peter Eade and the clerk, William Miles, were present. The service was short and the sole surprise was when Samuel presented Lydia with what had been his mother's ring. It must have been the last thing he possessed that had not been sold in payment of his debts. Even their furniture was for the most part what Will Goodrich had persuaded his parents they no longer wanted. It seemed out of place in their tiny cottage, too grand by half, and Lydia never felt really comfortable with it.

Throughout the brief ceremony, Mary Mallows, Lydia's sister sat stony faced with the three year old Johnny beside her. He was the son she and her husband seemed fated never to have. She and her husband had looked after him like true parents since his birth. After ten years of marriage, they were still childless and here was Lydia scrambling to be wed before she had two in tow. It was hard not to feel bitter.

"I know we only bin lookin' after him, so to speak, but should you ever need a home for any of your children, then there'll be a place up on Hill Farm" Mary offered as graciously as she could manage.

Lydia knew only too well what she was going through. She knew how it hurt to be parted from this child. She also knew that however much she cared for Samuel Blomfield, if he had not been prepared to take Johnny into his home, then she would not have married him - never in a million years.

Harriet was born at the end of May. Her aunt, Elizabeth presided over the birth. As she had found after Johnny's birth, for some time Lydia felt unbelievably tired. In an attempt to restore her health, she spent long hours under the apple boughs in the garden of their cottage, recovering. Her sister Mary would bring her the infant from time to time and she would feed it, whilst whitethroats warbled and skylarks celebrated. It was a blissful early summer, and gradually Lydia grew in strength.

It didn't take very long before Sam Blomfield's position at Church Farm began to change. In the early days, Will Goodrich's father assumed he was doing his son a favour, employing a failed pig-farmer, but little by little, he began to recognise the quality of the man. He had a good eye for a beast when it came to purchasing livestock, and he had an uncanny knack of keeping them healthy once he got them back to the farm. Often as not, the master would take Sam with him to markets and fairs, where he again proved his worth, knowing how to haggle a good price.

For Lydia, bringing up two children, this was a mixed blessing. Often Sam stayed away overnight and at times, she felt alone and abandoned.

The bonus, however, came in the form of extra money at the end of the week, and in the wonderful stories he would tell her and Johnny on his return.

"You never saw such a thing. Right outside the White Hart at Scole, these two coach drivers, come to blows they did."

Freshly back from the Norfolk border, early in June, Sam was recounting his latest tale.

"Seems as how the Phenomena Coach and the Times Coach had been racing all the way from Norwich, and one had cut across the path of the other, so when they reached the coaching inn, they stripped off and began battering each other senseless."

"What did their passengers think?" asked Lydia.

"Begun a wager, of course; and there was more wagers taken on which would be the first to London."

Another time, one market day in July, in Bury, a terrible storm had struck.

"Hailstones - you should'a seen'em, big as walnuts they were; trees stripped of their leaves, and I seen one house where every pane of glass was broke down one side."

"'Tweren't that bad here, though we heard the thunder away off over Bacton."

"Thunder - you should'a heard it - deafening it was, and the electric fluid lightened down all the while. A maid goin' up Guildhall Street got struck, and they say she still 'in't recovered her sight or speech."

"We feared for the corn, when the rain come."

"The farms round Bury 'in't got a blade left what's fit to harvest," said Sam, revelling in the telling of it all.

Was he exaggerating? She would never know. Lydia almost envied him the opportunities he had to see the world - or if not the world, at least a few miles outside the village of Cotton.

But they were happy enough, and come the harvest, it was all hands to the scythes and stooks, and they found themselves working side by side in the fields day after day, Lydia with Harriet strapped to her back much of the time, and Johnny with a tiny wooden-bladed scythe of his own, trying to mimic the man he now saw as his father.

Johnny was such a blessing to her. Now fully re-united with his mother, after years with his Aunt Mary, he was anxious not to leave Lydia, even for a moment. So he ran errands incessantly from house to garden and back, until convinced by this new arrangement, he grew ever more adventurous.

Perched on the platform afforded by a spreading oak, Johnny sat, king of a comfortably limited world. At one end of the garden, close to an ancient track-way the oak had once stood as a boundary marker and been stopped early so it divided about five feet above the ground, branching four ways. For three hundred years it had grown like that until now its massive outer branches threatened to pull it into quarters. A platform layered with soft peat was at its centre. This provided a perfect observation post for a boy who could climb this short distance. To aid him, others before him had created what were almost steps up the bark, so his task was made all the easier.

He was watching a man watching him. The well-dressed gentleman had been there some time before Johnny noticed he was there. Now it was unclear who was watching whom.

"Johnny!" That was his mother, She would need him to fetch her something. He made as if to rush, then decided to take his time. As he descended the tree, the man emerged from the shadows of the tree-lined track.

"Are you the boy Johnny?" the man asked.

"Yes sir," the boy answered, too polite even to be cautious.

"Are you a help and a pleasure to your mother?"

"I think so sir," the four year old replied.

"Then take pride in it and do it well, for she was ever most special to your father. Do you know who your father is, boy?" Now he was confused.

Still remembering that there was somewhere a man known as his father, nevertheless Johnny's recent experience was of a kind and generous father who had brought a warmth to his life that he had not known before.

"My father work for Mr. Goodrich. If you want to speak to him, you have to go up the farm."

"Yes, that is probably how it should be," Jack Hart uttered.

For it was Jack Hart, half-curious, half longing. A share of both emotions had brought him there that day. But, he was not to know Samuel Blomfield had arrived home only moments before.

Working close at hand, he had taken the opportunity of sharing his lunch break with his family.

"Johnny!" That was Lydia calling again.

This time, Samuel had come in search of the boy. He knew where to look. He could see what had delayed him. He recognised the figure through the trees as Jack Hart. He called out, "Go home Mr. Hart; my son has no further need of you now."

"I only came to look."

"Yes, and you needn't detain yourself," Samuel Blomfield said.

"I do still pay towards his keep, remember."

"An imposition you needn't bother with no more. I can mind after my family without your money."

"I heard things had been bad."

"You heard wrong."

"And if I continue to send the money?" asked Hart.

"Then it will be sent back," replied Samuel.

Jack Hart could see there was nothing further to be said and left them to it. They were now a family and his role in this was at an end, at least for the moment.

He found where he had tied his horse to the branch of a tree. There was little for him to do at Lodge Farm that afternoon, so he rode to Old Newton, where he knew he was sure of a warm welcome from Philip Turner, and a warmer one from his daughter, Maria.

Chapter 22

Spring & Summer 1825

It could have been a colourless existence. The monotony was there for all those who were prepared to accept it. Lydia could have resigned herself with a heavy heart to second best in all things, marriage, motherhood, life. But it was not in her nature to be like that. Since, as a tiny child, she had flirted with death and fallen from a tree, only to awaken revitalised, she had lived life to the full, and continued to do so. Sam, for his part, found it exhausting at times, just trying to keep pace with her, but he did his best, in the knowledge the fire that burned within her was what made Lydia special. As a family, they thrived on the 'out of the ordinary'.

On Shrove Tuesday, when Sam and Will were off to Lavenham Fair with horses to sell, it was Lydia, with the children, wrapped up warm against the cold, who drove the cart that would bring the men home. There were so many things to see, but you had to be on your guard. The place was alive with pick-pockets, and even those with money sewn into the linings of their clothes could find their wealth mysteriously disappear, if they didn't keep their wits about them. Some of the gipsy traders remembered Lydia from earlier times and it was like a grand reunion. They made so much fuss of her children, as she did of theirs.

One day in early April, Sam came home before breakfast with a secret. He'd earned a day off. Working largely with livestock meant labouring even on the Sabbath most weeks, so the occasional Tuesday to spend with his family was not unknown. On this particular day, he had a plan that he felt would show Lydia she was not the only one capable of springing a surprise.

"Get you ready gel," he called, a grin across his face from ear to ear. "Mary's lookin' after the babby, but the rest on'us (and here he tickled Johnny under the chin) are going out for a proper treat."

"Where we goin'?"

"That's for the folks as read the paper to know, cos them's the folks as finds out what's goin' on in the world."

Lydia blushed.   Somehow she had never got round to learning to read and write, though Sam could wrestle the odd story from newspapers he saw lying around at Church Farm.

"Don' mess about." Lydia laughed.   "How shall I know how fine to dress up if I don' know where we're a-goin'?"

"Got that number of fancy frocks have you?"

He knew she hadn't.   Still, he couldn't keep it to himself any longer.

"Pretty soon, master Will, he say, he'll take us to Mendlesham where Edmund Wood is a-runnin' a coach to Ipswich."

What he failed to tell her was the word 'coach' was altogether too grand a description for the cart that the local carrier used.   Still it would take them there and back the same day, and being lighter than a coach, would negotiate the poorer parts of the turnpike with fewer bumps and lumps along the way.

"But wass brought this on?" Lydia was still intrigued.

"You'll find out soon enough; thass if you're ready in time."

But of course she was; she was ready and away, and the three of them were soon trundling along the turnpike from Mendlesham to Ipswich, where they were set down outside the Cow & Gate, in Quay Street.   It was a bustling part of town; the air thick with the sounds of chains on pulleys and the whinnying of horses. But it was the smells of the docks that Lydia found strange and exciting; tarred rope and malt, fish and freshly-sawn timber; the stink emanating from the fellmonger's shop and the potent smell of the brewery. They could almost smell the heat of the iron-foundry in College Street as they made the short trek up into the town.   There were shops of every kind imaginable, including plenty Lydia had rarely, if ever, encountered.   There were pipe-makers, doll dealers, tallow chandlers and sail-makers.   There were countless music dealers, tea sellers, umbrella makers and even traders in antiquities.   There seemed no end to the fascinations of this place.   Yet, Lydia realised, she still had no idea why they had come.

"'In't you goin' to tell us what we're a-doin' here?" she asked.

Sam, never one for secrets, could not hold out any longer.

"Hev you heard of Madame Chew Swords?"

"You mean that French lady what makes statues?"

Lydia may not have read the paper, but she knew what had been on display in the Assembly Rooms for a fortnight or more. It was the talk of the county, even though most doing the talking had never seen the exhibition at first hand.

"They do say them statues is so real, you can't tell who in the exhibition is a statue and who's a person."

"Well, that may be true, but I don't see how we'd know unless we went to see 'em."

Lydia's excitement was uncontained. She wasn't the only one. Johnny, holding hands with both of them began to run, dragging Sam and Lydia with him.

"Here, hold you hard! You don't know the way," laughed Lydia. But he didn't need to: it was as if everyone in Ipswich was heading for the Assembly Rooms that day, and all they had to do was to follow the crowd.

All the descriptions they had heard of the Madame Tussauds exhibition were no exaggeration. It was as if the King himself was standing before them, and Napoleon Bonaparte - although Lydia knew perfectly well he was dead - he looked alive enough there. There were in excess of sixty figures and the family could have stared at them for hours, only the crowds made it difficult to stop for too long in front of any one figure, and they did have to get home.

All too soon, they were hurrying back to the Cow & Gate, and not a moment too soon, as Edmund Wood was harnessed up and ready to depart.

Johnny slept all the way back. He was exhausted. Lydia leaned back with her head on Sam's chest, feeling thoroughly contented. It was one of those magical days, even if it did mean a two-mile hike back from Mendlesham in the dark and the drizzle. It didn't matter. Nothing could put a dampener on a day like that.

In that gap that sometimes comes between haymaking and harvest, word reached Cotton that a company of comedians was performing at Eye Theatre for the summer season under the leadership of the famous Mr. Charles Fisher. It seemed a chance too good to miss, and Sam hired a carrier to take the whole family, including baby Harriet, as he was paying for Lydia's sister Mary and her husband Thomas Mallows to join them. It was a trip that started so well, but nearly ended in disaster.

The journey there was uneventful. It was a fine July afternoon, and but for the lack of shade, it was a pleasant enough drive. They were there in good time, pulling into the yard attached to the White Lion. The comedy was excellent, though hardly suitable for the children. Lydia was glad they were as young as they were. Harriet slept right through the thunderous laughter and Johnny found most amusement in some of the ludicrous costumes the performers wore. The jokes went right over his head.

The problem came when it was time to go home. Unbeknown to them, the carrier had been drinking across the road and received a better offer from a group of drovers keen to get back to Mellis. So abandoning the theatre-goers, he left the briefest of messages saying he was very sorry and would make it up to them some time. It clearly wasn't good enough, but there was nothing for it other than to spend half the night walking home. If they could have afforded accommodation for the night, it still would not have solved the problem of Sam and Thomas needing to be at work early the next morning. There was no chance of finding alternative transport at that time of the evening. All they could do now was to walk home - a distance of eight miles, in the darkness, and at the mercy of whatever footpads might lie in wait.

As they left the town of Eye, their intention was to cut across to Stoke Ash by way of the sleepy and now sleeping hamlet of Braiseworth. The adults agreed to take it in turns to carry Harriet, but Johnny, tired though he was, would have to walk as far as possible. He did his best, bless him, and it wasn't really his fault everything went awry.

In the darkness, they must have wandered into a farmyard, which set a load of dogs barking. Suddenly, there was light from a doorway, and silhouetted in it, a man with a gun. A large black dog was beside him.

"Hold you hard; stand still or I'll shoot; I mean it, I will!" With a shriek, Johnny let go of Lydia's hand and ran for cover.

"Johnny!" yelled Lydia, wanting to run after him, but unsure about the gun; unsure which way he'd gone.

"I told you to stand still," said the farmer, still brandishing the weapon. Somehow he appeared less of a threat, having not fired when Johnny moved, so slowly the group advanced on him, making appeals to his better nature as they did so.

When he realised his supposed poultry thieves were just a party of lost strangers, the tone of the farmer's words changed. In acknowledgement of his mistake, he invited the party inside. But he had failed to recognise one small problem. One of their party had disappeared and was nowhere to be found. Calling for Johnny didn't reveal where he had gone. Lamps were called for and a search instigated. It was an anxious few minutes. A deep moat ran along two sides of the farmyard. However, they needn't have worried. Not only had Johnny disappeared from the earlier scene, but so too had the black dog. Catching the child just a few feet from the water's edge, the dog was making certain he could go no further until help arrived. Funnily enough, far from frightening the lad, the adventure had been for him the best part of the whole trip.

"Can we get a dog?" he asked his mother, "a big black one like Prince?" That was a question he would ask a dozen times or more over the following days.

As it happened, they were fortunate ending up where they had. Their reward for nearly being shot was supper and a lift home, for which all kinds of promises were made, should their paths ever cross again. Though the promises were well intentioned, it is unlikely they expected to meet again in a hurry. In this respect, they would, quite soon, be proved wrong. They would meet again twice that year.

*   *   *   *   *   *   *   *   *   *   *   *   *   *

215

"Liddy, get yourself togither gel," called Francie Miles.

It was about midday, the first Saturday in July, and it became clear that there was quite a procession of people heading towards Wickham Skeith.

"Where's everyone a-goin'?" called Lydia from the shade of an open doorway. Harriet was strapped to her back.

"They're a-givin' old Isaac Stebbings the trial by water."

Lydia was dumbfounded. Swimming witches and wizards was supposed to have died out at least a hundred years before, but truth to tell, many still believed in the old superstitions, and in the old ways of dealing with them.

"He'll not be no wizard. He's just a miserable old huckster what don' know what time of day it is."

"Ol' Tommy say when Stebbings pass by his window, he can't get his wax to melt."

"Oh yeah," scoffed Lydia, "An' you'll be telling me next, some fool paid a cunning man to tell 'em who was the cause of all their troubles."

"I was going to say that," said Francie.

"An' they paid the cunning man three shillings for a load of ol' squit; an I ask you which one's got a brain on his shoulders, the one what parted with three shillings or the cunning man?"

"Now you put it like that...," started Francie. "Still, should be worth watching - so dew yew git a move on, like I said!"

It was irresistible, and the two found themselves holding Johnny's hands and following the crowd. Before long, the rhythm of their walking had lulled baby Harriet to sleep, oblivious to the chatter of the walkers. Lydia and Francie followed paths across by Hempnall's Hall to Dandy Corner, then past Wickham Abbey to Wickham village green. In the centre of the green was a large patch of water, too big to be a pond, too small to be a lake. So it was known as 'The Grimmer', its dark origins clouded in mystery. By the time the two women arrived, the banks were crowded with people from at least a dozen villages.

They were not a moment too soon, as they could recognise Isaac Stebbings being led down to the water's edge.

"Poor ol' bugger," said Lydia, "'T'in't right."

"They say he asked 'em to do it," replied Francie. "Cos he believe it'll prove he 'in't a wizard."

"Still 'in't right," said Lydia. "Just proves he's as daft as the rest on'em. How old is he, anyway?"

"Sixty-five or sixty-six," chuckled Francie. "At least he'll get a bath an' smell a bit more wholesome. I don' reckon he an' water have had a meetin' for many a fine year."

The crowd was bolstered by the occupants of the Swan. Fuelled by beer, they added weight to what was already a cacophony of sound. A cheer went up from the assembled multitudes as Isaac Stebbings, led by one of his accusers, entered the water. Fortunately, generations had passed since the last trial by water in that part of Suffolk and no thought had been given as to the accuracy of this historical reconstruction. Back in the days of the Witchfinder General, his thumbs and opposite big toes would have been tied together and he would have been cast into the deepest part of the Grimmer to 'sink or swim.' As it was, unsure quite how to proceed, the village elders managed to turn the whole thing into something of a farce. They sat on his feet, then on his middle. Finally, they sat on his head, but he was a large man and determined to float, whatever treatment was meted out to him.

Having watched patiently for a while, the parson and church-wardens denied the crowd any more entertainment by coming to the poor man's rescue. He came out of the water more dead than alive. Still not satisfied, there were those along the water's edge who determined that another should be found who was a similar age and size to compare how well the two swam at the same time.

"Get ol' Tom Wilden," a voice was heard to say. "Get Tom Wilden an' we'll try agin next Saturday."

There were plenty of voices in agreement, though whether from genuine belief or just wishing to witness another bit of mischief, it was hard to say.

"They'll not swim you again while I'm here," the parson was heard to remark. Isaac Stebbings, coughing and spluttering still, was in no mood to argue. Disappointed at an end to their sport, the crowd began to disperse. Lydia checked the still sleeping child at her back, before preparing to head back home herself.

"Well, hello stranger!"

Lydia turned, and there beside her was the farmer who had come to their rescue the week before. He looked quite different in daylight and she briefly had to ask herself who he was. But Johnny instantly recognised the big black dog he had become so enamoured with on that occasion.

"It's a long way to come to see some poor old sod get half drowned," said Lydia.

"It's on account of my brother-in-law, who's parish constable at Yaxley. I'm here to observe there's no breach of the peace, so to speak, seeing as how he can't come himself. We've had a bit of trouble nearer home - a nasty business - I won't trouble you with the details. So I'm the law in his absence."

"Weren't it important enough to come and stop a murder being committed?" Lydia found it hard to hide her impatience. "Or was some bit of petty-thieving in Yaxley more important than a load of bullies trying to drown a poor old man over here?"

The farmer looked uncomfortable for a moment, but he soon regained his composure and came back at her with a vengeance.

"A ten year-old boy blinded by a spring-gun is hardly 'a bit of petty-thieving' as you put it." He waited for his words to sink in before continuing. "Whilst landowners encourage game keepers to set man-traps and spring-guns, there's no saying what dangers will lurk in the countryside. They think that as they put advertisements in the local papers warning of what they intend to do, it'll stop accidents, but there's far too many of these kinds of accidents for my liking - unwary travellers losing feet in traps and getting shot for wandering a few feet off the path. Even the keepers themselves don't remember where they put the traps and end up blasted with their own pellets and shot. We have had maimings and even deaths as a result of thoughtless acts by men who ought to know better. That ma'am I would consider as being well worthy of the attention of the law."

This time, it was Lydia who was taken aback, but she still had more in her armoury. "Then, as you be the law on this occasion, how come you didn't put a stop to it?" she asked.

"What makes you think I didn't?"

"We saw it was the parson what made 'em stop."

"And who do you think asked the parson to intervene?" He looked at her and smiled at her confusion. "No, if I had told 'em to stop, they'd have ducked me, if not worse, and I'd have been forced to read the riot act and half the village would have ended up arrested. Far better to have a quiet word with someone the people respect and get things done that way. Now, everyone can go home having had their little bit of entertainment. Added to which, a man from the Bury Post was there. In a week's time he'll be telling half of Suffolk what a load of silly beggars there are in Wickham, and maybe they'll think twice about it another time."
But Lydia still wasn't convinced.

"This lot think they can prey on the likes of the old and the poor and the stupid." She paused before continuing. "There's farmers and smiths and wheelwrights and shoemakers all thinking because they can afford a church pew they've got a right to behave like heathens. Fine upstanding citizens!" she mocked. Lydia was well into her stride by now. "I knew a soldier once, thought he was God's gift, cos he'd fought in a war and they'd won, and he'd been cheered all the way from Harwich to here. But he got a decent girl with child and tried it on with two more. He weren't that special even if everyone thought he was. But it needed someone to stand up to him and tell him how heroes ought to behave."

She was, of course, remembering her brush with John Hubbard, the father of her sister Sarah's child, a man she still found it hard to forgive.

"So what now? What if old Stebbings goes home and dies of the cold an' the wet?" she said, as one last parting shot.

"Then we might have to talk to the ringleaders; but he looks a tough old bird to me. I reckon he's got a good few years in him yet." Even Lydia could not find fault in his explanation, and was left to mumble an apology of sorts.

"The next time we meet, perhaps you'll start by giving me the benefit of the doubt before you lay into me, full of righteous indignation."

His words sounded fierce but his smile made it clear he had enjoyed their banter. "I shall certainly know where to come when I need help with the righting of wrongs," he grinned. And with that, he drifted away, leaving Lydia, Johnny, Harriet and Francie to make their own way back to Cotton.

And, you know, he was dead right. Isaac Stebbings was a tough old bird. He lived another twenty-two years. But in all that time, there were still plenty that believed he dabbled in witchcraft, and bemoaned the passing of the days when witches and wizards were put to the test, and, if found wanting, dealt with!

Chapter 23

November 1825

To the figures approaching Thrower's Pightle, there was little trace of anyone being at home. Late into November, it was bound to get dark early, but this evening seemed particularly dark to two men who were not familiar with the area and having difficulty following such instructions as they had been given. At first glance, the cottage seemed dark and empty, but they could just sense the faintest glow within, such as would be supplied by one or two rush-lamps. Dismounting from their horses, they hitched them to an overhanging bough and fumbled their way towards the house.

Hearing their arrival, Sam Blomfield opened the door, but without the luxury of oil-lamps or candles, it was a poor excuse for a light that framed him in the doorway.

"Can I help you?" Gradually, his eyes picked out the two shadowy figures. One of the horses neighed gently behind them.

"Mr. Blomfield?"

"And who's asking for him?" There was a nervous pause, but in a matter of moments, all was revealed. Lydia, finding a stump of candle had lit it, and appearing at the doorway herself was able to recognise a friendly face - none other than the farmer from Braise-worth who had helped them back in the summer when they had found themselves wandering and lost on the way home from Eye.

"Come you in, don't stand out here, or we'll all catch our deaths," said Lydia, ushering them in.

Beside the farmer stood another man who became identifiable as a constable by the short staff of office that was attached to his belt.

"This is my brother-in-law I told you about when we met over at Wickham… Mr. William Sparke from Yaxley."

He was a tall man with a weatherbeaten face and a furrowed brow.

"What can have brought you here on such a night?" Sam Blomfield asked.

"It's something your wife here said when we spoke at Wickham. She said she knew a man as used to be a soldier, served with a regiment in Essex. We need to find that man. We need to move fast or a criminal of the vilest kind will escape justice."

Sam looked first at his wife and then at the two visitors, in hope of some kind of explanation. Gradually, the story unravelled.

"We are in pursuit of a man called Walter Peck," explained Constable Sparke. "Only a few days ago, he ravished a young girl by the name of Eliza Canham; she is just nine years old. But before we could apprehend him, he signed up with a marching regiment and is on his way to Harwich to embark for the continent."

"But how can we help?" asked Sam.

"We can follow him to Harwich, but we have no knowledge of the town or of the regiments that use it. We need a soldier who might be prepared to come with us to intercede on our behalf - talk to the officers if necessary, so they let us take him to face trial at the next Quarter Session. You did say you knew of such a man."

All faces turned toward Lydia.

"You'll be talking of a man by the name of John Hubbard - he's a man who owes the world a bit of decency and you can tell him I said as much. He's married now with a family and I'd like to believe he's turned over a new leaf. I can give you guidance as to where you'll find him, and maybe he'll go with you. He has a daughter nearly the same age as little Eliza Canham and every reason to wish to rid the world of men like Walter Peck."

"I'll come with you," said Sam, pulling on his boots. "I'll show you where Hubbard lives and come to Harwich too, if you'll wait for as long as it takes to ask my master for a horse."

Lydia desperately wanted to plead with Sam to stay. She had news she wanted to share with him, news she was sure would please and delight him, but also she knew he was determined to play his part in this venture. She could hardly expect things from John Hubbard, a man she loathed, whilst being unprepared to expect as much from the man she loved and admired.

As they prepared to leave, and she heard the sound of horses' hooves fade into the distance, the glow from the rush lamps seemed dimmer than ever. Lydia sensed the danger that awaited them there. Embarkation towns were such lawless places. She had been meaning to tell her husband there would soon be another addition to the family. Now it would have to wait until he returned... if he returned.

Give him his due, John Hubbard was a very different man from the swaggering war hero of ten years earlier. He was now a family man with responsibilities, and shouldered them with strength and purpose. He needed no second bidding, nor reminders of his past peccadilloes; within minutes, he was saddled and the four were on their way to Harwich.

They rode through the night, arriving when all was quiet. Even the inhabitants of the dockside taverns had drunk themselves into unconsciousness. The sky had cleared somewhat and the moon had appeared to give light to a forbidding kind of place. There was no friendly air to Harwich. It remained dark and uninviting, yet it was here they had execute their mission, tired though they were. Daniel Defoe, in visiting Harwich a century before, had found it much as they did now, 'a town of not much gaiety and pleasure, its inhabitants extravagant in their reckonings.' A cold wind blew from off the sea to remind them they were not welcome in a place like this.

Through the half-darkness, they could make out the masts of ships; tall government ships ready to convey soldiers to the continent, sea-going sloops which ran as packet-boats to Holland, fishing smacks lined up ready to face the capriciousness of the North Sea in their search for herring; and a fossilised relic of a bygone generation... a once proud Dutch privateer captured and left to rot with its mainmast broken and its partially furled sails in tatters and hanging in threads. Out away on a promontory of land known as Beacon Hill stood a lighthouse, a marker of a safe haven that shone out through the darkness.

On the Suffolk side of the bay behind a fort with its battery of guns guarding the approaches, lay a veritable shanty-town of tents. Here had to be what they were seeking. It was here that companies of soldiers gathered before embarking for a variety of destinations. Even at that time of night, the little party could hear the uneasiness of the horses in the camp. There was too the bleating of sheep and clucking of hens that would travel with the enlisted men. Armies needed feeding.

They found it easier to dismount and lead their horses. Here the road became firmer but more slippery, taking on the surface of baked clay. Past the inns and taverns, past the sleeping houses they went, tired but determined to see this through. The guards at the entrance to the camp were suspicious of them, but seeing the constable's truncheon, permitted them to pass and showed them the way to their officer's tent.

He was none too pleased at being roused so early, but received them civilly and listened to what they had to say.

"We believe, sir, you have been recruiting in the vicinity of Eye in Suffolk?" asked William Sparke.

"Indeed we have, and in a handful of other towns in your county."

"We also believe you have in your numbers a man by the name of Walter Peck?"

"I cannot say without checking; my recruiting sergeant has the list. What if we have?"

"The man is guilty of a diabolical crime. We are here to see that he receives justice."

"You want to deprive His Majesty of one of his soldiers on the strength of a mere accusation?"

"This was not just any crime. This man sought to deprive a child of her innocence. Another child was there to bear witness." He looked at the officer. "Do you have children? Perhaps a nine year-old daughter?" Here he knew instantly he had hit on a soft spot, for the officer's tone of voice altered somewhat.

"There are those who would say sending him to fight for his country would be punishment enough. He could even be killed."

224

"And he could come back a hero." This time it was John Hubbard who spoke. "He could come back with a reputation that was built on the blood of others more deserving, and be twice the devil he was before he went away. I once knew such a man. He served with this very regiment. The sins he committed may have been different, but the end result was the same. Fighting for King and Country was not what put him on the right road. What he needed was someone to make him understand natural justice. And I think we be more fitted to do that in this case... sir!"

Somehow he conveyed to all in that tent the fact he knew, better than any of them, what he was talking about.

"And yet, fifty years ago, the sentence he would have received for such a crime would have been to press him into service with the army or navy... however, I understand how you feel," said the officer, with a sigh. "Doubtless, among those that have taken the King's shilling, are all kinds of ruffians. We hope to make better human beings of them and turn them into fighting men. Still, I would rather your Walter Peck was not among them. You shall have your prisoner, gentlemen. But should he be found innocent, perhaps you will return him to us."

At this point, a sergeant entered the tent clutching a book. It did not take long for them to find the name of Walter Peck. They had feared he might have registered under an alias, but confident he would be well clear of danger by the time his crime was discovered, he had taken no such precautions. Within the space of a few minutes, he had been located, arrested and put in chains. The little party of four accepted the officer's offer to sleep and to have their horses attended to, before making their way back to Suffolk.

It was with a gentle feeling of triumph they reached the White Horse at Stoke Ash before parting and going their separate ways. The constable and the farmer carried on up the turnpike with their prisoner. John Hubbard and Sam Blomfield rode a while together along the road to Wickham before they too parted. They said little, but both knew that Lydia would know soon enough that Hubbard was a changed man, and a good deal of that change had been wrought by Lydia herself.

No-one can describe the sense of relief felt by the little family as Sam rode back to his cottage at Thrower's Pightle. First he called in to embrace Lydia, to cuddle Johnny and kiss little Harriet. Then he had to return the horse he had borrowed to the farm, taking care to look after the animal after its long night's exertions.

Only then was there time for he and Lydia to share the pleasure of her news. Another child... maybe a boy of his own this time. That was what Sam really wanted, though he could hardly voice it in those terms to Lydia, and certainly not to Johnny. Johnny was so much a part of their family, he was almost Sam's own son. Almost...

In November 1825, Johnny's real father, Jack Hart, married Maria Turner at Cotton. As with Lydia's marriage, no banns were called. They married by Bishop's licence. Partly, it was a statement of status that said, 'if we are rich enough, we can pay to ensure no one dictates how long we should wait before we tie the knot.' But it may also have been due in part to the fact Maria was already three months pregnant when she walked up the aisle; though no one in their hearing was prepared to accuse them of indecent haste.

Just into the new year, at the Ipswich Quarter Session, Walter Peck pleaded guilty to a serious assault on a child. He was sentenced to twelve months hard labour. After that, he returned to the regiment with whom he had enlisted. He was sent on an expedition to Holland from which he never returned.

Chapter 24

June 1826

It was a mystery why William Cuthbert, member of the Royal College of Surgeons and an outstanding student at the time of his graduation ten years earlier should have elected to serve out his days as country physician in the village of Mendlesham in the depths of rural Suffolk.

It was true, his father before him had ended his career in a country practice, but his contemporaries had expected so much more of this brilliant young man. However, since he had settled in the village adjacent to Cotton, he had taken to the role of country doctor with a will, accepting the post of Registrar to the district and also buying land and property as it had come onto the market.

The reputation he had begun to earn was to serve his family well. Both his son and grandson would continue to practice medicine in the village until the turn of the century. Of course, it was to the rich he ministered mainly, his fees being well beyond the means of mere agricultural labourers. However, he was known to be a compassionate man and would on occasions treat the poorest and most needy with no intention of demanding payment.

A guarded respect existed between William Cuthbert and Elizabeth Saunders. Robert and Anne's eldest daughter had built a life around offering affordable services to those who could least afford to pay. Though Dr. Cuthbert may have questioned her moral turpitude, he had to admit she was a fine midwife and a remarkably successful healer. It was not unknown for him to consult her regarding old herbal remedies when his own chemical concoctions failed to have the desired effect. Only with a great effort of will would he take himself from his comfortable house opposite the church to the squalor of her hovel in Back Street where she wet-nursed screeching brats in conditions of questionable hygiene. But it was usually worth the effort, he had to admit.

Elizabeth, for her part, recognised her limitations, especially since one of her own children had died in spite of all her frantic efforts. Elizabeth now knew that there was a time to admit defeat and enlist the help of the trained professional.

With so many sisters, Elizabeth could have filled her time ministering to her family alone. Though Tom and Mary Mallows were childless, Robert and Sarah Head, Anne and Will Oldridge and now Lydia and Samuel Blomfield all had growing families. Added to this, Robert and Anne Saunders suffered from the kinds of afflictions that restricted their movements and rendered them for long periods housebound.

But Elizabeth had three children of her own to care for and plenty belonging to other people. She had always been independent in spirit and the poor of half a dozen parishes relied on her wisdom and good sense. They also relied on not being billed for her services. Even if she had been able to write, that would not have been Elizabeth's way. She knew her customers would pay what they could in their own good time, or the parish would pay it for them.

William Cuthbert was awaiting a call. Maria Hart at Cotton Lodge was expecting her first child. He would be expected to deliver it. This was a modern minded couple - no embarrassment over a male doctor attending to a mother giving birth. None of that prudish and dangerous practice of hiding the mother's nether quarters beneath a sheet and expecting the physician to deliver the baby by touch alone as if blindfolded. Thank heavens! But it was a first child, and they were always a concern.

Elizabeth Saunders too was expecting to drop everything to attend to her sister Lydia. It would be her third child - no reason for caution then; with two successful deliveries already encountered, one boy, one girl.

So, less than a mile apart, two very different families prepared for a birth. It had been uncommonly hot and if anything united the two mothers-to-be it was the shared experience of discomfort they suffered.

Maria Hart, young and pampered, couldn't hide her irritation at the situation in which she found herself. Her mother, who might have seen fit to offer some comfort and support, simply reminded her this would probably be the first of many. She had given birth to thirteen and was hardly sympathetic.

Lydia, on the other hand, had taken to cooling off by lying naked on her bed during the heat of the day. Samuel found this slightly disconcerting, but could understand why she did it.

Ever a prudent man where money was concerned, Samuel Blomfield worried that with his wife lying-in and not earning, he would be unable to support his family. Lydia, however, in spite of her wanderings was still regarded as a Cotton girl and the Overseers of the poor were called upon once more to support her.

Samuel for his part was working long hours in an attempt to prove that his master's confidence in him was well placed. If he did but know it, he had already proved his worth many times over.

He would be glad when this child was born. It had been a strange pregnancy. No sooner had they realised Lydia was expecting than she had grown very cold toward him, and though as her time drew near, they were now close again, it had knocked his confidence for a while. Whilst it may have been a result of her pregnancy, it did cross his mind more than once, her coldness might have coincided with Jack Hart's marriage to Maria Turner.

Two households, just about a mile apart as the magpie flies, made ready for a birth. At The Lodge, all was a-fluster. This was Jack Hart's first child, his parents' first grandchild, as far as most in that house were concerned. The other potential grandparents had also arrived to oversee things. Philip and Mary Turner had a host of grandchildren already and regarded themselves as old hands at this. For all that, they were hardly a calming influence.

Maria Hart had begun her contractions during the night. Now, by early morning, they were stronger and Doctor Cuthbert still had not made an appearance. Activity in the house fell only just short of panic.

Things were only slightly calmer at Thrower's Pightle, where

Samuel Blomfield was about to hand over responsibility to Lydia's sister, Elizabeth, before hurrying off to mind Goodrich's livestock.

Elizabeth had brought with her Jochabed, her eleven year old daughter whom she said might prove useful. She assured Samuel as he left for work she would send the child for him if there were any problems. She foresaw no reason for anxiety. Lydia had already given birth to two fine children, one of each sex, and appeared herself, to be a picture of health.

Lydia's pains had begun in the early hours of the morning and a neighbour had collected her two children, Johnny and Harriet, before sending word to Elizabeth that the time was near. Knowing how babies had a habit of coming more quickly the more the mother had, Elizabeth had wasted no time in making her way along the lanes from Mendlesham to that part of Cotton.

Dawn had broken soon after she had started walking and by the time Elizabeth and Jochabed had reached Lydia and Samuel's cottage, it showed all the signs of being another hot day.

As Elizabeth was unpacking the herbs and tools of her trade, Doctor Cuthbert was, with an irritating lack of haste, guiding a small carriage into the lane that led to Lodge Farm. Again, he had no reason to believe this should be anything other than a reasonably uncomplicated delivery. He saw no need to hurry. It was a first child and would, in all probability, be a false alarm.

Still refusing to be rushed even with the encouragement of two sets of expective grandparents, Cuthbert took his time, only to discover that his prediction was correct and they could all take tea. It would be some hours yet before the child would show itself.

With all males except the doctor banished from the house, Jack Hart, his father and father-in-law went for a walk around Lodge Farm. If you had seen them as they discussed the state of the growing crops, you would have described them as being like lords inspecting their domain; but it was all merely an attempt to calm their agitation and to put their minds to other things.

At one point, where Heigham land abutted that farmed by the Goodriches, Jack Hart could see Samuel Blomfield moving sheep onto the remains of a newly harvested field of lucerne. The two men acknowledged one another courteously. They didn't have to like one another, but like brothers in arms they recognised a shared concern.

"Your wife's time is here then?" Blomfield deduced.

"The physician is with her now - and yours?"

"Elizabeth will be there."

There were no comments about 'good luck.' It was a natural process beyond the laws of chance and something that had enabled these two men to communicate on an equal footing. The meeting was brief and each returned to his separate undertaking.

In the meantime, Lydia's labour was well advanced and Elizabeth was rapping out orders. Jochabed, though little more than a child herself, was well versed in such matters. Elizabeth recognised in her second daughter much of the enthusiasm and skill she had possessed from an early age and valued her help.

When the birth came, it was unremarkable and fluent. Elizabeth took the child, gave it cause to cry and showed it to its mother before taking it off to clean it up. It was a boy. Though she said nothing, Elizabeth was a little worried, for the infant was small and pale and had taken several moments to draw breath.

"You wait there," she instructed Jochabed, "...for the after-birth to show, then you can bury it in the garden." She took time and care to check the baby's airways and to examine the child. She needn't have worried: he was colouring nicely and looked a fine, if small, boy.

"You got that afterbirth yet?" she asked Jochabed, returning with the baby? "It 'in't come yet. Is that a problem?"

"Oh I don't reckon. It prob'ly be waitin' for the baby to be put to the breast."

She passed the child to Lydia, who by now knew enough to prompt the child to suckle. "What will you call him?"

"It's a boy then?" Lydia smiled.

Elizabeth realised she had not said, and drew back the cloth that covered the baby's nether regions for his mother to see.

"Samuel did say we should call this one William, as Will Goodrich will be god-father."

231

"William he is then. Should I send the gal to fetch Sam?"

"He'll be back soon enough. Let him get his work done first."
Lydia yawned. "I feel right tired. 'In't that afterbirth come yet?"

"There's still some bleedin', but placenta 'in't shown."
Jochabed replied. Elizabeth smiled at her daughter's use of the
correct word. She was training her well.

"Don't you worry. Some takes longer than others. Get you
some sleep. We'll wait awhile."

It was only after another half-hour when the bleeding continued and the placenta had refused to yield itself up that Elizabeth
began to fret. Normally the action of feeding the child would
encourage the body to complete the process. Still she continued to
bleed.

"I'll have to wake her and get her to try feeding the child
again," she informed Jochabed.

"The blood flow's less."

"Only 'cause she 'in't got so much blood no more."

Lydia was hard to waken. Weakened by loss of blood and tired
from the labour, she attempted to suckle the child, but without
enthusiasm. Elizabeth knew what had to be done.

"Dew yew get yourself back to Front Street and fetch Doctor
Cuthbert." "Who'll pay?" asked Jochabed.

"Don't be burdened by that right now. Say we need him and
tell him the problem."

Jochabed sped off down the lane to Mendlesham, unaware that
Doctor Cuthbert was otherwise occupied, but closer than she
thought.

"We need the doctor!" she shouted to the housekeeper,
gasping, for she had run most of the way.

"He is attending Mrs. Hart at Cotton Lodge; he'll not leave
there till her child is born and mother and child are adjudged safe."
Without waiting to argue the case, Jochabed set off at haste along
the back road to Cotton, choosing the most direct tracks and paths
to bring her to the rear of Lodge Farm.

Skirting the moat, unattentive to protocol, she went to the main
door and hammered on it with her urgent fists. Sarah Hart having

been drawn away from the imminent arrival of her first grandchild was largely unsympathetic at the sight of this frantic girl gasping and demanding to speak to the doctor.

Fortunately, William Cuthbert, hearing his name mentioned in all the commotion came down to see what all the fuss was about.

"It's Auntie Lydia," Jochabed sobbed. "We 'in't got the afterbirth and she's still a-bleedin'."

"How long has it been since you left her?" Cuthbert asked.

"Oh - an hour or more."

"Listen, go back and tell your mother to make your Aunt Lydia drink. She must get as much liquid into her as possible. I cannot come right now."

From upstairs came a cry of pain: clearly Maria Hart was in the advanced stages of labour.

"As soon as I have discharged my duties here, I will drive with all haste to see your Aunt. Don't worry, she'll not perish for loss of a trickle of blood and you'll probably return to find her sitting up in bed having parted with the afterbirth and feeling a whole lot better."

"Should we find a carriage for this child?" Sarah Hart was showing her practical, caring side now.

"No ma'am; I'll be quicker on foot by the fields and foot-paths." Jochabed replied.

"As you will."

Sarah Hart caught a last glimpse of Jochabed, long hair streaming behind her, heading for Lydia's house. Further cries from above brought her back to her own commitment.

"I think he looks like his father," Maria smiled as her son was shown to Jack. He had been born ninety minutes after Jochabed had come hammering at the door. The doctor had left soon after, to the distress of Philip and Mary Turner who felt he should have stayed longer.

"When you pay his bill, I hope you take account of the fact he didn't really complete the job," Philip Turner commented acidly.

But mother and child were both well. Maria felt remarkably

pleased with herself.

"I'm sure I'd prefer he had his mother's looks." Jack Hart sought for the right words to say.

"All that hair - I never saw a child so hairy. And of course we'll call him John." Maria gushed.

"I already have a son called John," Jack Hart replied before he could stop himself.

"Not as you can rightly lay claim to," Maria snapped. "I'll have no discussion on this." She lay with the child beside her. "We'll christen him John like his father and his grandfather."
And that, she was sure, was the end of the matter.

Jochabed had not returned to learn that all was well. Far from it! Lydia lay, pale and anaemic, whilst a tortured looking Elizabeth fought to spoon water between her lifeless lips.

"The doctor's at Lodge Farm. He say he'll come when he can." Jochabed explained.

"You done well. Carry on with trying to give her water and I'll do what I can down here."

Jochabed could see her mother had anticipated the doctor's other instruction over administering fluids. But there was no staunching the weak but relentless flow of blood and they both feared the worst.

In all her years as midwife, Elizabeth had become resigned to losing mothers and babies; sometimes both. But this was a sister, this was the irrepressible girl who had sung and danced and played and laughed and loved. She deserved more than this - to fade out of existence while her new born child cried to be nursed and those who loved her, sat by helpless.

It was hard to say exactly when Lydia died. Just before Doctor Cuthbert came, her pulse had become so faint it was scarcely more than a flutter. He could see she was beyond his care, and was more of a mind to console Elizabeth and Jochabed, assuring them that they had done no less than he could. Samuel was sent for and if Elizabeth's grief was sore, his was far worse.

Elizabeth placed the new infant to her own bosom. Her milk

234

still flowed, thank goodness. Four children in eighteen years had ensured a continuous supply. She would feed and wean young William Blomfield. It was the least she could do.

Doctor Cuthbert returned to The Lodge the next day, which was when Jack Hart heard of Lydia's demise. The news struck him as if he had been shot.

He took a walk outside. It was still hot and dry. At one end of the moat, the water level had dropped, exposing the silt. He could see something glinting, so picking up a long handled net that lay nearby, retrieved the object. He recognised it at once. It was the key to the chapel; the papist's church that lay hidden behind a still locked door at the northern end of the big house. He took it inside and used it to enter the secret room for the first time since he and Lydia had done so seven years before. He sat in the centre of the room on the floor, oblivious to the peeling paintings that once must have decorated the walls. And he wept whilst upstairs they argued over how and when the one-day-old John Hart Junior should be baptised.

"We must have the baby baptised without delay," said Sarah Hart. There was always a fear a child would succumb to some early ailment and face the ignominy of an unbaptised burial.

"As the marriage was only in November last," observed Philip Turner, it would be unfortunate to say the least for a baptism to be listed before, shall we say, August at the earliest."

He had a point. Then, as with so many decisions in his life, Jack Hart would rejoin them to discover another choice had been made for him, and in his absence. They would probably forbid him to attend Lydia's funeral. Unused to going against the will of the family, Jack was nevertheless determined this was one occasion when they would not stop him.

The burial took place two days after Lydia's death. It was hot and the sooner a body could be committed to the earth the better. Delay was undesirable.

With a baptism, it was different. It would indeed be a further two months before John and Maria Hart's son was entered into the register as being baptised in Cotton Church.

Chapter 25

June 1826

Lydia's final journey was not an easy one.   Following tradition, the coffin had remained open overnight in the front room of their tiny tied cottage.   Samuel's employer, Mr. Goodrich had lent a horse and cart to transport it up the half mile of lanes and tracks to the church gate.

From the cover of the surrounding trees, Jack Hart watched the cart arrive.   He had absented himself from home that morning without a word as to why; a move that was bound to be unpopular. He saw the crowded churchyard empty itself into the ancient building. It was the signal for him to make a move. He came to the porch to be, as he believed, alone outside the closed door.

"I see you turned up then."

It was Lydia's eldest sister Elizabeth. She had not entered the church but chosen to remain outside in the porch. He could see why. She was suckling the child they were all trying so hard not to blame for Lydia's untimely death.   It was the least she could do. Openly, in full view of his gaze, she put the hungry infant to her breast as if to advertise the service she normally expected to charge for.

Everyone knew, along the road in Mendlesham, Elizabeth Saunders plied a debatable trade as nurse, midwife, wet-nurse, layer-out of the dead and comforter to the living.   She had felt the need to witness her sister's last journey but had no intention of taking the two-day old child into church.

"I guessed you'd be there somewhere. Bit late don' you think? Hadn't you best be returning to your own?"

He felt dismissed, and lacking any kind of excuse or answer, waited until he could sense the service was at an end before retreating to the safety and obscurity of the churchyard margins.

As if there had been a rehearsal, though clearly this wasn't so, people filed out in logical order, Rector and family first. Next came the coffin bearers, four fit young men who had known her and loved her. Each in his turn had reason to regret her passing.

Robert Head called the others to lift together. Thomas Mallows, John Hubbard and Will Goodrich lifted with him. As they raised the coffin to their shoulders, it was with such ease that each must separately have marvelled at the lightness of his burden. It was as if the coffin was empty and they all half wondered whether Lydia might appear, lovely as ever, beside them. But the match-wood-thin box and her frail haemorrhaged body were borne to an unmarked corner of the graveyard where a mound of earth lay beside a pit lined with evergreens.

Then as the coffin was lowered, village children tossed in posies of wild flowers and sprigs of thyme. There were the ritual-istic words and many tears. No one seemed inclined to move away. Least of all, Jack Hart, all the while, unseen by the rest, remaining hidden among the trees.

Feeling conspicuous; better dressed and looking more well-nourished than the others, he had not ventured inside the church. Instead, he had chosen to pay his respects at a distance. He removed his hat as the body was laid to rest, before tears clouded his view of the still crowded graveyard.

After three weeks of unremitting June sunshine, the overcast nature of the day must have come as some relief to the overdressed congregation. Ominously it remained hot and stuffy. As the first drops of rain began to fall, those at the fringes of the throng were just starting to move. Most were expected back at work within the hour.

All at once, a month's rain fell and the mourners scattered. Samuel Blomfield stood rooted to the spot oblivious to the elements. Robert and Anne Saunders reached for the hands of their grandchildren. Harriet went willingly, but young Johnny wanted to stay with Samuel at the graveside and had to be pulled kicking and screaming away.

Soon, there were only two of them; Samuel, his borrowed best clothes wringing wet, and George Wilden filling in the grave as fast as his spade would allow. He began to tire. The mound of earth had grown heavy from the now receding downpour and was more than the old sexton could manage. Samuel removed his jacket, and shovelling like a madman, completed the task for him.

Samuel still had the task of returning the horse and cart, and finishing his day's work on the farm. Will Goodrich was waiting for him at the gate to the churchyard.

"I'll take you home" he said. "You're not to come back to work today. I'll straighten it with my father."

"But I told Mr. Goodrich as how I'd be back after lunch."

"You're in no fit state - and anyway you need to sort out your family. You've got a new baby…"

"He'll die - they all do when their mothers die - to tell you the truth, I can't bear to pick him up right now."
Samuel seemed resigned to tragedy.

"He won't die. Elizabeth will see to that. She's raised more on her own than Doctor Cuthbert for all his money and surgical knowledge; and anyway, there's Harriet and young Johnny."

As he spoke the words, Will knew he'd said the wrong thing. A look of panic crossed his face, as Samuel produced the reply he had feared.

"I'll look after Harriet as a father should but I'll not take young Johnny; not now. Lydia was never well after having him. If any-thing killed her, it was giving birth to him."

He looked William in the eye. William was his master's son and in all ways his better, but William had known him longer than most and had proved more a friend than any of his peers.

"I'll take him to his father. While Lydia was alive, I said I'd look after him. No-one can say I di'n't do my bit. But he's his father's responsibility now."

The horse and cart steadily moved away in the direction of Samuel's cottage and Jack Hart watched until they were out of sight before riding back along well-rutted tracks where the hard clay of summer had filled up with the recent rain. The docile old chestnut he rode that day had hooves weighed down with mud but barely

238

faltered as she trod the familiar lane to The Lodge.

At least Samuel Blomfield had the sense to change out of the stiff saturated funeral clothes he had borrowed from Will Goodrich. It was only a short step across the fields from his cottage to the hamlet that had grown up around Lodge Farm. Just beyond, in a hovel, barely fit for human habitation, Lydia's parents, Robert and Anne Saunders had lived for a few pence a week so long as both had worked long and hard for the Harts. They had, in spite of all the difficulties involved, brought up a family there. By the time of Lydia's death, well into their sixties, they were housed instead, at the parish's expense in a terrace of thatched cottages near the church. Still, however, they worked a few hours a week for their old employers. Old habits died hard.

Within The Lodge, that afternoon, John Hart was expecting visitors and an air of panic pervaded the place. They took a pride in the entertainment of guests that bordered on the fanatical. With two of the house-servants missing at the funeral, there was too much to be done and too few people to do it.

That was what Jack Hart returned to. His parents made no secret of their irritation over his absence. It wasn't good enough! Where had he been? He had been missing for a good part of the morning, before arriving back soaked to the skin. His young wife Maria, with a baby newly born, was lying-in and hence, in no position to help. Sarah Hart couldn't see how they could hope to be ready on time.

At least the food had all arrived. Unwilling to slaughter their own animals at quite the wrong time of year, Sarah had reluctantly purchased a pig carcass from Saunders. Who knew from where he'd obtained it, but at least it smelt fresh and would feed them all well enough. She supposed he needed the money for his daughter's funeral, but guessed in all likelihood it would be poured down his throat. She felt sorry for Anne, having a husband like that, but perhaps it was only to be expected with those kinds of people.

Jack Hart did not hear Samuel arrive. He was still changing out of his wet clothes when there came a hammering at the door.

Aware of something of a commotion, Sarah Hart was the first to head in that direction. Servants who had been busy preparing for the visitation had stopped and were staring from the top of the staircase.

"Get back to work - this is not for your eyes!" Sarah snapped, recognising the two characters framed in the open doorway. Sensing his own involvement in this, Jack was soon there. Samuel had his hand tightly clasped around the wrist of young Johnny. He had collected the boy from his grandparents on the way.

"This one's down to you now … sir," he stammered, in spite of his anger, feeling slightly intimidated.

"I've whully looked after him while his mother b'in alive. I've b'in the father to him what you never was. But right now, I can't do it no more."

Emerging from a door off the hall, Jack's wife, Maria's voice could be heard calling to know what all the fuss was about.

Sarah, recognising there was something that needed saying, spoke out.

"Look - I'm sorry your wife is dead - we all are, but can't you see, we can't do anything about this right now. And anyway my son paid for his mistake. For five years, he paid your wife for the upkeep of the boy. As for our looking after him, that's quite impossible."

"I don't think you understand, ma'am."

Samuel Blomfield raised his cap. The boy was beginning to whimper.

"He's not my son; never was; and I 'in't having him no more. With respect sir…" he uttered, turning to face Jack Hart. "…you'll have to do with him as you see fit. There's no way the Parish'll make me take him back."

Then, retaining as much dignity as he could, he turned away, unable to look the boy in the eyes - those eyes that looked so like his mother's, he couldn't bear to face them any more.

Almost as a mirror reflection of the same act, Sarah turned and uttered, "I don't care what you do with him, but he's not living in this house!" Then, slamming the door of the room from which

Maria's questioning voice continued to come, she turned her back on the situation.

Someone had to make a real decision, at least for the time being, so taking the boy by the hand, Jack made for the open door.

"Take him to his grandparents," Sarah called. They'll have him if your father tells them to."

That was not his intention.

"No: I'll have no son of mine brought up in that house!" Jack said, emphatically. "I'll take him to his Aunt Mary. I'll pay her to look after him until we decide what's best."

And without further ado, pulling the still tearful child, he half-walked, half-dragged him across the moat and down the lane to Hayes Corner where he knew he would find the road that led to the cottage of Mary and Thomas Mallows.

It was not the way it should have been. Lydia had been dead for just two days and already her three children were scattered across the parish.

It was still only midday.

The afternoon of June 27th 1826

All the reluctance to be a part of the game of 'pass-him-on' had gone from the boy. Though only six and already half-orphaned, he knew he was going to his Aunt Mary where he would be comfortable and loved and wanted. *Why then, did I still feel I owed him my commitment?*

He couldn't understand why he no longer had a mother and was being rejected by the man he had come to call, 'father'. If he had viewed his own reflection, he would have seen how like his mother he looked and maybe begun to understand how Samuel had been unable to face this reincarnation of his dead wife day in, day out.

Safely away from The Lodge and still holding Johnny's hand, I spoke to my son as a true father for the first time.

"You'll not mind going to your Aunt Mary?" I asked him.

"No sir."

"I expect she cossets you and makes much of you."

"I think she is sad she has no son of her own," replied the boy. I remember thinking he showed remarkable maturity.

"Then you understand I am not really sending you away?" The boy didn't answer.

"So much in my life is not of my own making," I tried to explain. "I have not rejected you, nor will I forget you are my son."

"No sir."

"I will tell you this now because it may be some time before I can come to you again," I continued. "When you are a young man looking for work, you must come and speak to me and I will see the best is done for you."

"Yes sir."

"It will be some years in the future, but you won't forget?"

"No sir."

"And who knows, as I replace my father at Lodge Farm, so should you replace me. For you are my first-born son and this is my promise to you."

"Yes sir."

He looked and sounded so earnest.

"Have you anyone to teach you read and write?" I continued.

"No sir."

"Then when you come to me, I will see you are coached in the skills you require to be master of Lodge Farm after me."

The boy continued to acknowledge my words as we walked past Hayes Corner and on towards Hill Farm where Thomas and Mary Mallows lived. It is to be doubted to what extent he understood the promissory words I uttered that day. But he did tell me, in later years, he remembered the earnest tone of my voice. I am glad, because I meant every word, and as I addressed him it was as if I was, at the same time making a belated promise to Lydia. At that time, I did not know how I would provide a birthright for this son of mine, but I was sure I could make a difference.

And in years to come when asked what work he expected to seek, he was prone to answer, "I will go to The Lodge, for there lies my future."

In the Census of 1841, John Saunders was listed as a servant in the house of John (Jack) and Maria Hart and their nine children.

He married in 1848 and began a family of his own.
In the census of 1881, he was living at Cotton Lodge as Bailiff of Lodge Farm.

A Genealogy for this book

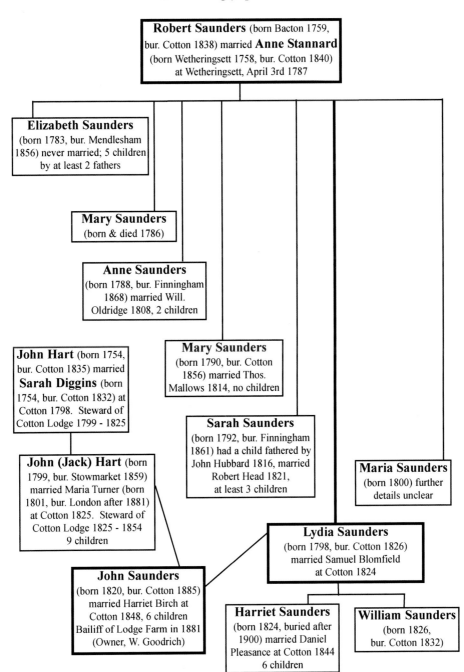

Robert Saunders (born Bacton 1759, bur. Cotton 1838) married **Anne Stannard** (born Wetheringsett 1758, bur. Cotton 1840) at Wetheringsett, April 3rd 1787

Elizabeth Saunders (born 1783, bur. Mendlesham 1856) never married; 5 children by at least 2 fathers

Mary Saunders (born & died 1786)

Anne Saunders (born 1788, bur. Finningham 1868) married Will. Oldridge 1808, 2 children

John Hart (born 1754, bur. Cotton 1835) married **Sarah Diggins** (born 1754, bur. Cotton 1832) at Cotton 1798. Steward of Cotton Lodge 1799 - 1825

Mary Saunders (born 1790, bur. Cotton 1856) married Thos. Mallows 1814, no children

Sarah Saunders (born 1792, bur. Finningham 1861) had a child fathered by John Hubbard 1816, married Robert Head 1821, at least 3 children

John (Jack) Hart (born 1799, bur. Stowmarket 1859) married Maria Turner (born 1801, bur. London after 1881) at Cotton 1825. Steward of Cotton Lodge 1825 - 1854 9 children

Maria Saunders (born 1800) further details unclear

Lydia Saunders (born 1798, bur. Cotton 1826) married Samuel Blomfield at Cotton 1824

John Saunders (born 1820, bur. Cotton 1885) married Harriet Birch at Cotton 1848, 6 children Bailiff of Lodge Farm in 1881 (Owner, W. Goodrich)

Harriet Saunders (born 1824, buried after 1900) married Daniel Pleasance at Cotton 1844 6 children

William Saunders (born 1826, bur. Cotton 1832)

A map of the villages mentioned in this story

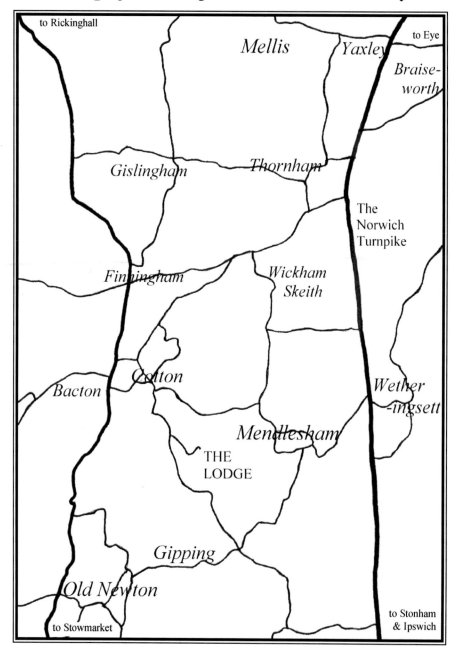

to Rickinghall

Mellis

Yaxley

to Eye

Braise-
worth

Gislingham

Thornham

The
Norwich
Turnpike

Finningham

Wickham
Skeith

Colton

Bacton

Wether
-ingsett

Mendlesham

THE
LODGE

Gipping

Old Newton

to Stonham
& Ipswich

to Stowmarket

A map of Cotton in the early nineteenth century

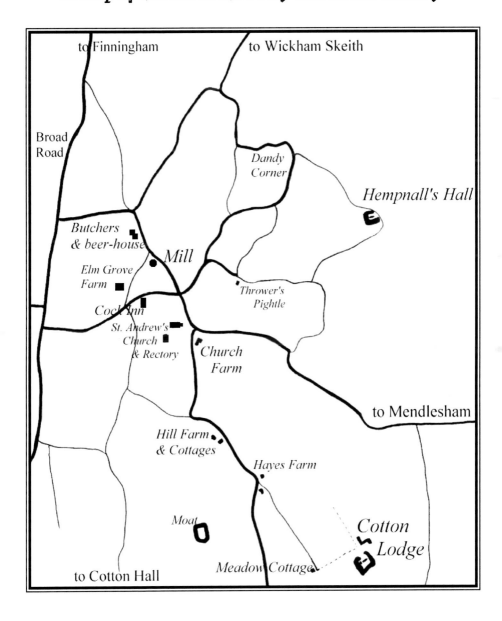

to Finningham

to Wickham Skeith

Broad
Road

Dandy
Corner

Hempnall's Hall

Butchers
& beer-house

Mill

Elm Grove
Farm

Thrower's
Pightle

Cock Inn

St. Andrew's
Church
& Rectory

Church
Farm

to Mendlesham

Hill Farm
& Cottages

Hayes Farm

Moat

Cotton
Lodge

to Cotton Hall

Meadow Cottage

In this book, Lydia and her family are all known by the surname **Saunders**. In reality, the name appears in parish records in a number of other forms, in particular **Sanders** and the name carried by Lydia's descendants today, **Alexander**.